THE HOUSE OF LIGHT & AIR

Printed in the United Kingdom
First Printing, 2024

ISBN: 978-1-0687840-0-2 (Paperback)
ISBN: 978-1-0687840-1-9 (eBook)

Alexia Daniels
Southsea, Hampshire UK

Prologue

September 1888

The air is thick with the stink of offal and rot. It clings to the fabric of my clothes and ingrains my already grimy skin. It overwhelms already city-dulled senses, landing at the back of my throat as a tangible foul taste. I pull up the rough-knitted scarf around my neck with a free hand in a vain attempt to cover my nose. In recent years, the stink has lessened, but some days, it fights back. The sack is hanging heavy and low against my back, forcing me to hunch forward to counteract the load. The earlier rain has done much to clear the detritus from the streets, but in the end, everything, everyone, like me on this chill night, travels to the river. My feet are leaden with exhaustion, and I consciously place my solid, dull boots down in places clear of suspicious rivulets and trudge onwards. Thousands of busy feet have worn the cobbles to cup shapes, and I fight to keep upright on the shiny, slick surface.

I am moving like a single, insignificant blood cell travelling through the arteries and veins of the city. The blackened and filthy networks have pumped disease and endless liquid filth through rotten organs and onto *the still-fetid gut of a river, which lays on her back, exposing her stinking underbelly to the world without shame. Vulnerable but mighty, she begs, demands my attention, devouring all who stray within her grasp. And I, her child, one of the millions spawned by an ungrateful mother, hide within her stinking folds. You could put sewers along each river bank, pump houses north and south, but the bitch of a city was born of the mud of the river and fire. She has been baked hard and forgives nothing.*

Tonight, the fog is mercifully light, enough to feather the edges of the dockside buildings that claw at the hidden sky with broken fingers. However, despite the world's edges being soft, it is not enough to choke and blind.

I shift the weight of the sack and reposition the load so it nestles in the small of my back with hands that are still stiff and sore. Exhaustion is trying to claim me, but I will soon be done, and the sleep afterwards will be deep, dreamless and cleansing. For one night, just one, I may see colours other than the red, which usually floods my thoughts.

I had surfaced by Whitehall and then crossed the river. I am nearly there. It doesn't really matter if I am observed; no one cares about another figure with a sack on the streets of Battersea at this time of night. Even if they do the assumption will be someone up to no good, and that suits me. People who don't ask questions don't get an answer they don't want. If accosted, I could brazen it out, but not if they looked in the sack. Even I would be hard-pressed to explain that.

My heavy steps have taken me steadily to within sight of the wharf. The last stragglers of this night have dissipated and vanished. It is now too late for the activities of darkness and too early for those of dawn. The city is suspended between worlds for this short time, like the moment before a deep breath. Perhaps the breath before a scream. The omnibus ceases at midnight, but the poor and the able walk. She is a city of cobbled pavements and shoe leather, and the quiet of this turning time between night and day feels thick and unnatural in the air.

Wisps hang over the grey water, and the peaks and troughs of little waves belie the force of the pulsing current, which snatches and claws just below the surface. The tide is high tonight and is heading back towards Woolwich, flowing out to meet the open sky at the coast. It will draw the sack away from here and maybe put it to sea. Perhaps it will dissolve into nothing. Maybe it will be found. Either option has its charm and thrill.

I imagine for a moment that the contents of the sack move, just a little, against my back, and a shiver of excitement arcs down my spine, crackling like electricity. I pull a deep breath down into my lungs and let it fill me with a moment of rare peace. Like her, I am suspended between worlds before I finally swing the bag in a wide arc and let go.

The sack hits the water, the sound amplified by night, bouncing off the structures jutting into the now blackness. But it is too late; others are making so much more 'noise' than me. Nevertheless, I have left a small gift in the building rubble at the new Bow Street Police Headquarters as a small mark of my... respect.

The sack bobs, riding and falling, greasy with oily water. It rolls and journeys away, away from me and my city.

For a moment, I am happy.

Chapter One – October 1888

I t was a favourite moment, standing outside the front and absorbing it all. Fanny closed her eyes against the morning bustle around her and drew in a deep breath of cold air. It was always good to be standing on familiar ground, the rolling landscape of London.

New bridges had spanned the river since her absence, and urban sprawl reached out, grasping across what had once been green fields. She thought of the tendrils reaching out to Hammersmith in the west and the invisible one which tied her to her family and her tiny daughter. Pausing, she felt an unexpected tug in her core.

The Gaiety Theatre sat east of Trafalgar Square and Charing Cross, running parallel to the Embankment in the smoky heart of the Theatre District. Behind her, she could feel the chill wind as it rode the Thames to Kew and broke around Waterloo Bridge. Even in her absence from London, Fanny could barely recognise the square mile of Theatreland, which had continued to emerge from the network of rookeries and small alleyways that clustered around it. The monumental Somerset House had been fettered by the new Victoria Embankment and pushed back from the muddy waters that used to lap against its skirts. But behind the clean curves and etched lines squatted the raw city, and even now, Fanny saw the subtle darkening of the white stone as a cloak of grime was starting to claim her as one of its own.

§

Fanny had taken a cab to the theatre, the black leather seats polished against the fabric of passengers being ferried to destinations across the city. She had taken the most direct route, knowing that should tonight be a success, the journey would need to be set in stone to preserve whatever conjunction of circumstance or luck had made that success a reality. It would become one of the rituals which would maintain that fragile bubble of success for the run of the show, and to deviate might spell disaster. Stan had offered to come with her from home, but Fanny had gracefully declined. He would not be able to accompany her for every journey, even though she knew it was his fierce need to protect her against murders in the dark. The Gaiety Theatre was only six miles away from Whitechapel, and even from here, she felt the looming presence of the horror playing out in the east.

Fanny had peered out of the foggy window of the cab as the horse jinked her towards the theatre, hooves clattering on stone and metalwork, jumping and sounding with each movement. Usually, she found the rocking soothing, and this brief time inside the cocoon of the leather and the lingering smell of tobacco was her moment to reflect and prepare before the chaos of the performance. But Fanny found the motion sent her mind wandering towards the outside world, and she wiped away at the condensation on the window, causing water droplets to bead and run down the frame. She had looked out at the streets crowded with bodies bouncing between unknown destinations and those who paused to look in wondrous and new smooth plate glass windows that revealed vast displays of goods. The distraction of seconds was all that a small, birdlike hand needed to pick a pocket and for feet to carry the bounty away into the rat runs of alleys and side streets behind the bewitching facade. A flash of movement drew her eye to an alley dwarfed between two soot-coated buildings. An agitated man was being pulled by the hand into one such dark place by a woman nodding encouragement. Fanny caught a glimpse of the woman's lined face as she passed and saw the hollow cheeks and dead eyes of the part-time prostitute, the Dollymops her father had called them, or Ladybirds, women who had only one thing left between them and starvation.

Fanny felt lucky she had enough to rent a house and create a comfortable home. Stan had scolded her that she could afford something larger, with more staff, instead of Mary, the nanny, maid and cook. But something deep down stopped her, and it was the fear of that same bubble that could burst at any moment. Fanny knew well the uncertainty of her life, and while she would be happy to spend £100 on new music, which was an investment in the future and added to her safety net, she knew the bubble could be burst at any time and by anyone. Fanny had felt the bite of poverty, and even the thought caused her stomach to lurch with the memory of the cavern of emptiness that went beyond the rumble of a missed meal. She blanched at the hollow memory and shook her head to drive it away.

Those who could afford to had taken advantage of improved transport and moved to the less compressed suburbs, leaving the city centre to businesses. The wave of those poor left behind was slowly being pushed east, along with the pervading wind carrying the pollution of industry. In the east, where the poor huddle into crowded streets, the Dollymops were being hunted by a man they were calling Leather

Apron. Fanny shuddered. The press had been comprehensive and lurid in their descriptions and had drawn images of 'horrible' murder and mutilation. Fanny found it hard to push from her mind the feeling of nausea and the thin feeling of rolling fear. She wondered just how desperate you had to be to carry on walking the streets, knowing there would always be the potential for a flash of a knife in the dark.

The city continued to lure people into her folds, those from the country and those seeking safe haven, work and perhaps anonymity. Even in her short time back, she could see the different faces and languages of those who had broken upon foggy shores. Pockets of Irish, Welsh, Chinese and Yiddish-speaking communities were settling in the city alongside those with ancestral roots torn out by traders in people who abandoned them, penniless, under strange skies, all adding their culture to the ever-growing blend of people. The voices bled into the carriage, and she felt the wave of the familiar and new washing over her in a rolling tide.

As the winter light had started to fade into early night, Fanny saw them in the open space of Trafalgar Square, the lost people. Unlike those walking with purpose, in the corners were the creeping figures of the destitute, those even without money for a temporary roof. They were not difficult to miss for those who looked. The hunched and shabby figures of people who had slid under the grinding wheels of the city but still gravitated to its centre and would hide in the corners of Trafalgar Square or the embankment out of the worst of the cold and rain. This was their last vestige of fiercely held independence before the place of last resort, the Poor House, with its grim regiment of shame and control. Fanny felt her gloved hand touching the window grow cold as the temperature from outside leeched through, seeking warm flesh to draw upon. Tonight would be bitter, and some of those people, whose lives had spiralled beyond their control, would never wake and be discovered pale and still in the first light of the morning. There were stories of actors who lost their jobs, homes, and all means to survive and found themselves here as each domino fell, within reach of the places that once knew their names but were now a lifetime away. They were ignored but not unseen. The fortunate, huddled in carriages and crushed on the wobbling omnibuses, knew the road to the street was short and brutal. While society fooled itself into believing this was the wages of sin, and benefit Variety Shows to raise money for actors in poverty were often held, the reality was a mixture of luck and fate. It was a city of constant motion, and to stop was to fall beneath and be lost.

§

Fanny opened her eyes and returned to the moment. The carriage had come to a stop outside of the theatre, and opening the unresisting door, she carefully stepped down onto the pavement. Here she was, The Gaiety Theatre on the Strand, an old friend; in that time, they had both changed beyond recognition. The initially inauspicious frontage of the theatre, as it drew in the audience through two sides of the sumptuous restaurant, had evolved from the original Music Hall and was split into two distinct faces, huddled together, one in light and one in dark brick. Each window was generously covered in bright striped blinds, which could be rolled out in awnings, reaching out to the observer and giving an impression of the Mediterranean. The main door rose on columns like a temple arch, adding drama to the frontage and drawing in passers-by to the colourful billboards promising wonders inside. She tipped her gaze upwards to the three circular plaques of faces black with pollution and indistinguishable from each other. She had always imagined one would be Shakespeare. The Gaiety was climbing towards legitimacy from commercial burlesque, and to do so, it would borrow what it could to narrow the gulf. Efforts had been made to draw the language of the two disparate buildings together with a flower motif on the door of the darker building, which was repeated above the windows of the lighter. Cleverly hidden amongst the decoration, a novel ventilation system drew fresh air into the building from the outside, flushing out the constant pawl of tobacco which would rise into clouds above the vast auditorium, slowly descending towards the audience and curling in a hot choking vapour around them. The clearer atmosphere allowed the new arc lighting to flush the place with colour and vibrancy, bringing the stage into sharp focus. The overall impression was of an inviting place of pleasure, romance, allure and comfort. It was a magnet of enchantment; for this reason, it was known to many as The House of Light and Air.

She stepped lightly across the crowded pavement and picked past the mass of bodies, wrapped up warm against the biting cold. Snow had only just departed, and the pavement was covered in a brown and grey slurry that splashed and turned to water underfoot. Pulling up her skirts in an attempt to preserve the hem, she noticed a small woman wrinkle her perfectly pink kitten-like nose at a brief view of white-clad knees and petticoats. Fanny smiled as she saw the poster for the show "Faust Up to Date" adorning the front of the theatre. Below the lettering of the title which dripped with letters of blood hung the artist's rendition of the dapper demon Mephistopheles. The demon hung like a spider from a scarlet parachute against the background of the fires of a volcano and hellscape. Below was a detailed cast list and playing Young Faust, was her, Fanny Robina. After tonight's opening night, the kitten-faced woman would ask for her autograph.

A reference to Spring Heeled Jack, the legendary menace and now folk hero, framed in the door. "Faust Up To Date" covered the top of the poster in a banner heading dripping in blood, followed by the cast list, detailing the brightest lights of satirical burlesque in London,

Fanny was returning to the Gaiety as a star. Not so subtly, the production alluded to the current fear gripping the city and the person everyone called 'Leather Apron'. But some started calling him Jack after the folk character 'Spring Heeled Jack'. Whatever 'he' was, the London Theatres were not above taking current affairs and riding the very edge of the present tide. Mr. Mansfield's particularly grizzly version of "Jekyll and Hyde", recently playing at the Lyceum, had scandalised and intrigued audiences drawn to horror. Perhaps later, the more ghoulish audience member may take a murder tour of Whitechapel, even seeing carefully stage-managed puddles of pig blood. Fascination sold tickets, and it kept money flowing. As distasteful as it might be, the women were dead, and to lose employment could lead very quickly to huddling in a dark corner of Trafalgar Square. Some deaths, one cut at a time, could be worse than a quick knife to the throat. She had known more than one who curled up in a frozen corner and slipped away with the dawn.

But Fanny knew her place. She headed round the side of the block to Wellington Street and to the stage door, where the decoration ran out, and the functional part of the theatre life began. Front doors were traditionally for guests and bailiffs, staff and actors used the back door. She'd seen countless stages and halls, and they were all the same; she could always navigate them blindfolded. They were always the same, just in a different shape.

Chapter Two

*T*he voices are always tangling and echoing around my head. I have tried everything to silence them for a lifetime, but they always roll and build, prying into every corner of my mind, and I feel the chill jolt of falling into darkness.

Each time the voices become louder and I tear at my hair, scratch broken fingernails down my temples until the blood oozes and the torn flesh stings like the cuts of thousands of silver daggers. It is the building of pressure which threatens to break me apart and I want to tear off my skin and step out, bloody and exposed.

And in that moment when I am finally engulfed by the crescendo of cries, I hear her.

Chapter Three

F anny placed her square, capable hand on the chipped wooden stage door and pushed. It was rough, and flakes dropped off in response to the pressure. The sound of paper drew her attention to her left as she stepped past the coffin-sized booth of the Doorman. Part bouncer, part concierge, and mostly moustache, Albert Lightly peered above his habitual newspaper.

"Miss Robina fine day." Said Albert, lips moving invisibly below the immaculate mustache. On the counter was a sharp whittling knife and a small off-cut of wood. The piece seemed too small to work with, but she could see a smooth line already emerging from the rough surface. Albert's attention was focused on the object, and in each pause before making another cut, he pursed his mouth, a movement which seemed further punctuated by the facial hair.

It was a magnificent, carefully waxed moustache that rose slightly at the edges into a curl and always appeared to enter the room before its caretaker. It was surrounded by a wiry man in old-fashioned but functional and immaculately mended clothes. His accent betrayed the straw and hayseed of someone with origins outside of London, drawn by the prospect of something other than farming. A clay pipe sometimes protruded from his moustache, alight with aromatic tobacco, causing the doorway to sometimes appear like a demonic inferno. Albert was a veteran of the army, the boxing pits and other illegal street brawling. He was often underestimated, and only his large hands, that he cracked absentmindedly when not clutching a paper or whittling offcuts of wood, hinted at someone well suited to keeping reason and calm at the door of such a noble emporium of entertainment. Fanny had never seen him in action, but she suspected it would be economical. He wasted nothing, not even air.

"Fine indeed." She didn't ask if there was anything for her. Had there been, Albert would have employed more words than his usual few at greeting.

Fanny paused before heading up the stairs. "Albert?"

"Yes." He looked up, watery blue eyes meeting hers.

"Could you order me a cab for midnight, please?"

Albert nodded in affirmation.

"Tosher is walking the ladies staying at Mrs. Love's boarding house back home, and Mr. Free is insisting all ladies have a male escort home."

"Oh, no. Just a cab, please."

Albert regarded her for a moment and then nodded again.

Fanny's feet slapped up the stairs to the first floor and the single dressing rooms. Allocation of rooms always ran on a system dominated by a theatrical hierarchy; the higher up the bill, the nearer the stage. The result was a plush room given to those who spent the majority of their time on stage, and those of the chorus with multiple scenes and costume changes would be clattering up and down to cramped quarters somewhere near the attic or be forced to strip down to change in the wings if the change was too fast. In another life, she recalled peeking into this dressing room doorway to the chaotic court of Nellie Farren, undisputed Queen of the Gaiety. Wafts of scented powder would always fill the heavily pollinated floral air. The day she had walked in here a week ago, it had been eerie, as if she was trespassing on hallowed ground. The room had been empty, but the echoes of Nellie Farren remained imbued into the heavily wallpapered walls.

Fanny pushed open the door, and a figure in the black and white of a maid jumped in shock. "Oh lord, Miss Robina, you fair scared the life from me."

"Sorry, Mercy. I wasn't thinking."

"No," came the reply, and Fanny was unsure if she had heard a slight trace of curtness.

Mercy wiped her hands on her crisp apron and bumped an open drawer closed with her hip as she walked to Fanny with her hands outstretched. "Can I take your hat and coat Miss?" she asked, smiling keenly and with no trace of anything other than a genuine request to assist.

Fanny nodded, and Mercy helped her remove her feathered hat and blew dust from the colourful feathers, carefully placing it on a side table. She reached back for the coat, and Fanny handed it to her before taking a seat at the dressing table and removing her gloves.

"Miss, I've been asked if I can help with Miss StJohn tonight as well, as her maid is poorly. I hope you don't mind, but I have laid out everything for you, and I can come back and help you dress just before the first call."

Fanny nodded. "I'm very able to manage myself, Mercy."

Mercy curtsied. "Thank you Miss. I know Miss StJohn will be grateful."

As Mercy left the room, Fanny snorted. Grateful? Unlikely. It was more likely that Mr. Free was attempting to keep Miss StJohn from exploding and sending emotional shrapnel through the cast on the opening night. The last rehearsal had not gone well, and the opening night had been delayed by four days with Miss StJohn wound tightly enough to snap. Fanny was unlikely to see Mercy, and after years of managing for herself, she didn't feel it was a hardship.

It was opening night, and Fanny had to focus. She wasn't on stage for the first ten minutes, her role being the magically young manifestation of Faust after his deal with the demon Mephistopheles. Old Faust and the demon would spend a whole song designing his younger self, at which point Fanny would appear as if by magic. It would go unmentioned that one of the significant changes was Faust becoming young and somewhat female.

Fanny's dressing room, habitually devoid of personal items, had an exception on this occasion: a small article cut out from a newspaper attached to the gilt frame of the mirror. It was her one deviation from her usual ritual of a space devoted only to the current show's costumes, map and props. The clipping was part of the press for the show, and Mr. Edwardes, owner of the Gaiety and impresario, had started releasing information to the press a month before opening, increasing the advertisements and tidbits of information in a steady stream, using exclusivity and whispers of confidence to create enthusiasm. This article had amused Fanny greatly when Stan had shown her at home, and she had made the exception to keep it to remind her.

"A sacred lamp in a temple of Burlesque?" Stan had read, his shoulders shaking with laughter. He had scanned on and finally broken out into a guffaw. "Has anyone told Miss StJohn she is a Chief Priestess?"

"My darling, I suspect Florence StJohn thinks she's God", Fanny had responded, waggling her nose at her daughter, who giggled appreciatively and raised small pudgy hands to Fanny's cheeks.

"Yes, dear. I recall her affinity with worship from others, but it appears her style verges on the 'piquant' and 'charming'." Stan also wrinkled his nose at his daughter, who reached out her arms to her father and made urgent noises to be released by her mother.

"Proof positive the author has yet to meet her." He said, lifting his newly released daughter into practiced arms with a grunt of surprise at the weight. "My darling, we need to stop feeding this child rocks."

"Of course darling, I will ask Mary and cook to stick to gravel." Said Fanny, absently picking up the paper. An arched eyebrow raised. "You failed to mention I was one of the two 'leading virgins bearing her company."

"Yes, beloved, but we had established already the author is an idiot."

As the sound of excited steps clattered along the corridor Fanny found herself drawn back into the present, smiled and slid the clipping back into the frame around her mirror. She took a brief look at her face, her canvas, noting the small lines starting to creep in around her eyes. The familiar flutter of nerves ran along the bottom of her ribcage as she pushed her hair away from her face and started to apply cold cream to remove the day. Opening night, this was it and she could feel the air starting to spark with the electricity of show.

Chapter Four

I *try to forget, but at night, it comes unbidden, and I am dragged back. I am looking down, and my feet are small and square, the soft, fleshy feet of a child. There are what feels like endless gaps and crevices in the cold, splintered floor, and I can feel the biting daggers of cold air across the bare limbs which poke out from beneath the frayed hem of my stained nightshirt.*

I feel numb inside and out as my eyes are focused completely upon the black tower of shadow before me as the unfamiliar shape twists and lurches. It rises in shouts which tangle into the harmony of two voices competing to be heard before they lose all articulation, becoming screams which fill the room.

Two had become one image of flickering terror, noise, a single twisting mass. I can see one limb detach from the mass and kick over a chair, which skitters across the floor to a halt before landing on its side. I feel terror, so thick it feels like I can reach out and dip my finger into it.

A flash of light from the dwindling fire caught the edge of a long knife, and then the world erupts in red, and the screaming stops.

Chapter Five

It sounded awful, but it always did from under the stage, where it distorted and competed with other noises. The theatre was designed to channel the natural voices of the actors over the orchestra and out into the audience. Underneath, Fanny was subject to the crashing of feet and sotto voce comments of the stage crew as they signaled instructions and hauled heavy hemp ropes, which moved pieces of the stage in swift and magical speed. The singing and music covered the masked swearing and cursing, so hand signals and gestures evolved into a language of necessity.

"You stupid bugger!" hissed a voice as a young stagehand failed to move an errant foot and squealed as a pulley thumped into the plank floor. The free-falling rope was caught and ceased its uncontrolled descent into the darkness with the ease of a master, and callused hands pushed the boy into a pile of sacks. "Just sit there and watch me."

§

The crew almost outnumbered the cast. Behind the bright lights, above, beside and below the stage was a disciplined army of dressers, seamstresses and crew who swarmed around the action on stage above, to the side, behind and below. Most hummed happily along to songs and periodically grimaced when a line had been missed or a word incorrectly delivered. They watched and missed nothing from the dark.

Fanny smiled. She liked to get to her entrance point early to listen to the show and get a sense of the audience. In this case, it was in the traps under the stage. Down here in the heat and darkness, it was a four-story labyrinth of wooden spars and frames, holding together layers of ropes and pulleys which sat under the stage. It was like standing in a giant loom at night and just as unpredictable and dangerous. One wrong foot and the fall would end abruptly, far below the surface on a mixture of packed earth, rubble and in the domain of the rats.

The mechanism to push actors from the dark below the stage and into the light lay below the trap door which was cut into the stage floor. It would open seconds before, and they would be thrust upwards into the action above. Two iron safety pins kept the platform in place so it didn't move when needed but could be rolled away when not, giving the crew more room to move. Fanny glanced to check before she mounted the platform. Failure to put in the pins, a last-minute shift, forgetting to open the trap, or a mistimed push of a lever could result in her impact on the trap door above or falling down into oblivion.

"Faust Up To Date" was a bespoke theatrical extravaganza, and no expense or innovation had been spared, from Mephistopheles' entrance from the fly tower hanging below a scarlet parachute to the hot air balloon spiriting the lovers away at the end. The complexities had meant the opening had been delayed from the Friday to the Tuesday, and nerves were taut. Press had reported mechanical delays, some had reported Miss StJohn being poorly, and others had put the delays squarely on the millinery department. However, management strongly hinted at each reason as part of the drive for perfection, and this kind of publicity only built expectations to more dizzying heights. Indeed, the house could have been filled twice more tonight. The queues were vast and drew more excitement and attention.

Every night was different, but the opening night was the one where nerves twanged with tension, tempers flared, and at the end, relief made pieces of her soar above the applause. Appreciation wasn't always guaranteed; Fanny had experienced her share of failures, but once on stage, she read the audience like a trainer reading a wild animal. She was never out of danger, and the inconsiderate move of a fool could result in the delicate balance being broken, but once she held them in her hand, she could make them sing. She pushed her eye to the hairline gap between the trap and the stage floor. Above the stage, she saw the tangle of ropes and set pieces ready to descend to transport the audience to another place for each scene. Hidden amongst it all would be Mephistopheles himself, waiting for his cue.

§

Directly above Fanny, Mephistopheles, or Teddy Lonnen, looked down from the heights of the fly tower and gulped. It really was high up here. Below was the swirling spectacle of a chorus of dancers in what was supposed to be an Italian Exhibition in Nuremberg. The real great exhibition at The Crystal Palace had been more than forty years ago, but it had lodged in the public consciousness as the wonder of the age. Nuremberg thought Teddy, the reason for that was less clear to him, but it was a job to do and not his job to ask. He knew he was good. He wouldn't be descending onto a London stage while hanging from the bottom of a parachute if he wasn't. His stomach made a lurch, but it was excitement. He lived for this moment of exhilaration and it was something that had not been done before. *Here is immortality'*, he thought, *'particularly if I fall off this damn thing and leave a bloody great hole on the stage.'*

Peering down between his pointed shoes and the dark planks of wood beneath his feet, he saw the bob and sway of the cast 'boys and girls', most of whom, irrespective of gender portrayed, were girls. Burlesque had changed the landscape of the theatre, and where there had been casts of young men with few women, the pendulum of time had swung the other way, and they were now being largely replaced by women, men being relegated to older character roles. Teddy felt grateful that he had the expressive face of a character actor. It meant the world of opportunity was more extensive, and his career would be longer. However, the clock was already ticking for many of the young ladies below.

They were working hard, arms raised and feet thumping down on the wooden stage. He looked around at the crew as they watched; the lights reflected in their eyes.

"Oh, their nimble fingers certainly must be sore,
With thumbing so,
And strumming so,
All the live long day.
Eh, you mandolinists, timidly we implore,
Cease thumbing so,
And strumming so,
Those guitars you play."

Bright faces were all turned to the audience as the chorus sang, and the dance commenced with arms and legs flung out in what appeared gay abandon but had been hours of late-night screaming matches and aching feet. Spontaneity took a lot of effort and many, many rehearsals.

Teddy knew that after the opening number, there was the romantic hero, Valentine's scene with the girls, and then Old Faust and his side-kick Seibel before he would need to drop down onto the stage. Once Teddy had done his demonic deal with the old man, the new, younger version, played by Fanny Robina, would rise from the traps as the old Faust, Harry Parker, would vanish off to his dressing room for a pint until the end. It was a nice part, thought Teddy, playing a character who was in the show's title, doing a scene at the beginning and not coming back to the end. But he, Teddy, played the demon Mephistopheles on the posters covering the front of the theatre, the master of mayhem and, for some reason, using a parachute and arriving from above.

As old Faust launched into his monologue, crying, "Oh, the pretty souls!" Teddy shuffled forward onto the small standing board that jutted out from the gantry into empty air, holding the parachute handles firmly. The harness around his chest was too tight, taking up his weight and being firmly held by two crew members, their faces grim with concentration. But he was grateful for it, and as he heard his cue, "I'd give my soul to be a youth again", he stepped off into the void.

§

"Get off my damn foot!" hissed Alice, yanking her boot out from under the considerably larger boot of George. He, playing Valentine, and his Soldier companions were now mumming upstage and in the background of the current action. The stage directions had been to continue ribald drinking and talking at a low enough volume to ensure both actors playing Old Faust and his slimy and equally decrepit companion Siebel were audible. At the same time, they unsuccessfully flirted with a pretty barmaid played by young Mabel. With one ear open to remember to laugh on queue at the action, they had time to recover their breath and take a look at the audience.

George had thrown himself down on a chair, which had made an alarming creak as he leant back, legs wide and hand resting on his thigh.

As he had done so, he had placed a foot directly on that of Alice, who had gone pale and tried to keep smiling.

"Bloody hell, it's heaving out there." Hissed Emma, throwing a smile at her soldier colleagues and clinking glasses with Alice, who was rubbing her foot against the back of her other shin to massage some life back into it.

"They seem to be laughing in all the right places, thank god." Alice smiled back, slapping George on the back with a seeming bonhomie and taking a little pleasure in the wince of shock on his face as her hand impacted between his thick shoulders.

"Steady on," he muttered and went to punch her arm in retaliation, but Alice dodged and broke out in a genuine laugh, which earned a small glance of annoyance from Jenny, who was currently at the front of the stage playing Seibel with Harry as Old Faust.

"Oops." She looked down, knowing Jenny would be very unhappy come the interval and make it abundantly known to all that she had been 'upstaged'. Drawing attention was a cardinal sin and was actively frowned upon in the strict hierarchy of billing. A pre-emptive and profuse apology to Jenny at the interval would smooth this one over, but had she done that to Miss StJohn or one of the other stars of the show, she would have been in real trouble with management.

As Faust muttered the immortal lines, "I'd give my soul to be a youth again", Teddy made his demonic entrance as Mephistopheles. Alice found herself holding her breath as he descended onto the stage. His cape flapped around him, and his legs dangled like a spider in a cloud of red smoke. The singular gasp which erupted from the audience was like a gust of wind as the parachute seemed to float down to the stage, and as he landed, he said, "That's right! I'm down; the blessed thing ain't bust!" and wiped his forehead in mock relief. The roar of applause temporarily stopped the show as Teddy raffishly winked at the shared joke and took a florid bow. Now that, thought Alice, was a showstopper.

"Show off," muttered George, raising his tankard to his lips. From the smell of it, he had managed to fill it with beer again, and Alice wrinkled her nose in distaste. She caught the eyes of Emma, who nodded back at Alice, clearly realising they would need to steer him carefully towards the final curtain and intercept any stashes he may have hidden around. Opening night, thought Alice, and we've already had to postpone. Could he not have waited?

Mephistopheles was a joy to watch, and Alice had to remind herself to stop staring. The lights across the back of the stage had dimmed, and Old Faust and Mephistopheles were in a pool of yellow light downstage right. To her, this meant her right as she looked at the audience; to the audience, it was the front left. It was another excellent example of the topsy-turvy world of the theatre and the language of the stage, where downstage meant the front of the stage, upstage meant the back, right was left and left was right. The tower above the stage was the Fly Tower, or Fly for short, and the space under their feet was the Traps. Some of the names and reasons were lost to history, but after a while, it became as familiar as breathing, and she no longer had to remember to translate in her head. Alice watched the scene and felt her mind dance along the rhythm of the familiar lines, hearing the odd missed word and changed phrase like the wrong note in a familiar melody. She and the rest of the cast would eventually improvise and play around with it as the show started to become more familiar. It kept things fresh and maintained that tingle of excitement and play, removing the risk of things becoming stale. Eventually, they would throw volleys at each other, and the trick was not only to respond but to improve and outdo before sending it back. To have a moment on stage where dialogue was hit back and forth was a moment of magic and communication on a level far deeper than verbal. Then, you saw something truly special, and the audience was swept along with the tide, lost in the flood of marvels.

Alice relaxed. One more song from Marguerite, the leading lady, a little business with the new young Faust, and she would have around two pages before she had to be back on stage. Alice took a deep breath. Damn stairs.

§

Below the stage, Fanny heard the entrance of Marguerite, played by Florence StJohn. In her mind's eye, she could see a figure in white walking onto the stage, seeming to ephemerally glow in the lights. And she heard—no—she felt the surge of a loud cheer, a deeper roar and then thunder of feet pounding on the floor in exhilaration. The applause continued, and Fanny knew Florence would stop and smile, pausing in a winsome position of arms clasped together across her heart and a leg pointed out behind her in a semi-balletic pose. Florence would wait until she judged the peak and signal to the conductor to start. The trick was never to let the applause run out, and stopping at the peak gave the impression that it would have continued indefinitely.

§

Alice sighed as Florence started to sing to the strains of "I'm a Simple Little Maid." It filled the auditorium with liquid noise and floated across the audience.

"I can hear the whalebone creaking from here." Emma muttered a little too loudly, and George snorted into his mug, sending froth up his nose and causing him to cough, which he turned into an appreciative cheer as she continued to sing.

"I never go to balls
Or to the music halls..."

There were titters in the audience as Faust and Mephistopheles, acting as her chorus, repeated the refrain.

"How old do you think she really is?" whispered George. "I have a bet on thirty-two and a half."

"A half?" said Alice.

"Gives me the numbers on either side if no one else takes them."

"Oh," said Alice. "How are you going to find out?"

"Mercy. That girl can find out anything. I'm feeling lucky."

"I'm in," whispered Emma. "Judging by the thickness of that makeup, I reckon about thirty-five

"Blimey," said Alice, looking at the pale shoulders as Florence raised her arms to receive the thunderous applause.

§

Fanny moved to a crouch on the trap platform. The build-up to Old Faust's deal with Mephistopheles was now in progress as the forgetful old man, played convincingly but somewhat larger than life by Harry Parker, offered his soul for youth. Harry was a fine comedy actor, adept and belying his youth with thick powder, dark overpainted brows and perfect curls, which he would arrange in a mix of lard, zinc and ochre along his brow. He had a dimple on his chin, which he accentuated with shadow and a nose made bulbous with the application of wax and more powder. He refused to buy the new greasepaint, and in the slightly more forgiving light of the Gaiety, his face had sufficient shadow to hold the depth of wrinkle needed to play a doddering old man. But his physicality was incredible. His back hunched, his hands clawed, and his body shook with a palsy, which he used with a stuttering speech to create the illusion of extreme old age. Harry's caricature was designed to make the transformation to Fanny's young Faust, gender aside, even more startling. He would soon leave the stage, holding court in a shirt and braces in his dressing room until his final appearance at the end.

Fanny's cue dropped into her subconscious and rang a bell. This was the moment, and the deal was struck. The old man and demon had designed the perfect man, Fanny. She squared herself on the trap door to maintain her balance. Arriving in a pile of tangled limbs would be career death, and she made sure the stagehands at least liked her. She winked at Tosher, who was standing by at the trap mechanism, and struck a pose of amazement as a cloud of white smoke enveloped her. Old Faust swiftly departed as the cloud covered the stage, and she rose at speed into the blinding light.

Chapter Six

O nce the dream has me, I am bound to it until the end. In the beginning, I fought it, trying to bury the recollection, but now it is different.

I still remember the blood filling my open mouth, and the sensation as it drenches me, causing my nightgown to cling uncomfortably to the silhouette of my body. It tastes of metal, both wet and dry, flowing and sticky as it pours down my nightgown and throat, driving out the air from my lungs.

But underneath it all, the beast is there with its long-banked fury that also chokes me. A thin vibration, which had always been the background rhythm to my childhood, was somehow familiar and always swimming in the air. This old and tangible presence starts to mirror the beat of my pulse and amplify it, pouring off the figure which now crouches over the other. I can almost see it as it rolls across the soaking floor in a broiling wave, and it rides on the blood that covers everything, moving inexorably towards me.

The fury soaks into my skin, infecting me and grows in intensity, driving mingled blood around my body like a drumbeat; it pours in and out of the places where the demon had pierced my scarred skin. Old wounds break open anew and causing sharp stabbing pains, mortifying my flesh.

I look down at my arms, small and thin with hunger and under the red, I see the familiar bruises that have always moved and slithered around under the surface of my pale skin. The bruises are the almanac of the moods of another, rising to chronicle yet another impact and injury, changing colour like leaves as they continually fade, only to be replaced by the new impact of a fist. But blood, this was different; it had risen from the woman who had been my mother, and I had been christened in it. Now, I was confirmed. It was inside me, rising like a leviathan from the deep.

I was reborn in crimson, and now I crave that feeling like an addiction.

Chapter Seven

A t the interval, Fanny repaired her makeup and re-set her hair under her pillbox hat. The lamps' heat always fought against powder, fabric and voice, but she was used to it by now. The new floor lighting had finally solved the problem of the thick curtain of hot gas from the old front lamps, and a walk down to the front no longer meant minor scorching. Being a boy, or Mashing, had the advantage of fewer layers and less restricted movement.

A louche figure appeared round the door of her dressing room. With the tight red body suit of the devil Mephistopheles bagging at the crotch and armpits, Teddy slid onto the lumpy chaise lounge, pulling aside the edge of a cape that had trapped his arm. He removed his hat and pulled at the side of his hood to let in the air.

"Bloody hell, it's hot out there. Have they lit every lamp in London? I thought we were supposed to be less likely to be catching fire under this 'spectacular' new illumination."

Fanny raised her hands, forming a banner in the air in front of her. "Arc Lighting is the wonder of the age," she said, and then she poured out a foggy glass from the tray left by the maid. "Water?" She said doubtfully, offering it to Teddy.

"I do bloody wonder. I thought we were supposed to be getting fresh air in there. I'm cooking. You know Savoy's gone completely electric, and everyone's face looks flat as a wet shit." His lip curled in dismissal at the cloudy offering. "I'll drink that when the fish get out to use a toilet," he said, reaching under the seat until he returned with a brown bottle. "Ah, ha!" he exclaimed with glee, thumbing off the stopper and taking a long drink. Fanny watched in dismay as her post-first night treat vanished.

"So, dear boy," said Teddy with a sigh of satisfaction. "How do you think it's going?" He ran a long finger down the edge of a crimson boot, having a scratch.

"Not bad", said Fanny. "Everyone appears to be on form."

"Can you have a word with that young chorus girl for me, dear boy? Mabel is it? If she gets any further front and centre, there's a risk she will end up in the pit. And fascinating as her hat is, if her pretty head is between me and the audience one more time, I am going to push her in myself."

Fanny sighed. To be noticed was to attract better roles and wealthy patrons. She had never been interested in playing the coy miss and batting her lids at any man who sent flowers. But she understood the hunger to succeed with whatever measure of talent was available.

A roar of laughter came from Harry's dressing room at the end of the corridor.

"He really only has one volume, doesn't he? Do you think they can hear him in Croydon?" mused Teddy.

"He's done his bit, and we don't need him till the end. Stop moaning. Besides, you speak to Mabel. She gazes stars at you." Fanny applied a loaded powder brush to her forehead. "I'm a respectable woman and above all that such things."

"So am I! ..... Well, man......and only above things when I'm hanging from the ceiling. I might wait for Florence. She's very good at spying out and shooting down the competition. Besides, I hate being the villain." he grinned. "I appreciate the irony of the costume." He took another swig from the bottle and sighed. He looked at Fanny as she repaired her lipstick. "You and I could have been Romeo and Juliet, but alas, I think Stan is your Juliet."

"I met him years before you and I met and about two thousand miles away on tour."

Teddy rose and stretched. His saggy red suit dropped slightly, and fibres relaxed further by the heat.

"Ah, the Antipodes. Spiders, snakes and salaciousness. I do admire you for having a go at the Australian theatres, but it must be good to be home. Plus, a little bit of exotica from time away from smelly old England always helps. I did six months on a tour in Newcastle last year, but it just doesn't have that level of glamour." He looked down at the sagging crotch of his red suit. "Do you think Mrs. Freeman and her magical team of seamstresses can do anything about this? I don't want anyone thinking it's empty down there." In the distance was the sound of a bell approaching. "Time to go young man."

Fanny stood and readjusted her waistcoat. "Are you going to re-member my cue this time?"

Teddy pointed at his horns. "Demon." He raised perfectly painted eyebrows and strutted out.

§

Fanny followed the baggy figure out of the dressing room and swam against the tide of bodies exploding in different directions in a chorus of rustling fabric, hurrying to Act 2 starting positions. The small figure of a boy of around eight bobbed past her, dodging between people and random baskets of props, tearing down the corridor towards the prompt side of the stage where Mr. Free always took position. A skinny arm arced a bell as he ran, the noise filling the corridor with sound and each performer with the electricity of the show. Fanny felt her heart give a familiar flutter. It never went away, and as she stepped from the dimmed corridor light to the thick door of the stage, she heard the susurration of the audience taking their seats. It was the moment they ceased to be individuals and started to become a single organism.

The famous Pas De Quarte would happen in the second Act, and as she heard the tap of a baton bringing the orchestra to attention, she felt the audience slow to silence and anticipation.

Fanny pushed her way through the door into the wings on either side of the stage, looking up into the fly tower way above her. Hanging like sheets of washing were backcloths painted with bright scenes. Each setting flanked with a painted scene and side panels, set slightly forward to provide depth. Subtle increases in scale would send the last cloth further into the distance, and the slight rake of the stage, which caused an almost imperceptible tilt of the floor down towards the audience, added to the illusion.

Hanging from this great loom was the parachute that brought Mephistopheles down from the sky and the Hot Air Balloon, which would draw Faust and Marguerite upwards and away at the end. This meant Fanny and Florence would climb into a basket and be hauled by teams of stagehands up into the dark nest of pulleys and ropes while her knuckles blanched white on the handrail and a rictus smile was fixed on her face. She never got used to the lurch of the first movement, the sensation of her stomach being torn away from the ground and the alarming sound of a woven basket under tension. She only ever started breathing again once she had made the perilous step onto the platform at the top to the accompaniment of the final applause of the crowd and made the walk across the walkway to the solid brick of the wall and the metal ladder bolted to it. As she descended each night to ready herself for her bow, she thanked the heavens for a good solid stage. Well, tonight would be the first time in front of an audience.

"Oh damn," she muttered, her stomach lurching in anticipation.

Chapter Eight

*T*he secret of London is not in its streets; it is in the spaces in between and below—the hidden places, places in the dark that have slipped from memory and time.

The new sewers, embankments, and underground trains have bitten into the layers of the city and, like an anthill, exposed and disconnected these ancient spaces. Eventually they have been forgotten again. But anyone who dares venture into the dark can find out the secret, and that is—London exists below as much as it does above, and a determined person can rule it.

Initially, I had roamed around, finding a gap one night in the side of a railway cutting, waiting to be re-covered into a new tunnel. Old cellars and sewers had been opened to the sky during the works, and by dodging the brutal, hard-bitten gangs of navvies, I had slipped in and found myself in a whole new world.

It took around two years and the odd beating when emerging in the wrong places, but by then, I could travel some distance without being seen on the street. Initially, it was my playground, a space to explore, but *eventually, I realised that I had been led here for a purpose. So I cleared pathways between spaces and tunnels, chipping away at loose bricks and marking patchwork paths through the labyrinth.*

But it was only when I finally stumbled in to the vaulted space which had passed far out of memory, that I realised my steps had never been my own and she had guided me here.

Chapter Nine

The chorus room fogged in the cramped and untidy shared space in the lofty heights of the backstage. Identical sets of shoes were strewn on the floor, and chairs laden heavy with petticoats, skirts, and chemises tottered dangerously backwards when one of the women stood up. The weather outside was cold and found its way through every gap and crevice to blow small cold kisses at bare shoulders and necks.

The first night was finished, and Mabel carefully wiped away her makeup. Unlike the other girls, she was careful not to pull at her skin. Her mother had been adamant her appearance would earn her coin. A brief try at wearing her long hair down, brushed to a glossy shine, caused a hiatus as she was forced to pass Mr. Edwardes, the theatre's owner, to get into the wings that enveloped each side of the stage. She had been early for her entrance to build her reputation for keenness, and just before she was due to go on, he had caught her arm and told her to tie it back immediately and put on her bonnet. As she ran at lung-bursting speed up the stairs to the dressing room, Miss

StJohn had passed her, handed her a soft fabric bonnet "You forgot this I think." Mabel's face had gone scarlet with embarrassment and humiliation.

The audience had cheered and applauded, but she had been stuck near the back. Not quite one of the faceless chorus, but not in a place she could stand out. Everything she had tried to make herself different had been spotted and crushed. The frustration she felt and the anxiety of what her mother would say was causing a hard ball of tension beneath her tightly corseted rib cage.

"Allo, sweet lady," said a voice behind her. "Fancy a kiss," and the sound of smacking lips fired little pouting kisses into the air just behind her head.

"Knock it off, Emma," said Mabel, returning to her mirror. It was one of the smallest but surrounded by dried flowers and cards. Most of the cards had arrived in a flurry tonight and were in her mother's handwriting, but people noticed what was delivered to the stage door, and a few fictional admirers might lure some real ones worth having. Her mother, Mrs. Love, was perched on a chair behind her, industriously darning a stocking. It would be Mabel's. Mrs. Love had arrived at the theatre with her daughter and insisted on being with her backstage, always ready with a brush or needle to ensure her daughter would appear perfect. The Loves were an old theatrical family, and Mr. Edwardes tolerated the additional and unpaid presence of Mrs. Love more out of respect for the family name than usefulness.

"That went well," said Alice, wiping a blob of cold cream from her face, causing a shiny trail, which she wiped again with the back of the cloth.

Mrs. Love walked to the dressing table, where Mabel was pinning up her hair. She leaned down to her ear and placed the darned stocking on the cluttered surface. Mabel felt the hiss of her low voice in her ear.

"It's *'she left the town _not_ many years ago'*. Make sure you get it right tomorrow." Mabel nodded mutely, and Mrs. Love took the pin from her hand and started to ram them into her daughter's hair, causing Mabel to wince subtly.

"You were wonderful, dear. The audience loved you." Mrs. Love said to Mabel, loud enough for the room to hear.

Emma caught Alice looking at Mabel's face reflected in her own mirror. It was grim, and Emma understood. Mrs. Love had the force of a storm.

Emma at down and rubbed her foot. "I'm exhausted." She said, trying to rub some life into her stockinged toes.

"Emma, we've got five more changes than you do," a voice said from across the room.

"It's true," said Alice. "No sooner as they're kicking their legs in the air, they have to spend a whole song being a Madame Tussaud's Waxwork. I'd be breathing like a broken bellows and topple over."

"Well, at least I had the right hat on and didn't have a glove sticking out the back of my skirt Lilian Price," Emma said to the voice in the corner.

"Balderdash," came the response, followed by a wave of laughter through the room. The exchange wasn't enough to earn the level of mirth, but it felt like a release of tension.

"Ta-ra-Boom-De-Ay," Emma started to sing. Her voice was rich and strong as she bounced along the nonsense words, punctuating the 'Boom' with a stamp. Alice joined in, and as each woman started to sing, the room filled with whoops and cheers. The song ended in a crescendo of shouts and more cheering, some breaking into a hum as they continued to change back into their street clothes.

"Oooh la." Said Emma, throwing herself into a chair that creaked in protest. "Better get dressed and out, or Leather Apron'll get you..."

She laughed and started to pull her boots. But it was a laugh tinged with something else. The girls didn't need to check; they all felt that sensation of danger in the air.

"Better than being blown up by the Fenians. I hope they've got a sense of humor, or that Irish dance at the close'll be a death sentence," said Alice.

"Precious, they're too busy trying to blow up the police to worry about a girl with a well-turned leg in green." Said Emma, finally pulling off the boot with an 'ooof'. "Besides, we're more likely to end up Mashed by a Johnny on the door. Everyone going to Mariette's for a drink?"

There would normally be an immediate clatter of affirmative responses, but tonight, the denizens of the chorus dressing room paused.

"Mr. Edwardes has said we can't go out without an escort." Said a voice.

"How'd'ya know your escort won't be 'im?" Emma replied.

"Who?" said Alice.

Emma rolled her eyes. "Leather Apron!"

"Oh," said another girl as she paused while wiping off her face. "Suppose it could be anyone. How would you know?"

"Nobody does." Said Emma. "That's the point, or they would have caught him by now."

"How do you know it's a 'him'?" asked Alice.

"I don't think a woman would do that. Would she?" Emma said, and it was clear she was putting some serious thought into the realisation before shaking her head and saying, "Nah."

"Do you think it's the same one that's been leaving those... bits of people around in the river and that? There was even a leg and the rest in Whitehall. It's almost on our doorstep." started Alice, and she stopped as she caught sight of Mabel's mother, Mrs. Love, who was frowning at her. Alice and Emma exchanged glances, and the room suddenly bustled with activity.

Alice winced in recollection; the previous year, pieces of a woman had been found over a period of two months along the Thames from Pimlico, turning up in rough sacks on the foreshore, and now mutilated pieces of corpses were turning up with terrifying frequency in Whitechapel. A rumour was rife there was a madman, or men, stalking the streets with sharp knives, and any man seemed a stranger to be feared.

"We are The Gaiety Gals," said Emma. "We don't walk in fear, and to us, the rules don't apply." She raised a glass of water in a mock salute, her face determined. "We dance on a tightrope between the saint and the sinner, and we are free." Emma placed a hand on Alice's shoulder.

Alice looked around the room at the women and girls around her, some so young as to be only just women. No one met her gaze.

"I hear those women weren't all on the game, said Lily flatly from across the room. "That's what the police want you to think. It could be anyone, Fenian, Pole, madman or the vicar!"

"Stop it," said Alice, cutting the atmosphere dead.

"Is anyone unclothed?" came a voice from outside. It bit into the pal and smiles of recognition broke out around the room.

"Yes!" came the rehearsed cry from the ladies of the chorus.

The door burst open. In it were framed two male figures in dramatic pose.

"Oh damn," said one in disappointment, looking round at the hurriedly clad girls and gales of laughter.

"Miss Estella Spague and I, Miss Fan-Fan Greville, more parochially known as Earnest and Frank..." there was a cheer "...would consider it an honour if you would accompany us to Mariette's as your burly male escorts to join the management. This is for a brief aperitif, and possibly a larger drink, to celebrate our magical opening night for the lucky 'stay at home' Gaiety Troupe. We," he motioned at himself and Earnest, already showing some five o'clock shadow across the exquisitely painted jawline, "will guard you against the disreputable..." He paused. "The *more* disreputable elements."

"And," he said with far less theatrical flair "rumour has it, old man Edwardes, our illustrious leader, plans to put his hand in his pocket for champagne before he departs for America tomorrow, so you'd better get a wiggle on as I hear they're quite shallow and he might hit cloth before you get there."

"Yes," said Earnest in a formal pronouncement, hand clutching his lapel, "We, the 'Stay at Home' Gaiety Troop, unfortunate enough not to be joining the great Miss Nellie Farren, and the usual Gaiety cast as they stupefy America with their sell-out tour, shall do our best to mourn their departure and tonight's spectacular success with alcohol." He waggled his eyebrow and smiled, showing a row of slightly crooked teeth.

Frank waved a large bottle of champagne, and from behind his back, Earnest produced glasses. It had taken minimal persuasion for Frank and Bertie to become chorus members Fan-Fan and Estella, names which they currently used both on and off stage to their colossal amusement. The reference was apparent to those in and around the Strand. Faust Up to Date poked fun at the established and renowned Gunaud's dramatic Opera Faust and, along the way, took many satirical swipes at popular culture. Very little was out of bounds. Including the tale of Thomas Earnest Boulton and Frederick William Park, known homosexuals, or Molly's, of well-heeled semi-noble families who had famously attended the local theatre together as Fanny and Stella. Despite the tolerances associated with wealth, however, their exuberant evenings on the town finally resulted in arrest and trial. While the case remained known to those attending theatre, Frank and Earnest had been written into the show's cast as two larger-than-life chorus girls, appearing in full and respectable female attire next to women in tights and corsets playing men. The comedy was obvious, but the darker legacy after Boulton and Park walked free was up to two years of hard labour if convicted. The world Frank and Earnest faced was less forgiving outside the sphere of theatre, and the swing to what was considered respectability was starting to crush those who failed to fit the mould.

But in the theatre, where the world shimmered between poles and danced on the thickness of a cobweb, like the women dressed as men, Frank and Earnest could cloak themselves in satire and leave the rest unsaid. The beast could turn on them, but their present refuge was in plain sight.

§

In a small nook to the side of the stage, a bowler-hatted man scratched at the curly black hair on the side of his face. A stump of a largely missing index finger moved in phantom motion with its neighbouring digits as they scratched thoughtfully. Around his neck a black, dotted cravat was tied with care around his immaculately barbered neck.

"Boy!... Mouse, here!" he said, using his free hand to thrust a broom at a small, fragile, passing figure who took it unquestioningly and commenced sweeping the empty stage.

He ceased his musing scratch and picked up a discarded sword. The blade was blunted, and the metal chipped. The hilt daubed with gaudy gold looked cheap and useless close-up, but on stage, it was bright and, if not expensive looking, impressive. It had been liberated from the stores and lovingly re-purposed to serve as weaponry for Valentine, but the actor, George, had a habit of waving the sword around to impress the chorus girls and on this, the first night, had knocked a pronounced notch out of it. Probably drunk again, he thought and sighed. It was becoming a problem, and George's last chance was rapidly vanishing. It was a shame, Mr. Free mused; he was so talented, but his love for performing paled against his love for drink and cards. He muttered, running his finger down the edge of the now dangerously compromised weapon. It was likely whatever patches he put on it wouldn't survive many more nights of George.

Around him, the stagehands and people of the dark corners reset sets, manhandled flats of movable scenery back into place for tomorrow, cleaned down the stage and turned off the lights. Early tomorrow, he would be back with Mrs. Freeman to make repairs, hers to costumes and him to the stage and props. While millinery, costumes and sets were designed by known artisans with exceptional reputations, the Freemans would remain as the unknown, those who existed to manage alteration and repair.

In contrast to Mrs. Freeman, who demanded the full title, he was known as Mr. Free, the rest having fallen away years ago in the rush of live theatre where complicated names presented intolerably long pauses to action. Looking down at his hand, he knew the price to be paid for inattention and lack of speed.

Mr. Edwardes, owner, producer, and impresario, and Mr. Harris, Company Manager, demanded a theatre that ran as a coherent organism and not the often chaotic democracy of he who shouted loudest. The Gaiety had a tight schedule with few 'dark' nights when the stage was empty, but what was sent on stage was always rehearsed. A show may look like chaos and a series of divine acts of near misses, but it was timed to the second.

It was a world removed from the Gaiety's first show under Mr. Hollingshead, where the stage remained swarming with workers, carpenters and choking debris on the day of the first night. The curtain had risen to a cast still having alterations to their costumes in the wings. The company Stage Manager at the time, Robert Soutar, had been under significant stress to 'finish building a bloody theatre' in less than two and a half hours before the curtain rose. Mr. Free remembered the chaos but the night's excitement and the wave of relief when Mr. Soutar pressed the button, and the curtain went down. Upon leaving the role to return to acting, Mr. Soutar handed Mr. Free his keys and left hurriedly before they were later given to Mr. Harris. But Mr. and Mrs. Freeman were the heart and soul of the company, taking in apprentices who would be unlikely to receive an opportunity elsewhere. The rich diversity of knowledge, experience and gratitude from the staff had created a tight-knit, unconventional family.

Mr. Free felt the weight of this production in particular. Mr. Edwardes and Mr. Harris were both leaving for America to meet the touring company once the London company had finished opening night. The publicity of a triumphant tour (and it would be reported to be, even if they had performed to single-person audiences) would draw interest from those hoping to catch a glimpse of glamorous performers fresh from America. Mr. Harris had confided that it didn't hinder interest either to have a certain amount of scandal trailing Miss StJohn upon her chaotic and dramatic arrival, fleeing from her marriage. But in the meantime, Mr. Free would be in charge, back and front of the stage. It was a responsibility and an opportunity of which he was adamant he would make a success.

Chapter Ten

*I*t is always under the surface, bubbling away and sometimes rising like an unstoppable leviathan through the earth. But even when it sleeps, it is still there and liable to stir and rise unbidden. Without that flame of energy, I am motionless; I cannot move. It drives me.

Anger is fuel, and time is the road it takes me along. It is my constant companion. Sometimes, I consider it an unwelcome reminder, but it is increasingly a friend. I have no illusions; I know it for what it is, and I know what I am. I will never forget, never forgive, and always hold it like a dog, waiting for an opportunity to unleash it. I remember everything, every scrap of information, every action and reaction, and I keep score. While some may wish for the scales of justice to balance, I am not as short-sighted and naive as them.

I have to succeed, and I don't care about the cost.

Chapter Eleven

Tosher emerged from the traps, wiping callused hands down the sides of his trousers and stared across the dark dressing room doors to where he knew Ida would be working. Over time, through hastily snatched glimpses from hidden corners, he had memorised her to the point a perfect facsimile would dance across his dreams at night. Ida never seemed to realise that as she concentrated, she would bite the lower corner of her lip, causing it to blanch subtly. Her curly hair, which occasionally fell into her view, would be hastily pushed back out of her way with a pin until it was a nest of pins and tangles. On the rare occasions when daylight filtered through the grimy windows into the wardrobe it turned her red hair to flame.

"Penny for 'em."

Tosher turned to see the oval face of Mrs. Freeman as she winked at his rapidly reddening cheeks.

The curtain was down, and the stage being re-set for the next performance the following day. Mrs. Freeman was a short woman of rounded and soft curves that were currently hidden by a pile of petticoats held in her arms.

"For the love of God, ask her out, "She looked down at the pile in her hands. "One night!" she said in exasperation. "One night, and it looks like they've cleaned the stage with them."

Tosher, a big man with hands worn to leather from a career of pulling ropes and operating scenery, unconsciously rubbed his palms down the sides of his trousers and looked in danger of wearing through the cloth as his uncomfortableness threatened to overwhelm him.

Mrs. Freeman leaned forward and Tosher caught the scent of carbolic soap. "Ask. Her. If the sighs and lingering looks coming from her workbench mean anything, she won't turn you down. Had I not cornered Mr. Free by the stage door and told him where he was taking me out to dinner, I think he'd still be shuffling around the wings with a spanner. Sometimes, someone has to break the silence. You can only look for so long, Tosh. You're a good man. Think about it." She paused. "And if you tell anyone what I said about Mr. Free, I'll fill your boots with pins. There's a good boy."

He watched her walking back to the dressing rooms, knowing she and Ida would be at the theatre until the early hours washing and cleaning. He heard a now distant Mrs. Freeman already busily haranguing Mercy, maid to Miss StJohn and Miss Robina, about some unfulfilled duty. He knew she was right. Somehow, he hoped Ida would corner him by the stage door and tell him how life would be from now on. Maybe he would wait and offer to escort Ida home.

Tosher looked down at his oversized hands. Everything about him was immense; he had spent his life accidentally colliding with a world designed for people much smaller than him. As a street child roaming the docks, he had become the bully he resembled in self-defense, and people more readily accepted fists than a man whose soul was out of step with his body.

§

Tosher had a vague recollection of this mother and the day she went to bed and didn't wake up. He remembered a pale woman who gradually faded away until that morning. Tosher could still feel the rising panic and the smell of cold and dampness in the air as he patted her arm and then her face, stretching up to reach and small heels leaving the floor to rise onto cold toes up to the bed. His mother had felt like ice, but she looked asleep still, eyes closed and her face calm and free of the usual lines of worry.

The landlord barked that his mother was dead, and the cart he loaded with her meagre possessions was what he said he was owed. Tosher, alone on a doorstep, the door locked behind him, was told to disappear before the landlord returned with his dog. He never knew where his mother's body had gone, maybe to a communal grave or into the river. On that day, he lost everything. Tosher didn't know his father; now, he would never have the chance to ask.

As the sun arced in the sky overhead, he curled up in a corner between two walls where the wind had less bite and fell into a fitful sleep, full of cold and the aching space where his mother had been. Tosher was numb inside and out, and he had been pulled away from the street by rough hands to be taken to a dark place with high walls and other gaunt children. He had not cried. He never cried. He placed his emotions in a box and buried them deep in his chest.

He was given a name based on where he was found when demands for his own failed to elicit a reaction other than bewilderment. Mark for St Mark's church and Silver for the Silvertown Docks deep in the east docklands.

Mark Silver was never really his name; it simply described a place he had once been. He lasted long enough in the orphanage to learn that charity and kindness did not always travel hand in hand. Tosher never knew how old he was and could only guess. The young child's rounded fleshiness had dropped away as his body had grown.

The lessons had been to instill virtue, industry, and fear of God. Tosher did not understand fear until the morning his mother had gone to hell. The men in black with beards who proclaimed morality and gratitude, as well as the pinch-faced women, had been very clear about that.

When the sickness struck and the boys around him, one by one, started to shiver at night, become stiff, tired and vomited, he heard the word 'typhoid', and the men and women in black began to hurry around and look worried. Tosher had been moved to another room away from the sickness. Still, when he felt the ache, he was moved back to a dormitory of eerie stillness, and time had slowed into the sensation of physical symptoms and the all-consuming pounding in his head. He had been unable to move or breathe through the unrelenting vomiting, which caused aches under his ribs like a vice as he drifted in and out of fire, ice and dreams with no end or beginning.

When he had started to improve, he saw empty beds and eventually heard the names whispered in sorrow. A tired woman clutching a battered black book with gold letters on the spine had told him that god had saved him and he should feel gratitude. He didn't feel any gratitude, only a sense of anger for the fifteen boys who had shivered and vomited to death in a bare room which smelled of bile. When he managed to stand again, he was just tall enough to look into the eyes of the dormitory master, who had informed them that the orphanage would be moving to the clear and healthy air of Watford and away from the disease and filth. Tosher took the opportunity of the chaos of the next few weeks and on a day when the trees were starting to show the buds of new leaves, he had slipped away. He was struck by how easy it was and regretted not doing it earlier. Perhaps it had not occurred to them someone would prefer the streets to rigid charity. He had nothing and knew he should be terrified, but he had felt the brush of the wings of death and survived. The air had been cold and thick on that day, with the lingering smell of the river, and he had taken deep lungfuls, knowing it as freedom.

Tosher was large and slow but still not a fully grown adult, so he could not compete with the stevedores unpacking ships at the wharves or at the markets. He had tried but was pushed aside and kicked with large, worn boots. He'd tried descending into the old sewer to tosh, seeking out dropped coins, jewelry and other valuables amongst the rotting remains of food, sewage and rats. He earned his new name in jest when he became jammed in an old sewer culvert on a stormy night and nearly drowned as the water levels rose against pipes which were overwhelmed. He found himself caught as the water rose towards his mouth and nose, stinking and powerful. Still, he fought his way out, the water rising around him in brown currents of bubbling intensity and dragged his aching body onto the steps by Wapping, coughing up foul water and shaking. Found by other toshers who managed to get him back to the relative safety of a flophouse, he was christened the 'best tosher' in London. He didn't remember the name his mother gave him, but he sometimes thought he remembered her mouth rounding on a name he could never quite hear. Tosher was a name as good as any other, and on the basis that you are what people call you, it stuck. He had never been Mark Silver and left the name down in the sewer with the rats.

Time and muscle rounded Tosher out, and by the time he felt the more prominent wisdom teeth breaking through the back of his gums, he was able to compete with the men who had once thrown him aside at the docks. He was accurate and relentless, slow to anger, and prepared to work for hours with no sign of fatigue. At night, he would use his size to earn extra coin with his fists.

On one of his frequent visits to the illegal fighting pits that floated around empty corners of the city, Albert Lightly had come up against a young mountain of a man with a punch of granite. Still, he had easily won with speed and cunning. Offering a hand to the waking giant he had left temporarily knocked out on the floor, Albert looked at Tosher and said, "What the bloody hell are you doing here lad? Get your coat and follow me."

Tosher had followed in bewilderment and some curiosity. In the last five years, he had never been beaten, and this small, wiry man had looked as if he wasn't even trying. Albert had led him through the dark streets, a stream of smoke pouring from the pipe clamped between his teeth as he rolled down his sleeves and put on his neatly patched coat. Reaching a chipped wooden door, Albert produced a key and opened the lock, walking straight in without looking behind him. Tosher hesitated but followed into the dark; a light had snapped on, and he had recoiled.

"Dark lantern boy. I always leave one going." He clicked a small metal door, and the light vanished before another click, and it appeared again. "Coppers are using 'em. The doors hide the light till you need it in a hurry, and it's safe enough to stop any little accidents. Handy. Keeps the ghosts at bay" he snorted and let out a puff of smoke which circled in the yellow light and drifted upwards.

Tosher felt rather than saw the space in the dark. The sense of something vast and open while still being inside, out of the London fog and rain. Albert had led him out onto the stage behind the curtain, and he had looked up into the unfamiliar shapes and ropes above like the rigging of ships that clawed at the sky along the crowded docks. Tosher had revolved on the spot, his mouth open. He gazed up as Albert's lantern played light and shadow across the void above. He had no sense of where it started and ended, the roost of unfathomable things he had no words to describe.

"Took me like that boy. Look at this!" Albert pressed the button to raise the curtain.

At that moment, Tosher felt his heart fly out into the auditorium and soar up into the gods. He felt elated, humbled and terrified, his face flickering between the rush of emotions both new and overwhelming. A tear had fallen unbidden from his eye for the first time, rolling down a smooth cheek and into the stubble of his patchy beard.

Tosher found his size suddenly became an advantage amongst the forest of ropes and pulleys, and the looks usually of wonder and fear turned to an admiration he had never experienced before. Albert became his colleague, mentor and landlord, and Tosher had found a piece of happiness in the lamplight below the stage.

§

Women had been a different matter, and Tosher felt the familiar sense of uncertainty and fear. He had avoided them as much as possible; even the professionals who would catcall him and ask if 'everything was as big'. Ida Palmer filled him with terror and unfamiliar longing, but he had no idea how or if he should tell her.

Ida was perfect, small with curly red hair and bright blue eyes that seemed to have a star of their own. She had come to the theatre a year ago as a protégé of Mrs. Freeman and quickly showed her talent with the needle and designing costumes that danced with light. Tosher knew Ida had grown up with the circus and had flown on the trapeze. He could imagine her small form sailing on through the air and her nimble hands catching the bar at the last second to send her soaring up into the roof of the tent. An accident had ended her career, and she had left. No one asked for details here. That was the unspoken rule, and what you shared was what you wanted to share, but Ida could not hide the limp of a poorly healed leg and the white line of scar which ran across her temple to a hooded eye before nesting in fiery red locks. He had noticed where the scar ran into her hairline and faded. Tosher could recall every detail of her with perfect clarity.

The rumbling of metal stairs grew louder, pulling Tosher away from the familiar world in his head as the company spilt down to the stage level. Loud giggles and excited chatter filled the space as chorus members checked hats, hair and dresses before they went out to meet the public. Miss StJohn would be sitting in her dressing room, replete with jewels and a perfectly made-up face, judging the right moment to maximise her leaving the theatre. She would not be diminished or hidden by preening hens and puffing cocks and would wait till midnight if she had to. And those outside would always be waiting for her.

"I know you're looking," Said Tosher, a smile parting his lips. He turned to face the small figure, skinny legs dangling from his seated position on the prompt table. In one hand, a half-eaten apple, and the other, a dog-eared Penny Dreadful.

"Get off now. If you damage anything, Mr. Free'll leather you." Tosher looked into a small, angular face and laughed. "Well, he won't, but he should little Mouse. Wise Mouse. What do you think I should do? Ask her out?"

The boy nodded furiously.

"Smart boy. But its words, little Mouse, they get all tangled in my mouth."

The boy smiled and jumped down from his perch, half-nibbled apple in hand.

"You going to hog that or what?" The boy, eyes wide, slowly stretched out a twig-like arm toward the tall man as high as he could. Tosher leaned forward, mouth open, as if to bite, his maw so wide it would swallow the thing in one. Mouse cowered as the man leaned in, and a second before he reached the apple, Tosher loudly said, "That pissy thing? It's just a snack for a giant like me. You keep it." And patting the boy on the head, he turned to the traps. "Follow me, little Mouse. I need a strong man to help me lift the backcloth."

As Tosher returned to the traps, Mouse followed him like a small shadow, mimicking the man's walk. Tosher jumped and changed feet without looking around, momentarily startling the boy.

"Too slow!" roared Tosher, breaking out into hearty guffaws.

Mouse's face split into a wide grin, and he followed in Tosher's wake to work.

Chapter Twelve

The first time I saw the Gaiety Theatre, it was like walking into a dream of lights.

I was crouching in the shadows backstage and felt myself involuntarily gasp as the curtain rose into the tower, and the light and sound poured onto the stage like syrup. I felt overwhelmed by the opulence of the gilded shapes and fixtures that caught the lights, the acres of deep fabric curtains, the shell-backed seats in neat lines leading off into the dark, and the faces. The light dazzled me. It terrified and thrilled me in a way only one other thing could.

As the auditorium finally emptied, silence and a cocoon of absolute red seemed to envelop me. I knew that I had seen something incredible and divine. I had experienced a moment of true religious ecstasy and found my church.

I saw the adoring faces of the audience and was drawn into the exact moment of their transformation into worshipers as they watched the ritual of scripted chants, lights, smells, songs and robes, and I saw it for what it really was.

For a moment, the audience had been one body, one mind and one experience.

Chapter Thirteen

F anny stood in the quiet of midnight, waiting for the cab, lost in thought. The rush of energy and surge of noise from performance always had a price, and that was an introspection which descended in the silence going home after the curtain. Each time, she would return to the obscurity of comparatively sombre dress and in that dulling of the spotlight always came a slight sadness and regret that one more performance was complete. Time would eventually rob her of this bauble of excitement, and she would move on to another. But now, in the watches of this night, she became Mrs. Stanislaus and mother to little Florrie. Fanny smiled; if you genuinely stripped the layers away, she was really Miss Cooper. The ring, carefully waiting for her in a box at home, had no certificate behind it, not while Mrs. Stanislaus was someone else.

As Fanny Cooper had become Robina, Frederic Stanislaus was not all he appeared. Tall, gangly son of a carpet weaver in Kidderminster, his mother Hannah Smith, with no connection to Europe other than an ear for the unusual, had given her children names that sounded exotic. Young Stanislaus Smith, however, did not need a distinctive name to stand apart from his peers. Stan had exhibited a singular talent for music and later, composition. He was a rising star, and when Fanny's gaze landed on him in the orchestra pit, crouched over the flautist with a pencil, making some last-minute additions to his work, she had, for the first time, come adrift from the lyrics. At the moment between the musicians realising they no longer had their singer and one by one coming to a stop, Stan looked up, and she was truly lost to everything. As soon as he had whispered in her ear in a languid Black Country accent, "Stan, my name is Stan", it was clear she had fallen. He was quiet, contained and a steadying hand in the firework life she led and filled her home with music.

It was past midnight now and had become colder, threatening snow. Unusual cold snaps had been a feature of the year, and heavy snow had descended several times, seeming to put a roof of brooding cloud over London. She pulled her velvet shrug around her shoulders and glanced into the shadows. It was never entirely still in this part of London, and there were always people darting from alleys, walking home or rolling out of pubs, but outside the contained frame of the stage, the world felt less predictable and unsafe. Fanny returned to the theatre to collect her thicker stole and was now waiting for her cab on Wellington Street by the stage door. Albert had sent a boy to hail a cab for her, and she waited in the pool of light.

Fanny Robina played the Masher, a woman who dressed as a boy. It was her speciality, and as a theatrical conceit, it had started as an opportunity for a young woman to show her legs when, for the majority of the time, she was contained under the voluminous and ornate fabric. It had been almost a fetish to see women act as men, still wearing corsets but in a parody of masculinity. However, the unexpected outcome became a kind of freedom for the women who assumed those roles.

Fanny smiled ruefully; the original male Mashers had been known as 'Lady-Killers', something which had taken on a more sinister connotation now. But before the cloak of fear had descended in the summer, the female Mashers had started slowly removing the pantomime corsets and tights and started wearing suits, taking on a recognisably male form and adopting a more aggressive and forthright manner. These 'impudent minxes' had moved from object to position of power. It was a heady drug and gave Fanny more freedom than most, but she recognised that tolerance tended to stop at the stage door, and here, on this corner, dressed as a woman, she felt more vulnerable than usual.

Three women were now dead, slaughtered only a few miles away and eviscerated by god knows who. Fanny shivered and drew the stole higher up around her shoulders. Who could do that to another human being? Only a madman would not only kill but slice and destroy like that. Was it one person or two? Was it a gang stalking London, hunting for prey? Who knew how many victims had not been found, how many were floating in pieces in the muddy water of the Thames or buried in packages in hidden corners? There could be hundreds killed for an unfathomable reason and abandoned like waste, leaving them nameless. Were they alive when he started cutting? Did they feel the cold of the blade and know this was the moment they would die?

"Can I help you, Miss?"

Fanny jerked out of her reverie, her heart giving one enormous thud as adrenaline thundered around her body in an instantaneous panic. Her head snapped in the direction of the voice, and behind her stood the familiar silhouette of a cloak and domed helmet of a Policeman.

"Oh, Robert, isn't it? You fair scared me. She took a large gulp of air and tried to force her heart to slow.

"I'm sorry, Miss Fanny. I didn't mean to." He raised his shoulders, shrugging. "Day job.... Night Job." He laughed and pointed to his uniform. "Albert has had me helping out backstage before I could walk. Well, as soon as I could walk! I would do it all the time if it paid better. So I can only help out when I can. A free hour here and there and my day off. It's on my beat, so I never really lose touch. But," he sighed, tapping his shiny polished badge," this is my real job. It's not a place to be standing here, Miss, what with everything."

He was a tall boy. Fanny stopped herself, man. The thick, dark uniform, matching cape and domed hat changed his shape. His shoulders, which appeared usually turned forwards as if to protect him like the armour of a crab, were rolled back, and he seemed much taller. His thick cloak seemed to absorb light, and the dark fabric drew him into the background; only flashes of light on the highly polished badge, buttons, whistle and chain marked him out. Despite her initial reaction, the sense of recognition at that unmistakable silhouette made relief flood her. Just as she had become an unremarkable woman waiting to go home, this familiar face had become something more than simple Robert.

"Do you float around in that cape?" Fanny laughed with some brittleness. "I didn't hear a footfall. You must fly around like a bat."

The side of Robert's mouth tweaked upwards. "Tyres," he said, holding up a foot to show thick soles cut and stuck to the bottom of his heavy boots. "The older coppers used to do it when they were out. They're all doing it now. Cut out an old tyre and nail it to the bottom of your boots. Dulls the sound, and no one can hear you. These old boots are suitable for years of wear, but the last thing you want is for the likes of Leather Apron to hear you pounding up the road from half a mile away. With these, I can be up behind someone, and the first they know about it is my breath on their necks." He laughed, sharp and loud, like a whip crack in the air.

Fanny looked at the officer before her. She felt she barely knew this person, and that look of what she had taken of humour, was it pride? The Police had few enough advantages, and a hungry young Constable might be off the streets before long and up the ranks. God knows it was clear his upbringing had been hard. Anyone who comes out of Whitechapel's maze must be smart to survive.

"Sorry, I missed the show. How was it?"

"Good", stuttered Fanny as the subject changed in an instant. From the Constable before her, she saw a glimmer of the keen face that had so often been caught by the lights in the wings. "Albert ordered me a cab. It won't be long," she indicated to the stage door. "He's just popped in to hurry up Tosher."

Robert nodded his head to Fanny. "Then I'll be on my way, and I will finish my rounds. Have a lovely night, Miss." He went to turn away and stopped. "I do enjoy the shows, Miss. They're like going somewhere else for a while. It's so beautiful, and it gets into your soul and lifts it. Nothing will happen to the girls here. I promise that."

For a moment, his face had become almost still and the usual twitches and ticks on the surface that indicate the mind's machinations below stopped in Robert. He looked almost serene, and Fanny's heart softened to this strange, earnest man.

"Come along tomorrow, Robert and I'll try to get you a proper seat. It's different from the front; all the sounds come together like they should, and you can feel the band through the floor. Here's a tip from my Stan, slip off your boots and plant your feet on the floor. He always does, and he says the way to enjoy music is to listen with your ears and feet. Try it."

Robert's face lit up. "Can I? Thank you, Miss"

"And bring a friend or a lady. I'll have two tickets for you. Call it a thank you."

"William, I'll bring him. We share lodgings. He joined up at the same time as me, but he's from up north." he paused momentarily. "Manchester, I think. So I've taken him under my wing, sort of. London might eat him up! You've probably met him. He sometimes helps out backstage. Face full of scars, looks every inch the villain," he grinned.

Robert nodded and walked off on soundless feet back up the Strand. The lack of sound was eerie, and Fanny involuntarily shivered as the figure moved through pools of light and into the distance. She didn't realise she had been holding her breath when the sound of horse hooves rang out on the cobbles, and the cab pulled up. Snorts from a velvet nose huffed white into the air, and metalwork clanked as the horse's head bobbed up and down. Fanny let out a sigh, got into the damp darkness of the cab and directed the driver to Hammersmith and home.

She didn't know why she had lied about Albert being nearby and admonished herself for being a coward. The contagious fear in the air was chilling her to the bone more than the cold, and it had been instinctual to say to any man that she was not alone. Fanny made a mental note to reserve two tickets tomorrow as a fulfilment of a promise, but also from guilt for an unfair thought. She would be relieved to get home and into the safety of her family.

Chapter Fourteen

*I*t had to be perfect, and time blended into a ritual of cleaning, replacing crumbled mortar around walls and polishing until it shone with the glow from the battery of candles on every surface and recess.

It is now complete, and in the centre of a glowing circle of soft yellow light, I remove my filthy clothes and bathe in the hallowed gold. The shapes around me remain visible in the light, but the colours are washed and muted. I look down at my body and gasp as I see myself transformed. My skin glows, and the scars blur to almost invisibility. I feel the emotion rising and the streaks of tears running down my face. I have never seen myself washed clean of them, and in a shard of broken mirror, I can see my face set free from the past.

I scoop a hand, breaking the dark surface of the contents of an earthenware bowl and rub what I gather in my hands over my naked flesh. As it makes contact, I shiver in cold and excitement. It is no longer warm and has already started to congeal into lumps of jelly, but the contact of my flesh starts to reinvigorate and transform it.

With two hands cupped almost in sacrament, I dip my praying hands into the liquid and start to cover my face.

Chapter Fifteen

S tan was awake when Fanny finally arrived home on deadened feet. Her body ached with the strain of unfamiliar routines, which, given time, would become second nature. But that initial period of unfamiliarity and hypervigilance was exhausting.

Withdrawing long pins from her hat, Stan helped her remove her stole and jacket, placing them over the arm of a chair. Fanny picked the jacket up quickly, tutting.

"It'll crease Stan. I can't afford to steam it every time."

"You can, my love. You are a star," he replied, gathering her into his arms and planting a whiskery kiss on her lips.

"No, dear, you of all people should know it all changes in a heartbeat. We can't be foolish."

"And there was me thinking you loved a fool."

"And look where that got us." She paused and looked up to the bedrooms. "Is she asleep?"

"Yes," said Stan, pulling her closer. "Everyone is asleep, and we are alone. Completely alone."

"Are we indeed?" said Fanny.

"Yes. Fancy being foolish?"

§

Fanny rarely slept well during the first week of a new show. She was bubbling with energy and would spend those first days awake at dawn. Mary, luckily also a light sleeper, had already swept in and grasped a newly stirring little Florrie and was presumably in the kitchen filling her with porridge and gravel. Fanny laughed.

There was no doubt Florrie had been a surprise for them both and, of course, a good one, but the circumstance could have been more auspicious. Stan had children from two other marriages. His first wife had died, leaving three older children who were old enough to start their own families. Stan had remarried, and it had not been a success beyond the production of two additional children. Divorce was expensive, and young children complicated things, but he had met Fanny on tour and simply did not return home, sending back money when he could. She knew she should feel guilt, but all it had taken was him sending regular cheques to his old address, and she now introduced herself as Mrs. Stanislaus. It had been surprisingly easy, but it was fragile, relying on complicity from both sides of Stan's life, and she hoped Florrie would never suffer for his choices. But the bed she was lying in was the one she made, and Stan was gently snoring beside her.

Stan awoke not long after and dressed. His routine was always to compose in the morning and, if he had an engagement, to work later in the day and evening. A career that touched on success with a promising directorship of the D'Oyly Carte B Company and his light opera "The Lancashire Witches" and the most recent "Palace of Pearl" had stalled, and he was now at forty-five years old. Fanny, while still madly in love with him, was realistic about the twenty-year gap between them and what it meant. She was a rising star and had time to hone her craft, but time was not on Stan's side, and she doubted in her heart that he would now achieve the heights he craved. While Stan still composed small love songs for her, always in bright but in surprising and unexpected key shifts, they were always the unspoken words between them.

Drawing her onto his lap and stretching their arms around her to continue touching the keys, Fanny leaned her head on his shoulder and closed her eyes. He smelled of soap and hair oil, fresh and warm. She breathed in slowly, pressing her face into the space between the rougher hair on his face and the softer skin on his neck.

"Do you think this will last forever?" she sighed, knowing it for its romantic naivety.

"I don't know, amore. I haven't finished writing it yet." His busy hands paused and changed to a new melody.

A child's laugh came from the kitchen and the sound of approaching, waddling feet pounding on the wooden floors.

"Porridge," Fanny said, sitting up in anticipation.

Stan wrinkled his forehead, thick eyebrows knitting together. "Hm?"

"I think that's why she's so heavy. Mary and Cook fill her with porridge every morning. She adores it." Fanny rose, kissing the thinning hairline just above the resplendent eyebrows.

"Maybe we should ask her to ...."

Fanny interrupted him, "No, darling." As the little girl appeared in the doorway, Fanny swung her into her arms and marveled again as little arms encircled her neck and porridge-flavoured kisses deposited on her cheek.

"No," she said again. She turned to her daughter's lips pressed to a tiny pink ear. "You will have whatever you need, Florrie, I promise. But first, you smell so good I am going to eat you," and to the delighted shrieks of the little girl Fanny and Stan chased her around the salon.

§

Over the subsequent two days, papers arrived, and as custom dictated, breakfast was moved aside to spread them out across the linen tablecloth.

Stan, sitting on a chair in the parlour, one leg crossed over another, and a shoeless foot waved to an unheard rhythm in the air.

"Ah," he announced, breaking the silence. "I have one. *The Morning Post.* 'Yet another travesty of the apparently inexhaustible legend....'," he read down the page, lips moving as he read "'Bowdlerized'" Stan laughed, his face wrinkling.

Fanny huffed. "Critics"

"There is more 'Miss Fanny Robina is a bright and lively Faust, who sings and dances with taste and spirit'. Well, beloved, your 'spirit' seems to be much admired. Although I admire other things." He wiggled his top lip, and Fanny laughed. "*The Daily Post London* also appears to admire your spirit, but Lloyds call you 'vivacious'."

"And *The Echo*?" said Fanny, buttering some toast to keep her hands occupied. She hated reading reviews, but she needed to know how her performance was being received. It also didn't hurt to know how she was received compared to others.

"They start by calling you young, so I think we can take what they say with a pinch of salt." Stan started and, having caught Fanny's sour expression, concluded, "'Not all together unknown... comes from Australia with a high reputation. She has a clear, fresh voice, cuts through with spirit' again, 'dances with grace and is full of business. Her reception was genuinely cordial.'"

Fanny paused to consider. "Australian? I'm as English as they are. I suppose 'cordial' is good." She said, biting into the toast.

"Ah yes, but what appears to come from further away is more exotic and therefore exciting. Don't be quick to correct them my love. A little illusion is always more exciting." Stan picked up *The Standard*. His thin finger scanned down the page, and he suddenly exclaimed, causing Fanny to drop the toast. "A triumph!" he shouted. "They call you a triumph."

Mary ran into the room to find the cause of the noise, looking in panic from face to face.

"Mary, your mistress, my marvelous heart, is a Triumph."

"Congratulations.....? Ma'am......?" bobbed Mary, looking again from Stan to Fanny in some confusion. She left the room, and Stan turned to Fanny. "I am so proud of you, my darling."

"Please remember, heart, good staff are hard to find, and we cannot scare her off."

The only negative review from *the Sporting Gazette* called Fanny 'unemotional', but Stan assured her that any publication, which should be concentrating on sport and hunting, was unlikely to have any expertise in theatrical criticism. Fanny hugged him, knowing that the word would stick in her mind more than the good ones, but glad she had Stan and his relentless enthusiasm for what he called her 'star quality'.

Chapter Sixteen

*T*here would be no time for shock, fear or curiosity.

I have done this many times, but I realise now that what came before were the clumsy fumblings of an apprentice and not the actions of a master. At first, I was indiscriminate, relishing the moment, led by opportunity and circumstance. I was carried away in that ecstasy, working anywhere, foul and fetid corners and skulking like an animal.

But then I found this place and made it worthy of the task. A space which was mine in a way no other had been. This space within the tunnels below, nestled under the theatre, is where I can indeed be and touch the face of a god.

I practiced the motions until I was sure I was ready. But it had not gone according to plan, and that was unfortunate. I failed to complete what I needed and eventually had to roll the still-resisting woman into the river, where I watched her finally become still and silent from the pig-like shrieking that had pierced the air. I watched in some relief when she sank beneath the dark water into merciful silence and was carried away.

What had gone wrong? The awful shrew had clawed my face and bloodied my nose with the arc of a fist. Had she been sober, the bitch may have beaten me to death. In the darkness, I soaked my injuries and covered them so I could explain them away. It wouldn't be hard, but I need to be more careful.

So, I will go back to watching and planning before trying again.

Chapter Seventeen – November 1888

Robert stopped across the street from the theatre, absentmindedly buffing his dusty shoes on the back of shiny trousers, the tickets from Fanny clutched in his hands. After his shift had finished he had run home to change out of his uniform. Breathing in, he took in the coloured awnings, polished brick and the lights, which seemed to reach out like a siren song. It held the promise of excitement, and he felt the contagious thrill through his body as he stepped into the light. For a moment, he imagined stepping from a carriage to awestruck faces lighting up in recognition as he graciously greeted them, apologising he could not linger. Still, he must have time to prepare himself. But as a rough shoulder barged past him, his reverie was broken, and his descent to reality punctured his usual passive smile.

"Come on, Bill! I want to be in the seats so we can watch everyone arrive." He hissed at the more prominent figure behind him.

"William!" he muttered. "Not Bill."

Robert sighed dramatically. "Oh, all right Will-ee-am", he responded, stressing the syllable like explaining a complicated term to a small child. "Let's just get in there, shall we?"

Robert led the way, swimming upstream via the crowd of people milling around the restaurant at the front of the theatre, a pathway for those not dining beforehand snaked between tables and towards the back where the theatre proper started. Diners sat in intimate pairs or larger groups of men and women in excited gaggles, loudly joking and laughing in a swell of noise which felt like a rough sea. It felt almost tangible and vibrated in the hollow of Robert's chest, running up his jaw and into his head. He felt alien and unseen, and when another figure cut across his path, barely glancing at him, he found himself shouting, "Oy. Watch it!"

A brief drop in the hubbub led eyes to search out the voice which had cut through the joviality, and as eyes fell on him and the moment passed, a peal of laughter across the room broke the spell. Blood flushed across Robert's face, burning his ears. He dropped his head and pushed past the stairs and towards the landing to the theatre. Humiliation dogged his steps, and he paused opposite the saloon, William following in his wake.

"Bastards," he muttered and pushed onward towards the auditorium.

The entrance to the auditorium was decorated with thick, hand-woven carpets, and the walls flocked richly and elaborately as framed pictures lined the corridors. It fogged with the warmth of lights, humans in close proximity, jostling and chatting excitedly, drinks in hand and spilling onto the floor, discolouring satin shoes beneath jewel-coloured dresses. Energy, darted between parties like a golden arrow, curving and increasing in speed, sound following behind it. Robert watched, an observer apart, and felt a prick of jealousy.

He caught William's lumbering form, his muscled bulk pushing a path through the crowds. William kept his head bowed as he tried to weave his way through, scarred face drawing a gasp from a woman as reality impinged on this world of illusion. Feeling momentarily embarrassed by his colleague, when William raised his hand in acknowledgement, Robert turned without a word and moved on towards their seats. Miss Robina had been good as her word, and as he stepped into the gilded space, he felt the pressure of the corridor suddenly lift and fly upwards towards the sky blue painted ceiling. The stage, still covered by the safety curtain, would eventually lift to expose heavy red swags and drapes, looking from the front as perfect and expensive. He knew from the stage that behind they were ripped and shabby, and this knowledge made him smile like the magician who knows how the trick is performed. Everything that looked outwards towards the faces of the public was illusionary and exotic, but those with absolute power and knowledge knew the hard-working glitter was never gold. It just worked harder.

The theatre was flooded with light, and the air that moved through the space gave the shock of the atmospheric change from the restaurant's smoke through the hallway and suddenly into a place that felt cavernous and open. The air smelled warm and fresh. It had only been 20 years since the theatre evolved from the original building and the space before that, but this represented the entirety of Robert's life, and he looked at the place as his life's almanac. The heavy safety curtain, quickly painted with a pastoral scene, had been installed only 12 months before, after the sister theatre in Exeter had caught fire. The fire had been initially contained backstage while the actors had continued to perform to distract the audience, but panic finally broke out. In the crush of bodies trying to reach the only fire exit, 186 people had been killed, some even unable to escape and burning or choking on acrid fumes. Robert looked around at the space and imagined flames licking the pillars surrounding the stage, the faces around him blooded and crushed, charred and lifeless. The gas had been cut off in an attempt to cut the fuel to the fire, but it had plunged the place into black, and everyone had died in darkness, hiding from the deadly light of the fire. Robert closed his eyes and took a deep breath. A sudden change in the air next to him heralded a panting William.

"Thanks for waiting." He muttered with some sarcasm. "Look at this!" He exclaimed, eyes wide." That's fair mint....I mean......" when words failed him, he whistled through his teeth appreciatively.

"Yeah," said Robert. "It's....... 'Mint'." He smiled and looked at William and met his gaze with a wink. "Bet you never saw something like this in the mills."

"Stop it," said William

"Well, consider this another day of education. Your horizons are about to get bigger."

The seats were narrow, and Robert felt every spring through the thin padding. Next to him, William was crushed between slim armrests, his shoulders up by his ears and his knees spread on either side of the curvature of the seat in front. He gave a small smile when he caught the faces of other patrons, and as the person behind him made an audible sigh at the view of the back of William's head, he tried to slide down further into the seat, his feet leaving the ground as his knees slid up the wood.

"You look like something in a zoo." Muttered Robert out of the corner of his mouth, smiling at the man behind William in sympathy.

There wasn't much difference in their heights, but in frame, William was muscled, whereas Robert was slight. William had come down to London from the Industrial North of Manchester, his accent broad and flat when he was distracted, but Robert had noticed significant effort being made into adopting the sharper vowels of London. He enjoyed the periodical dig and emergence of new words and phrases exclaimed and would often try and push him into slipping. 'Mint' had been a new one.

Robert considered the man beside him to be the same age but the polar opposite. Both had joined the Police together and been assigned to the City Police Division, working across the Strand and touching the F Division at Covent Garden. He had sighed in relief not to be assigned to the pressured H Division at Whitechapel. Rounds had been increased to 30-minute meet points with colleagues due to the Leather Apron murders and the local unrest bubbling up in mobs attacking anyone looking vaguely different. Vendettas were masquerading as vigilance, and the atmosphere was friable.

An additional point of relief in his assignment was to be near the Gaiety and away from the overpowering presence of his father, Napper Challen, Constable of H Division, born in Whitechapel, forged in the army and a spectre looming large in the streets he owned. Growing up, Robert had been used as his father's ears and eyes. Running in the streets, listening at doors and passing information back to his forbidding father, he realised he had joined up then, and the uniform was a final flourish on a path already chosen. But childhood had carved his adult bones, and the legs in front of him had a slight bow to them.

The theatre had started to fill. Diners had finished and joined the audience as the fire curtain rose to reveal the sea of red. Robert knew the theatre from the stage, and if he closed his eyes, he could see it now. But in his view, plush, scallop-backed chairs were always empty, and the searing lights were at working level. He had imagined the red obscured by the patchwork fabric of the audience, faces all looking towards him with excited expectation.

Robert had always enjoyed crouching in the dark sidelines just behind the spill of light from the stage towards the wings. The sharp line between the dark and the stage lights illuminated the bridge between watcher and watched. He sometimes placed a tiny toe into the light, imagining it illuminating his whole body and drawing him onto the stage. But Albert would be there, never moving or making himself overtly obvious, but his presence would radiate a 'no' which Robert would sheepishly obey.

Albert and his fussy, shiny moustache's kindness had evolved into a reciprocal relationship of small jobs behind the stage in payment of food. Robert suspected his father knew but chose to ignore it. A boy couldn't live on air, and had he been caught stealing, he knew his father's wrath would have been more terrible than any law. Robert was held to a higher standard, and brass knuckles and no mercy would have punctuated the usual blows. It was an unspoken relationship between Albert and his father, born from the comradeship of war. It had not forged a friendship; it formed kinship. Kinship was obligation from shared experience. Friendship was more ephemeral and about being liked. His father was not liked, he wasn't even respected, but he was feared. His father's career had been limited to the streets, and he told all that would hear he chose to be where he could do the most, but he was a loose cannon and barely tolerated. Retirement had been forced upon him at the age of sixty with a minimal package of thirty-fiftieths of this pay with no additional amount for merit, and talk of his fury was leaving white hot trails across Whitechapel and the surrounding districts. Robert suspected some of his colleagues would rather face Leather Apron than his father's legendary rage.

Chapter Eighteen

*T*ime *has become meaningless down here in the candle-lit chapel within the earth's embrace. In silence, it is easier to listen and be guided to the right one. I know now it could be something in the voice, the way she moves, something about her face, but it will ring out like a clear note in an orchestra. The powdered, preening birds that flock in Westminster and The Strand radiate artifice, and fashion renders them indistinguishable.*

I finally heard the note. It rang out in the crowd, and I found myself seeking the source like a dog catching a scent in the air.

It was the worn brown boots of a woman as she stepped into the puddle, and it had been the splash which had somehow cut through the constant background noise of the city and drew me to her. The dark brown stain of the filthy water had bloomed across the toe and, as she stepped away, leaving a trail of single wet prints I knew. The heels were worn on either side and rolled her ankles outwards as she walked with purpose towards Fleet Street, holding a bundle against her chest. The wet prints gradually faded, but now I had her scent, and I followed her with a sense of quickening excitement.

Chapter Nineteen

William hated mornings. Sharing his room with Robert, he stood testament to the fact he barely slept and would always be silently staring at the ceiling in his bunk well before the knocker upper tapped with a pole on the window to indicate the night had passed. But the morning always brought the chill of rising and placing bare feet onto the icy floor. An inexpertly made rug fashioned of old rags by William's bed was made in the hope of dulling the shock, but instead, it introduced the sensation of standing barefoot on marbles to his early rising. William had found an old blanket beyond repair and had coiled and stitched the rug, hoping for a reasonable size. What he created was a compressed muddle of lumps which held the dirt and vaguely smelled on damp mornings. He sighed and swung his legs out of the bed.

William stepped tentatively to the grate where two pairs of polished boots stood as ready companions for the long trudges of a Policeman's day, and every trace of metalwork on his thick, coarse tunic, coat and hat was shining. Both, so carefully and often cleaned, were already starting to show patches of wear as if, when cleaning them, he was trying to eradicate the raised designs.

The stove was always unlit until both men returned from their respective shifts, and was a luxury in the morning they could not afford. Mrs. Rudge, the myopic and perpetually squinting landlady, demanded a window be left open at all times, winter and summer, to "Stop the build-up of the poisons and killing us all in our sleep". To this purpose, she kept a miniature, sad canary in her room. The poor creature, thought William, held in a cage, its only companion a rising face, pressed periodically against its cage and muttering, "Not dead yet". He was convinced Mrs. Rudge felt it was a matter of time before they all died in their beds. Perhaps the Canary was a replacement for Mr. Rudge and his original purpose.

William pulled on his thick trousers, grateful for the warmth and wiggled the braces over his shoulders. He barely had to think now as he slowly dressed, his feet settling into the internal grooves of his boots. He had already worn the right side of the left foot, where his gait turned inward a little. He would be on foot for long periods, walking in hour-long patrols which sliced the day up into well-trodden pathways, checking in with colleagues at pre-assigned meeting points and starting all over again. It had been a year, and he had stopped dreaming of the route, but it had somehow settled into his feet, and he no longer had to concentrate and so could release his thoughts to other things. As his boots beat away on cobbles, he would let the steady sound become a background noise, and he would watch.

§

Robert's eyes snapped open as the door closed behind William, and he rolled out of the bed onto his feet. He grabbed the breakfast left on the table and pulled on his clothes. In minutes, he was out of the door and striding off. He was glad to be on different shifts to William; it gave them a break from each other and reduced the tension between two people living in close proximity. Slightly more than a guinea apiece per week for six days didn't go far to keep a man warm and fed, and there was talk of unions and strikes for better conditions. William had seemed keen, but Robert doubted it would make any difference and he didn't plan to remain on the street for long.

Robert kicked at the gutter as he strode down the streets. In his head, "Faust Up to Date" rolled out in colour, sight and sound. The riot of colour in the auditorium was carved into his head. William had seemed spellbound and had spent long minutes, head resting back on his shoulders, staring at the blue-painted dome which floated way above them. His mouth had been wide open in a perfect O, reminding Robert of the fish he would see frozen in a last gasp at the various markets. As he passed such a stall, he caught the eye of a young woman who winked and broke out into a gale of laughter. Robert nodded and walked on, feeling the hot flush rising on the back of his neck and around the curve of his ears.

Robert drew in a deep breath. He knew he had things which needed to be done today before his shift and could not be put off, however distasteful. Mr. Field, a neighbour to his father, had come to his lodgings and suggested Robert visit as soon as possible. The man, wiry and small, his fractured teeth framing words of concern and, Robert readily recognised, fear. Robert steeled himself for the encounter. It was never easy, and poked at scabs, which never healed.

As he drew closer, the blank looks from people started to tinge with recognitions and the odd but predictable call of "Hello stranger", which passed as hardcore humour around here. Robert had spent his childhood outside mostly, hiding in corners, running errands and acting as his father's eyes. Some of these faces had occasionally thrown him charity, and he felt the sting of humiliation. That tall figure, looming through the smog, was the daemon of his nightmares and the chain which tied him back here. Robert Challen hated Whitechapel and its filthy crime and poverty. He had scrubbed it from his skin, but it had tattooed him in ways he would never be able to escape from.

Robert had met William here all those months ago—two barely qualifying adults, more accustomed to streets than anything else. William, living behind a shop, had shared his ambition to join the Police and Robert, who had allowed himself to be pulled behind him in William's wake. It was ironic that his escape had been provided by what had blighted his life.

Robert realised he was swinging his leg from the hip in the energy-saving Policeman's walk, and to his surprise, he was doing so in the middle of the street. Before, he would hold close to the shadows, making it easier to duck and cover when needed. The world had changed, and maybe he had changed enough.

It wasn't far from the Whitechapel road when he turned into the maze of dark, crammed, stained brick houses, populated with wooden stairs, walkways and haphazard extensions. The house he was walking towards consisted of shared stairs that clung to the side, the top floor being Mr. and Mrs. Field and the next floor down, him. It came back to him like a punch to the gut, the stink of people, filth and familiarity. It lingered on the nose, filling the senses, taste, touch, and sound. It overwhelmed and polluted.

Robert felt the change in sensation of his foot moving to the wood of the stairs from the street and the dull thump as the structure reverberated with his motion. He had run up and down these stairs as a child and could see the patches of softness and rot which were now threatening to take over. He skipped the second to last stair, the one his father loosened so the sound would alert him to visitors. But he knew by the time he reached the door, his father would be expecting him. Knocking, his knuckles chaffed at the shards of wood and flakes of paint peeling all over the surface. The military precision of the inside never reached the door. It seemed unimportant to him.

Without waiting for an answer, Robert entered, knowing the door would be unlocked. Napper Challen never needed to worry about thieves. His campaign medals were the only things he owned that he genuinely cared about, and he had hunted and nearly killed the last person who had tried. Bad news, like a copper with a short fuse, travelled.

"Sir?"

He was sitting at the table that dominated the room. It was scrubbed clean and recently, if the bucket of sand and the fresh redness of his father's scarred knuckles were to be believed. Napper was sitting on an equally immaculate chair, legs spread apart in his version of relaxation, the picture of a soldier at temporary ease in his bare barracks. Robert hated the place; it was surgical, lifeless and cold. He walked to the grate and placed his hand against the black surface. It was cold, so cold it had clearly not been lit for days.

"It's freezing in here." Robert shivered. "Sir?" he asked again when he received no reply.

He looked around the room, taking in the familiar yet unfamiliar space. "I ran into Mr. Field." Again nothing.

Robert pulled out a chair, which made a shriek across the floor. He winced, pausing for a moment to see if he would get a response. He sat.

"Father?"

Eyelids flickered, and rheumy eyes rolled in their sockets before settling on Robert, who felt a brief moment of fear. He instinctively jerked back in his seat but forced himself to maintain his position.

"Father?"

The man's body did not move as if frozen in time, but his eyes hunted out the details of his son, and his mouth opened, splitting the beginnings of his unkempt beard with a cruel slash.

"Why are you here?"

Robert opened his mouth to speak, but it wasn't a question.

"Why. Are. You. Here." Came the growl.

Robert took a deep breath. "I had some concerns. Mr. Field tells me you have barely been out during the day since you ..."

"It's none of his fucking business!" came the roar, pitched loud enough to satisfy any curious ears on the floor above. "I don't bother him, and he should keep his nose out of my business."

"Albert tells me you have been missing at the pub."

"So?" said the man, his body barely moving below the neck, but Robert noticed the bunching of muscles below the sallow skin. "I do what I like now. I am... I was...... retired." He spat with venom. With a sound like the cracking of a whip, Napper Challen stood, the chair falling away behind him and hitting the ground, accompanied by the two meaty fists which struck the table. "Who do you think you are, coming here and judging me, boy? You and your shiny, clean uniform stinking of righteousness. Look at you, a child playing in a man's clothes. You earn that uniform boy with your own blood and, if necessary, the blood of others. And you are all fucking shine." He breathed in, nostrils flared and eyes narrowing. "Fear is respect, boy, but they must be pissing themselves laughing at you. Have I taught you nothing? You disgust me."

Robert said nothing. His father's eyes seemed to be boring through him now, focusing on a place way behind him and a lifetime away. He felt small, like a pebble being kicked down a street. He knew where this would land, and it was only getting worse.

Robert barely felt the hand hitting his face but did feel the impact of the wall and the fall to the ground as his body rolled and finally came to a rest. He didn't fight back; he remained silent. 'I am a stone,' he muttered to himself and sent his mind elsewhere as the blows rained down. And it did get worse. Heavy boots impacted his legs, arms and back. He drew himself into a ball and only dimly heard the other footsteps running up the stairs as Mr. Field and others burst into the room.

Robert refused helping hands, shoving them away with force. He leaned against the wall, blood running freely down his face from a split lip. He had been lucky this time, and the bull raging opposite him, held back by four other men, was roaring and pawing at the ground in his rage. He pulled against them, chest-bursting forward and legs cycling to propel himself forward against the arms which held him.

"Go, now!" cried Mr. Field. "We have him."

'Barely', thought Robert as he ran a hand across his bloodied face and looked down in detached curiosity. A hand reached out to Robert's shoulder, and he rolled it away. "Don't touch me!" he growled, walking unsteadily to the door. He paused to look at Napper, who appeared to have diminished, and Robert saw confusion breaking through the rage. He did not seem to see his son, and the tension rapidly left his body.

Robert lurched down the street, aching. He had undertaken a brief inventory, and apart from bruises, what felt like a sore rib, and a split lip, he had miraculously come away with minor physical harm. His jaw set as he straightened up and adjusted his coat and hat in the slow ceremony. Reassuming the slow pace, he continued back towards the Strand.

Chapter Twenty

I have found a rhythm now, one that guides my steps to the only woman it could possibly be in that moment: the hunt, the lure, the capture, the kill, and the other.

In my time in the darkness, I have perfected the swift kill on silent feet, the ropes and knots to tie and transport my prize in a sack into the places below and the byways and tunnels that represent my world. I am a god in the small hours when the streets are dark.

The unresisting body of a woman carefully tied into a bag could be anything, blending into the crowds and deliveries for the morning markets. I learned long ago that people look but do not see, and a nondescript person with a filthy, blackened bag is of no interest.

But these are only preliminaries.

Chapter Twenty-One

The name hung in the air like a knife; it punctured conversation and the atmosphere. Dan Leno was joining the cast of Atlanta as Leontes at the Strand Theatre, so close as to be visible from the foyer of the Gaiety. This was his first engagement in burlesque, and the excitement on the street was palpable. The news had carried from the Strand within an hour; by lunchtime, it was all over London. A bolt from the blue, his short notice casting, had surprised everyone.

It was at afternoon tea that Fanny, with the aid of a large piece of cake, was able to bribe Willie 'Pip' Warde, actor, dancer, creator of dances, singer, and most importantly, old friend and terrible gossip, to elaborate.

"So come on Pip. Spill the beans. Is it true?"

Pip regarded the fork in front of his face, laden with a soft sponge and the bulbous drip of jam starting to slide down towards his fork. He bit.

Fanny rolled her eyes, knowing this was deliberate. She leaned back on her chair and regarded him as he chewed, eyes closed in ecstasy and face set in beatific calm. To all viewers, Pip was hanging in a moment of bliss centred on the rich confectionery rolling around in his generous mouth. She was not fooled. The ecstasy was not just about cake.

Pip was part of the furniture and, more importantly, an Atlanta cast member. His reputation and skill gave the impression he was older than Methuselah, and his regular floating courts, held in tea houses, public houses and theatre bars, always drew the curious and ambitious to hear carefully curated pearls of information. Never enough to satisfy, but sufficient to keep the itch active enough for them to keep returning. Fanny snorted. If she managed to leave having only paid for one slice of cake, however generous the size, and a pot of tea, she would be amazed.

A small man, delicate of frame, sharp of features and receding of hairline, Pip was always in motion and this had led to the nickname Pip Squeak. Initially, a name given in mockery, he had relished it, and, to his friends, was now Pip. His left hand conducted an orchestra to accompany his taste buds; Fanny could feel his shiny shoes tapping out the rhythm on the floor. Slowly opening his eyes, Pip paused, smiled languidly and angled his fork for another attack on the mountain of cake.

Fanny caught his eye, radiating impatience, and Pip smiled sheepishly and made a significant motion of putting down his fork next to the plate and patting it. He sat back, expectant. Taking a deep breath, Fanny, who knew how the game was played, did not immediately jump in. She knew Pip was more than aware that he had the information she wanted, and she didn't want to appear too keen in case he asked to leave with a cake box.

Pip smiled and went to pick up his fork, and Fanny leaned forward and placed her hand on it. This breach of the court etiquette would have meant banishment for many, but Fanny was also an essential source of information, and he couldn't afford to alienate her. In addition, under this game was a long and productive friendship starting at the Gaiety when Fanny was understudy to Nellie Farren. Pip had been keen enough to spot something worth cultivating.

"Nice hat," he said. "Did you catch the bird in Australia and pluck it yourself?"

"Leno," said Fanny, ignoring him. "Tell me."

There was only one thing for Pip, more thrilling than cake, and that was the imparting of information. He placed two hands on either side of the plate as if he were standing and leaned forward like he was about to leap. Fanny leaned in.

"Atlanta has gone bad." He paused, knowing Fanny would understand but still relishing the moment. "Audiences are dwindling, and the cast is at each other's throats."

A production was a carnival of catastrophe which never quite happened. It ran along the edge, and mistakes or bad luck could destabilise it. If a play had become unlucky, it was near impossible to convince actors that it could be rescued. Worst of all, the stain of a failure could destroy careers and theatres.

"Well, Sir Charles is rampaging around the theatre like a bear, savaging anyone who gets in his way, and it sets everyone on edge. There are cast members hanging from the lights and trying to dig through the floor if they cannot identify another escape route."

Fanny's brow wrinkled. Considering the mental rewriting of the tale, which, of course, Pip was undertaking as he imparted the information, this still took quite the leap. She heard the gap in conversation and took her cue.

"Why?"

"Georgie wrote it. Sir Charles can't shut his own brother's play without a certain amount of familial disharmony."

"So he brings in a huge star and hangs the expense," said Fanny.

Pip pursed his lips, annoyed at losing his punchline. Flashing a lightning smile, Fanny took a sip of tea.

"So what now?" she said, putting down the cup with a chink.

"Cast changes, re-writes, all night rehearsals and a strong admonition to the cast to buck up or leave. It looks like Sir Charles is pulling out all the stops and plans to trample the competition. He's even had a song written called Mephistopheles. They're coming for Faust Up to Date, love, and mean to steal your audiences."

"Do you think he can?" said Fanny.

"I do. You and I both know people love novelty, and a bigger name is going to pull everyone our way, even if it feels like everyone is busy breaking mirrors and shouting Macbeth." Pip made a big sigh and lowered his voice. "I'm hearing other whispers as well. Telegrams across the Atlantic to America and a certain Gaiety Company Owner who is getting seriously jumpy and may decide to jump on a boat. If you get my drift."

"Oh god. "Fanny leant back in her chair and bit her lip.

"If the knives are out, your illustrious leader is going to come back with a bigger set and start chopping. In a town like this, no one is safe, particularly this far into a run when one's exotica may have lost its lure."

Fanny looked at him quizzically. "What?"

Pip tilted his head and looked directly at Fanny. "My dear girl. Novelty has a distressingly short life. However good you are, it's not always enough to last. Fresh blood may be needed."

"Have you heard something?" Fanny demanded. "Pip, please."

He sighed and sat back for a moment, looking into the distance. He seemed to reach a decision and mouthed, "Violet Cameron."

"Who?" Fanny wrinkled her nose.

"Oh, my love, you have been out in the sticks haven't you. Violet Cameron, flavour du jour, moderately talented and screwing an Earl." There was a lull in the hubbub around them and some disapproving glances. Pip continued unabashed. "Well, she's swimming in scandal and has been seen in the orbit of..." he finished by raising an arched eyebrow.

"Oh, but my reviews have been good." Fanny's heart dropped through the floor. "Maybe Miss St John is planning to leave." She reached desperately for a rationale.

Pip said nothing.

"What about you?" Fanny said with genuine concern.

Pip picked up his fork and stabbed at his cake. "Oh darling, like shit, I float." He sighed, putting down the fork, animated face for the first time stiller and less mobile. Fanny looked at him. The delicate, diminutive man who spoke with his hands was worried. It was only a fleeting moment, but instability and disaster were constant risks, and once your reputation was dented, it was almost impossible to mend. It was only later that she realised that the worry was not for himself. He had been right; scandal brought in audiences.

"Well, at least it's not the dizzying depths of Miss Agnes Hewitt, dear. It takes real talent to bring a successful play back from America and kill it stone dead in London." He snorted. "Apparently, Mr Haggard's the 'Immortal She' might live forever in a cave but can't last a month in a London Theatre."

Seemly buoyed by the misfortune of others, Pip crammed a large piece of cake into his mouth. Catching the eye of a passing waiter who raised his eyebrows with disdain, Pip held up an empty teapot.

Chapter Twenty-Two

*I*t is important to work slowly and methodically when starting to cut flesh, sinew, and open joints. The first hesitant tests to slice flesh from the thigh were hard, but they increased my confidence over time. But I knew knives and ran my hands over them as they lay on the oiled cloth. My inheritance. I had practically been born with one in my hand.

Each time I start to work, I enter a state of absolute peace and almost bliss, and before long, each square of carefully laid out paper in front of me is filled and wrapped into a neat package.

This one was almost perfect. I sat back on my haunches, my arms and legs raw and on fire. I saw in my mind the river turned crimson and faces that bobbed to the surface, crying out to the sky and slowly sinking. My arms had the last spots of dried blood on them; dust and mud-caked my naked skin. With some effort, I pulled two teeth from the skull and poured lime on the face. I held them in my hand, like pottery fragments which would dry and tinkle in the small pouch which continued to fill over time. I am here, your faithful disciple, your child.

Getting to my feet causes an involuntary groan as I stretch time-cramped limbs and stand in the light of candles pushed into crevices in the uneven walls.

My skin is barely visible under the clothes of worship I have made for myself, and the light turns carved sweat lines into silver

Chapter Twenty-Three

Napper stood, fists clenched and jaw so tight his teeth ground together audibly. The rage which had driven him for so long, too long, was creeping out, and his control was starting to fracture like glass. He had held this cesspit together by spit and wind for so long. The crawling effluent of these streets threatened to drown everything in a tidal wave, and he wasn't sure if he had the strength to hold it back. God knows he had tried. He had walked the cobbles until his boots wore through, letting in water and soaking heavily darned socks until the damp friction sheered the skin from his bleeding feet. He had fought the fight, and he had done it alone. Indeed, god must forgive and not abandon him now.

St Mary of the White Chapel, the church and spire that acted as a compass point to the whole district, where St Mary Matfelon, holy mother, watched, judged..., and ignored. Could his actions be any louder? Did he not offer his contrition with every arrest and demon removed from the street, consigning them back to hell?

He knew what hell was; he had been. Hell had a name, Crimea.

§

Sevastopol was the city of mud and death, mud that caked your eyes and concealed the remains of men who, too ill to move, drowned and rotted where they fell. The hell of water in your shoes, seeping cold into your bones and nowhere safe to sit in the hours of shifts in the living trenches of mud.

The start had been like any other siege—no worse, no better—but when the winter swept in and destroyed supply lines and isolated them, they started to freeze and starve to death. The summer was no better, as the cholera took over where the cold left off.

No one had fought in this semi-underground state before, and the mud walls, shored up inexpertly with rotting wood, would regularly collapse, giving snipers the perfect shot to reduce the head of the man on your right into red vapour and splinters. Dug in, some tried to sleep, but not being watchful brought its own risk and another man had turned in his sleep and been shot through the face.

It was horror on an industrial scale where men were reduced to meat. It helped to think of the man in front of you as that while you dragged what pieces you could out of the line of fire and that sick lurch when a leg or arm detached.

Surgeons during the war were desperately sought, so any who volunteered, whatever the experience, were hired. The assistants just had to be willing, take orders and learn. He'd been a butcher's apprentice, which was enough to temporarily reprieve him from the front line and take him back onto the hill. His stomach never voided at the sites and the smells, but instead, something in his head detached, and he could watch by sending his brain to a safe place far at the back of his head. In this place, he watched and listened to the screams of the patients of surgeons who didn't like to use chloroform and treated agony as proof of life.

He could still remember and relive every moment, even after all this time. He could detach, go back, and the world would fall away until he felt no pain. After a while, it became easier, and the journey back became harder. His will became an impulse that wouldn't let him rest until he answered the incessant scream to act. He had travelled so far away from himself he was lost and couldn't get home.

And it ended. He was sent to a boat and carried home, bewildered as the veil of smoke over London appeared on the horizon. For a moment, he thought they had turned back, and he would be flung back into the mud and chaos. It might have been easier.

Now, Napper had looked around at the wreckage of men around him. He knew he had left something of himself buried back there in the dragging and insatiable mud. The nights were dark in a way that was deeper and more ancient than a simple absence of light, and he pulled his coat around his ears to drown out the whimpers and cries around him. Periodically, he would jerk awake, mind torn back from the battlefield by the rolling of the boat, and for a moment, he would look around, bewildered, until he saw Ripper, who would nod. His friend was also hunched under waxy covers, shivering from cold inside and out. They had got into the habit of soundless communication. Noise gave away your position and got you killed.

§

He returned to Whitechapel, a civilian, used up and lost, looking for a balm to his raw soul. Those first days were ones of constant watchfulness. He blanched at every noise and was constantly on edge in case the next corner hid a sniper. Every bump or knock in the street would see him swinging around, fists raised and fury drawn. It was the first time he saw how he could cause fear, and he realised it gave him power. He was lost, but not so lost as to look up and lose sight of the tower of St Mary's Matfelon, an admonishing finger pointing up at heaven.

But despite all of it, people treated him no differently. He had gone to war a boy and come back, unlike so many others, and he had been absorbed again with no recognition of the profound change in him. There was still the same drunkenness, whoring, and theft, and on the day, a small hand dipped into his pocket to relieve him of his watch, only the four men who pulled him away prevented him from beating the boy to death. In his righteous fury, he had picked up the boy and beaten him until his face was pulped and distorted. Knocker Challen had rolled great shoulders, throwing off the moderating forces like toys and found himself in a widening ring of horrified faces, blood staining his shoes and covering his scarred knuckles. The boy had somehow managed to stagger to his feet, unable to speak through his bloody, broken face and spat teeth and foam as he lurched away.

Napper had heard about the H Division at Whitechapel and had decided this would suit him well. He needed money, occupation and, above all, distraction. Veterans had been sought and offered positions, men able to walk without fear in a profession where their existence was despised. So he had exchanged one uniform and battlefield for another, choking mud for slick cobbles and the streets which drew the dirt and excrement from the city like a low-lying sewer. He would spend his life fighting on a new battleground, and his sense of purpose returned. People still looked at him with wariness. News like Knocker Challen becoming Constable Challen spread quickly. Shifts at night and in the cold dawn were never an issue. His inability to sleep had become an asset, and his patrol, an hour circuit from beginning to end on each sweep, would be ruled in iron.

And they had retired him as soon as he was sixty with the added insult of no bonus for merit. They may as well have taken him to the

knackers and put him out of his misery. He had begged, pleaded, demanded and finally raged. Napper needed to make them understand
he was not finished and there was more to do, but they had taken his
badge and sent him home. He was too old, and when feigned sympathy
ran out, he was told he was a loose cannon and a relic of another time.
He had been a career constable who needed to be on the street, not
cowering behind a desk. There were streets in Whitechapel, like Ewer
Street, that coppers would fear to go, but he strode down them like
a colossus. Napper had a network of spies, bleats and moppets who
fed back information, but any who tried to operate too greedily in his
part of the Chapel would leave his good graces and enter a place no
one wished to inhabit.

The cold had been terrible the year he met her, his Rose amongst
the thorns. The frost had done what even heavy rain couldn't manage,
which was to clean the streets by hiding the usual filth under a cover of
snow and dampening the fetid air into a crisp cloud that bit at extremities. Napper had been patrolling his regular route, one his boots could
easily navigate without his conscious brain, and he had seen the usual
gaggle of the eponymously named Ladybirds, prostitutes, hiding in a
doorway and sharing a drink from cloudy bottles. He knew them all by
sight and name. Many fell on hard times when husbands left, one way
or another. He had heard the mitigating cries so often his sympathy
evaporated long ago, and offers of services in kind for a closed eye had
revolted him. Now, his reputation silenced such protestations, and
usually, the sight of his hat and cloak rising out of the darkness would
scatter them like cockroaches.

Rose had been like the rest at the beginning. He hadn't noticed her.
It was only one summer when he had seen her on the Chapel Road,
and her hair caught the sun. He had seen fire, and something in him
stirred.

It was not unusual for coppers to marry or something slightly south of marriage with these women, but Napper found himself obsessed. Rose Penny dogged his waking and sleeping, and when he finally woke to find her next to him, he felt his world changing. She had crawled under his skin and into his head in a way no one else had.

But it was a brief summer, followed by perpetual winter and the constant reminders of her. Napper had a son now, and Rose was gone. His home became a scrubbed barracks, and his son another informant. Napper had hardened into teak while his insides rotted. They still rotted, and he knew he would eventually collapse into dust.

Chapter Twenty-Four

*T*he river is a constant presence, carving the land and splitting London between north and south. But I know this town, the tributaries, the hidden rivers and the creeks; they run through the streets, under the streets and through my veins.

But time and tide do not always combine, and despite the best tides drawing things out to sea, on some occasions, in the depths of the night, I have to trust a rising tide in any direction and hope the packages would be accepted to mud and the deep. On those nights, I hand my gifts to her and pray.

Before I learned the tides I started throwing packages into the water in Wandsworth down amongst the meat factories, those which sold named meat and those which processed less favourable options, such as cat. It had felt appropriate to dispose of them in the already stinking water of the Wandle, knowing they'd travel north with the off-cuts to the Thames and onwards.

Meat and meat.

Chapter Twenty-Five

"Oh," said Emma. "I'm knackered", as she fell back into her chair. Her legs and arms hung around her, orbiting her tightly corseted middle like flaccid tentacles.

A short snort of disapproval from the corner resulted in the sing-song apology, "Sorry, Mrs. Love".

"It's not ladylike language," said the originator of the snort. "I do understand, though, dear. Mr. Edwardes works you all too hard. I've never known a show with so many performances a week. My Mabel flies straight home and falls into bed, poor love."

"He's a slave driver, Mrs. Love," said Alice, attempting to smooth down her frizzy hair with a wooden brush which was getting caught in her thick tresses. The frequent back-combing to achieve an extravagant fashionable bouffant had now caused her hair to settle into an unruly nest. "Ugh," she muttered in frustration, throwing the brush down on the table with a clatter.

Emma rose from her chair and took up the brush. "Sit still," she commanded and, with short strokes, started to untangle the worst gently. "You're lucky," she said. "You can stick a bow on it, wave a leg, and no one'll notice. This bloody hat," she motioned to the pillbox hat, which was part of her male attire, "perches on my hair like a pimple on a boil."

"The higher the hair, the nearer the gods," smiled Mrs. Love. "Even Mr. Leno can't compete with that. No one will notice a girl acting like a country mouse." She looked approvingly at Mabel as the girl combed out her shining, curly locks. Alice couldn't help but notice how it glided through from root to tip. She pinched her lips as she felt Emma shearing away at another knot.

"My Mabel brushes her hair one hundred times before she goes to bed. Don't you, dear?"

"Yes, Mum", Mabel whispered as various pairs of heavily painted eyes rolled in suppressed mirth.

"Is that while you're falling into bed, Mabel, or as you rush straight home?" said Emma with a smirk.

Mrs. Love made a small tight smile and continued to darn a white stocking. With a flourish, she bit the thread and handed it to her daughter. "There you go, dear. Perfect." She picked up a bag and started to collect her belongings from around her, stuffing them without ceremony into its capacious depths. "Well, I'm away. See you soon, Mabel. I'll be back tomorrow, girls, if anyone needs anything. She rose, and as her industrious figure bustled out of the door, she was followed by a chorus of "Goodbye Mrs. Love".

"Do you think we'll lose our audiences to Atlanta now that they have a bigger Star?" asked Alice. "I need this job."

Emma placed a hand on her shoulder and handed her the brush. "I'd get to back-combing then and start waving those legs around like an octopus." She looked around and noticed the other wide eyes looking at her, seeking reassurance.

"Ugh!" Alice replied and threw her brush at Emma, who caught it with expertise, before rooting around in a pile of costumes and standing up exasperated. Pieces of lace, petticoat and hastily doffed chemises littered the floor, evidence of quick changes. Finally, when the fountain of fabric ceased, she cried out in exasperation. "Has anyone seen my shoe? I swear I only put it down just now." Emma resumed her search with ever-increasing levels of desperation.

Mabel paused slightly in mid-brush and quietly sighed. When she got home, she would look in her mother's bag, liberate Emma's shoe, and smuggle it back to the theatre tomorrow.

Barely acknowledged by the departing Mrs. Love, a petite dark figure who had made a brief curtsy entered the changing room. "Mrs. Freeman asked me to pick up any washing or repairs." She looked around and sniffed. "I don't know why bloody Ida couldn't have hopped up here on her good leg. I'm supposed to be maid to Miss Robina and Miss StJohn," she finished, pronouncing the last name as 'SinJin' as if savoring a toffee. When no one seemed to offer validation of her situation, her carefully neutral tones slipped. "Well, have ya then?" said Mercy. Emma looked down and pulled out a shirt from the pile of fabric growing around her during her search. She held it up to the girl. "I got grease paint on it. Can Mrs. Freeman do anything?"

"So" said Mercy leaning against the door frame and regarding the proffered shirt with some distaste. "I hear the Ripper is an American who's be cutting up whores over there for years." She craned her head around the room to confirm she had their full attention. As horrified faces met hers, Mercy continued, "And I hear", she adopted a conspiratorial stage whisper, "he's moved onto cutting people up and throwing them in the Thames. They found a big bit up at Parliament Street and Embankment. Seven, they reckon, but how can you tell when they're in bits?"

The room was quiet. Finally two other items, a chemise and stockings, were silently handed to Mercy by other chorus members, who took the offending offerings at the end of two fingers as if handing a brace of dead mice. A cloud descended across her face and her nose wrinkled in distaste. "Smells bloody awful. I'm not carrying that." She turned abruptly, dropping them on the floor and stalked off the way she came.

As Mercy stomped down the stairs from the attic dressing room, she paused when judged to be out of sight and threw her body against the wall with a huff. "Bloody cows", she muttered. They all thought they were something special, and everyone knew they were mostly dancing whores, no better than the silly bitches being murdered. Taking some time to compose herself, Mercy straightened her apron, fixed a beatific smile on her face and, on lighter feet, went down the stairs. On the next floor, she meekly knocked on Miss Robina's dressing room door. Fanny was sitting on the chaise long, one shoe off and rubbing and aching foot.

"Can I get you anything, Miss?" said Mercy.

Fanny looked up at the neat figure and smiled. "A bowl and some hot water, please, Mercy. I think I danced through these shoes tonight."

Mercy nodded and gently closed the door.

Threading her way past wicker baskets with random props and fabric spilling out, she passed Teddy, who was busy pulling off a hood and Devil horns to the sound of muffled curses. The sound of Harry holding court as he scraped thick makeup from his face burst into the corridor as a door opened and someone departed. The rising and falling noise of a theatre alive with activity and intense energy always left a slight ringing in the ears when it ceased. Mercy liked the quiet hours at the end of a long day, but she enjoyed even more watching the chaotic dance of people. No one would recognise her on the street since they only looked at the uniform of black and white. If she had also shed the name, no one would know her from Adam. The anonymity gave her power, and she could pass almost unseen. Mercy smiled. Acting? They were all bloody amateurs.

Arriving at the room of George Stone, Mercy knocked and walked straight in. Looking up at this unannounced intrusion, George opened his mouth to protest until he realised who his visitor was.

"Ah yes," he said, fumbling in his pockets. "Here", he muttered, passing her a yellowed piece of paper folded in half.

Mercy took the proffered, lint-covered paper and opened it. She nodded in approval. "Four pounds. Goodness me, Mr. Stone, you must be sure about this horse. Any tips you'd like to share?" she smiled, putting the paper in the pocket of her apron and giving it an unconscious tap with her hand.

"No," George said flatly. He took a large handkerchief from his pocket and wiped his sweat-drenched brow. Mercy looked at the man. He was getting further from the handsome hero each day. His face was becoming ghastly white, and his jowls wobbled when he moved. He did not look well.

"Well, I wish you luck this time, Mr. Stone. It can't last forever. Ceasar'll place the bet tomorrow morning and I'll come back with the slip for 'ya. Minus, of course, our commission for shoe leather and time."

George looked away, shaking his head. Mercy could see he dearly wanted to put her in her place, but they both knew he couldn't, or approaching a betting establishment in person would result in awkward questions about current unpaid debts.

"See you tomorrow, Mr. Stone, and thank you for your business." Mercy bobbed a small curtsey and left George to a large and half-empty bottle of whiskey. She would have someone water the next bottle down when he was on stage—no point in letting the cow drink itself to death when there was still milk available.

Mercy moved back to the main staircase and down to the realms of Mrs. Freeman. On her way, she sought out the tiny figure of Mouse. "Boy! Yes you, stupid. One jug of hot water, a bowl and a towel. Second floor landing. Well?" she said as the boy hesitated. "Get on with it." she leaned down, caught the front of his shirt in a bunched fist, and drew him to her face. "Or I'll lock you down in the traps with the rats you dumb little shit, and maybe you'll finally learn to scream."

The terrified boy scuttled away, and Mercy turned back to the final destination of her journey. She heard the busy sounds of sewing machines before she entered the room. It was piled high with bolts of various coloured fabric, strings of brocade, feathers and glass jars of buttons. In the centre, orbited by this chaos of colour and texture, was Mrs. Freeman, crouched over a brocade jacket with a small needle. She peered up as Mercy entered. "Anything?"

"No. I did ask the girls, and they said to thank you, but there was nothing to do."

Mrs. Freeman nodded. "Thank you, Mercy. It was very kind of you to help. Ida couldn't do the stairs today, and Harry has somehow blown a hole right in the front of his jacket. What does that man do on stage? It looks like he's taken a bite out of it."

"Happy to help Mrs. Freeman." Mercy smiled.

As she mounted the stairs back up to the second floor, Mercy silently fumed at the likes of Ida. That useless girl sat flat on her bum in the wardrobe every day while everyone else had to run up and down the bloody stairs like trained monkeys. Ida was one of those travelling circus tramps who twisted their leg, falling off something—probably her own feet. Mercy felt the tide of injustice rise like bile, and she pushed it down. She just needed to bide her time, and as she picked up the jug, basin and towel left at the top of the stairs by Mouse, she gently kicked at the door to Miss Robina's with her foot, prodding it open.

"Oh, thank you, Mercy. I hope it wasn't too heavy on the stairs."

"That's what I'm here for Miss. It's my pleasure," she said, pausing for a small but theatrical gasp of air, and shut the door behind her.

Chapter Twenty-Six

*T*he idea came when I saw the deliveries to the Covent Garden market. Sacks and packages tied with twine. Inconspicuous working men carrying packages were plentiful and nondescript. With the right clothes, I would blend in and walk in plain sight.

By cutting a throat and letting the blood drain, bodies are always lighter, cleaner, and easier to transport. Once I've cut them, they can be covered in lime powder to stop the smell, and I have all the time in the world.

I've found a pattern of slicing and jointing with a row of knives I keep for the purpose in a niche in my space. They are wrapped in oilcloth, and I ensure they are cleaned and polished them until they shine. They are my brothers in blood.

Once the packages are carefully tied I buff the boots and finally clean the head from blood and smuts. I make them beautiful, more beautiful in the absence of life than when they swam in the filth of the streets. Both offerings must be perfect and finally I place them in niches and send them into the eternal darkness, sealed with bricks and mortar.

Sometimes, the river rejects the neat packages, but more often, they are accepted and either settle into the embrace of the mud or drawn out to the sea. They mingle with her life blood as it turns to salt at the meeting of the tides and my heart sings as I know she is smiling down at me.

Chapter Twenty-Seven

T he sense of unease remained in the air over the next few days when Mr. Free received a telegram from America. Mr. Edwardes and Mr. Harris had only been abroad a month, but would be returning early to the company and landing in Southampton in twelve days. The changes at the Strand had sent ripples across the Atlantic and caused sufficient concern to draw them both back to the Gaiety months before they were due. It wasn't even Christmas yet.

The surprise was a list of instructions for various individuals to ensure costumes were refreshed, the commissioning of three new songs and some re-writes. Mr. Leno was only a week away, but the bubbling word cross-pollinating between the casts and crew in bars, pubs and sometimes in beds all confirmed significant changes and unsubtle references to "Faust up to Date" itself. The new song 'Mephistopheles', heard by small ears sent to lurk under windows, had reported with a sad nod that the additions were indeed worrying.

"Spectacle wanted STOP No delay STOP", Mr. Free read from the yellow telegram.

Sucking the air between his perfect teeth the wrinkles around his eyes deepened a little. To a casual observer, he was merely absorbing the information, but to someone who knew him well, he was howling in frustration.

At the stage door, Albert, knife in hand and pipe in mouth, was whittling. He carved the dark brown wood with deft strokes, a small offcut picked from the floor in the traps. Holding the piece close to a rheumy eye, he considered the form and texture and made imperceptible changes, which slowly and surely became fins, scales and a sinuous tail.

Albert sensed the changes in the water like an angler and had noticed the far-off ripples, which now became a torrent raging along the Strand, and he knew change was coming. Audiences and reviews remained good, but they lagged behind the tide and by the time they started to decline, it would be too late. He did not need to see what was in the proffered telegram which came to the door. Mr. Edwardes would return and bring Mr. Harris, willing or not. Rubbing the light sheen of sweat from a growing forehead increasingly empty of hair, he considered the pending disappointments and distress that would arrive and depart past his desk. He would collect a supply of handkerchiefs for the inevitable hysterical cast and obtain some nostrums for the orchestra, who would, of course, be drowning their sorrows in the nearest pub.

Looking up, Albert saw Mr. Free's figure heading towards him, head down, still reading the telegram. He nodded, waiting for the reason.

"Re-writes and new songs...," said Mr. Free before looking up at Albert and meeting his eyes.

Albert nodded again, wincing slightly, but this time in understanding.

"Many?"

"A total overhaul," replied Mr. Free. "And arrange accommodation for a Miss Violet Cameron who will be arriving with Mr. Edwardes from New York."

"Hm," said Albert, carefully putting his work on the polished counter and his pipe in a bone ashtray. "To think it's come to this. Trouble I think."

"Yes," said Mr. Free ruefully.

"Well, it's touch and go with George, who seems to be permanently inebriated, but I can't see this Miss Cameron donning a moustache and shoving a pillow down her trousers. So one of our ladies is...." He raised his eyebrows unable to say the word. "If Mr. Edwardes is planning on getting rid of people, he must do the dirty work himself," he paused. "I'll buy some smelling salts and something to plug our ears, shall I?

Mr. Free nodded. He loathed publicity stunts. Technical set pieces aside, the show was clearly about to be significantly changed, and he imagined telegrams were already spiriting their way across the vast Atlantic to various people to arrange for new material and costumes. Indeed, they were probably on their way before either Messer's Edwardes, Harris and this Miss Cameron boarded the boat or sent a telegram to the Gaiety. Mr. Edwardes must be worried; telegrams were extremely expensive, and costs would mount up even in his familiar brief style.

As always, Mr. Free and the company would wait for instruction and make whatever anticipatory plans they could. He swallowed, suddenly realising a difficult conversation was pending with his wife. She was very unlikely to be happy, and without a doubt, the air in the wardrobe would be blue for some time. Shaking his head, he caught

Albert's eye as he donned his serviceable black coat and knew the old man was thinking the same.

Chapter Twenty-Eight

*S*ometimes, I can hear the music above me. I know each move, song, and step, and it plays across my mind as I hum along to the rising and falling melody as I cut.

Vibrations shake the walls and send small dust clouds down into my working area, snuffing out some of the candles, but it makes me smile as I work. It is easy to slip away and spend time down here. In the confusion of a show, no one misses one less person dressed in anonymous black.

From the sound above, I can hear that I have one more scene before I need to wash, clothe and be in time to help raise the final curtain, drawing a tired hand across a sweat-soaked brow and sharing a smile with the others, recognising another successful evening of hard work.

People are easy to fool if they underestimate you.

Chapter Twenty-Nine

"Fetch the boxes from back there and bring them up here," said Albert, motioning backstage. His head bobbed into the open wicker basket amongst the other boxes and props littering the stage.

It had been two weeks of chaos as the clock ticked away the final hours until Mr. Edwardes stepped back into the Gaiety. By the time his boat had hit the mid-Atlantic from America, the taut sense of anxiety had led to multiple meltdowns, cast members sleeping in corners after hours of additional rehearsals, and the usual jollity dimmed to a level of grim determination to survive another day.

Albert waved at a passing stagehand, piled high with fabric and unable to see his path. "There's a......" Albert started as a foot made contact with a broom, stopping the limb, but not the forward motion of the man who pitched forward and fell into a heap. ".....broom", Albert finished with a sigh.

"Albert?" came a voice from the wings. Mr. Edwardes strode across the stage in Albert's direction. He had arrived from Southampton, where his boat had docked last night, had probably harangued his way back to London and was already conducting the total overhaul of the show the following day. There was a sense of relief that he had finally arrived, but it was clear that this was the eye of the storm, and the rest was truly on its way.

"Are you out of your mind?" came a voice to the backstage. "I can't sing that!" Mr. Edwardes caught Albert's eye with a slight look of resignation, inhaled as if preparing for a sortie and made his way towards the din of protest and the quieter hum of futile reassurance.

§

Florence StJohn was standing on stage over a small piano behind which hunched a pianist who was making a spirited effort to slide beneath the keys in the face of the onslaught of fury and possible savaging. She looked up at Mr. Edwardes's approaching figure and opened her arms in pleading. "Eddie dear, I can't possibly sing that!" she motioned wildly in circles, holding sheets of music, some of which detached and fluttered to the floor. "It's parochial. I have three new songs Eddie, and lovely as that is, they are all the same. I need something special, Eddie." Florence continued her stream of consciousness powered by anxiety. "And I haven't even seen the new costumes! What if they make me look fat? It may have escaped your notice, I wear House of Worth" she motioned down at the exquisite green dress which fell in waterfalls of fabric to the floor. "I may be playing a sixteen-year-old virgin, Eddie, but I will not look like a milkmaid."

While this exchange continued, the figure of Teddy Lonnen was drawn upwards on a harness into the fly tower, a broad smile fixed on his face. To the side of the stage two crew pulled on the ropes, one with a pipe clamped between his teeth, which was removed by a frowning Mr. Free.

"Once we get him up Fred, see if we can counterweight him and get that fall to the stage a little faster." He waves up to Teddy who waved back. "Mr. Edwardes wants shock, drama..." he grimaced "... and no broken limbs."

Against the side of the stage, Alice and Emma were perched precariously on a tandem. Alice, both feet off the ground but leaning a shoulder against a pillar and Emma in a splay-legged gait, trying to pull the tandem to the vertical while trying to push off from the wall.

"Are you just going to lean there or help me? Ooff, bloody hell, girl, you are heavy."

"Rude," said Alice, placing a hand against the wall and trying to leaver herself up.

Finally, they managed to inch forward, and while Emma fought to keep the front wheel straight, they slowly gained momentum across the stage.

"How do I stop?" came a distant voice as the tandem came to a stuttering halt in the opposite wings and fell to one side, landing both women in a heap, to the explosion of laughter from the other chorus girls who rushed to help.

Another girl, firmly perched on single bicycle, passed them, a loud cry of "Woooooo" as she sped off back across the stage. Her legs locked out, and her feet flexed on either side of the speeding cycle.

"Whose bloody idea was this?" moaned Emma as she fought her way to the vertical from the tangle of limbs and cycle.

"Apparently, it adds realism and excitement." said Alice, crawling away from the tandem on her hands and knees before rolling onto her bottom and rubbing at her ankle.

"Really? And who, pray, is going to be there when I fall into the orchestra pit?" said Emma as a cycle roared back towards them as Miss StJohn cried out again in frustration at the chaos.

Mabel was standing demurely in the wings. Her hands idly played with black leather gloves. Harry stood beside her, watching the pile of tangled girls laughing in huge guffaws.

"I can suddenly see the attraction of cycles....." He winked at Mabel, who smiled thinly. She was watching Miss StJohn and Mr. Edwardes closely.

"I would do anything for you, and you know I would, Eddie. This is too much." continued Florence to Mr. Edwardes. "I have a reputation. I am a jewel, Eddie."

Mr. Edwardes sighed as the chaos continued to evolve around him. He had known she would win this round. He needed her, and she knew this too. Whatever songs they gave her would have to be show-stoppers.

"Florence, my dear, you, of course, will continue to be our star and will have music worthy of you. I would not expect you to have anything less."

Florence smiled with satisfaction and a hint of relief as the sound of a bell, crash, and laughter heralded an attempt by Alice to take Lily's place on the bicycle ended in a messy heap.

Mr. Edwardes looked up as a figure ambled towards him. It walked past the returning Emma and now disentangled tandem riders who were all supporting Alice and trying to push her forward, shouting instructions at each other.

"You are late sir!" Edwardes called out across the stage to the approaching figure.

George Stone puffed a cloud of smoke as he halted in front of Mr. Edwardes.

"So, we are going to do this then." It wasn't a question but a statement of appalled fact.

"Yes, you will, and you remain late," responded Edwardes, looking George up and down. He had put on weight, and his waistcoat buttons were clearly under strain. His face, consistently round, had become softer and fleshier around the bottom eyelids, which drooped slightly, exposing pink veins.

"Good god, man, have you been to bed?" said Edwardes, unable to stop himself

"Club," George replied. "Good game." he looked across the chaos of bicycles and spectators as Florence swept back up to the dressing rooms, passing Fanny as she exited. "The gods didn't quite smile on me, but maybe a few changes to the old show might perk up the spirit and make the lady smile down on my endeavours."

Mr. Edwardes sighed. "Ah, that would be the lady who concerns herself with luck." He pursed his lips in disapproval, and George beamed back unabashed. "And since you call upon the said lady, I imagine that means we are to expect unwanted visitors at the door seeking your fiscal attention."

George took a long puff and exhaled a cloud of smoke into the cold air, where it sparked. "I couldn't say."

A clatter from the direction of the dressing rooms stopped Edwardes in his response, and he shut his mouth with an audible clack of teeth. He strode back through the door, glancing at Fanny. As he passed her, she was sure he had given her an odd look.

"Faust, my dear boy", said Teddy, squealing from above the stage in his harness. "Larks!"

Fanny looked up at the dangling man and the worn soles of his brown shoes. "Larks", she muttered, unconvinced.

§

William, sleeves rolled up, dragged a trunk down the stairs to the wardrobe. He had been desperate for his one day off a week and some much-needed sleep, but Robert had promised both of them to Albert today to assist with moving around costumes and he felt he couldn't decline.

Behind William, as he struggled under the dead weight of the trunk, stomping down the stairs, cigarette in hand, was Robert who took a final huge pull, dropping the stub to the floor and crushing it out under foot. He gave William a brief smile and pushed his way past and into the room.

"Good morning, Mrs. Freeman. William and I brought this down for you. Where would you like it?" He walked back to the door, pulled at the handle by which William had been dragging the box, and pulled it into the room. William let go and rubbed life back into his blanched hand.

"Oh, thank you, lads", said Mrs. Freeman. "There, please." She pointed to a small floor space amidst the piles of costumes, hats and shoes. "Look at this mess", she muttered, disappearing behind a sewing machine and emerging with an armful of boots. "It would be easier to drop a match and start again. Changing costumes, new hats, new scenes, new script, and new songs - mid-run! I ask you! And not a beat missed, not a show cancelled, not a day dark. No, we keep going with one show while we...Oh gawd." She said, holding up a finger that had been pierced by an errant pin and had brought her rampage to a sudden halt. "Ida love, get me something to wrap this with. I can't bleed over everything."

Mrs. Freeman put her finger into her mouth and sucked at the blood. As Ida searched the room, finding nothing in the chaos of petticoats, dresses and feathers which rose in response to her search and then drifted down towards the marked and worn wooden floor.

"Not on the floor Ida!" warned Mrs. Freeman as Ida's hand caught a feather in mid downward flight and placed it on a chair. She limped towards a box of fabric scraps by the doorway where Robert leaned on the frame.

Robert had never seen Ida close up and he was surprised that she was pretty. He had always disregarded her due to the limp which overbalanced her as she walked and led to a rolling gait which made her look like a spinning top in its last gasps. Out of his pocket he whipped a handkerchief and held it up to Ida's face forcing her to look him in the eye.

"Madam", he smiled.

Ida responded with a small upward twitch of the sides of her mouth, which appeared to William, still behind Robert in the corridor, to be more out of learned politeness than a response to what Robert thought of a charm. He would be unbearable tonight, telling William in detail of the small, bird-like seamstress at the theatre who clearly liked him.

William had expected it, it was always the same, but it didn't stop his heart from sinking when her gaze met his, and her smile faded. She had seen the network of scars across his face. He pursed his lips and tried an assuring smile, raising his shoulder in a half-shrug, but she had already taken the handkerchief from Robert and turned away to hand it to a grateful Mrs. Freeman.

Mrs. Freeman, wrapped the handkerchief around her finger and looked up at Robert gratefully, realising William was also still there. "You boys been offered anything? Nice of you to come and help" she said, mollified.

Robert smiled, his face broad and open. "That's okay, Missus Freeman. I'd do anything for Albert, and William here, is an angel." He looked back at William and winked. William scowled in the darkness of the corridor, the shadows created by the scars deepened...

"Right," Robert turned back to Mrs. Freeman. "Things to do."

Robert lit another cigarette as they climbed back up to stage level. He stopped and leaned against the wall, regarding William. "Buck up," he said. "We're doing a good deed. It's balm for the soul. Brushes it up of all those dirty little smuts you get in life....."

William's rough hands pushed violently against Robert's thin frame, pinning him against the wall. William's face was thunderous with rage, and his lip curled, exposing a yellow tooth. He withdrew a meaty fist and punched hard at the wall immediately to the side of Robert's face, scattering paint flakes and masonry. Breathing hard, he stared into the smiling face of Robert, who put the cigarette to his lips and then blew a stream of smoke into William's face. William snatched the cigarette, threw it into the darkness, and pounded up the remaining steps. Robert took out another cigarette and lit it.

"Better do something about that temper of yours, Bill. It'll get you into all sorts of trouble."

§

William emerged from the stairs into the darkness of the wings, his head thumping and teeth grinding. The anger poured off him - it was thick, tangible and broadcast danger. He looked down at his hand where blood was pooling around sheered knuckles. Underneath were old scars, and he could see bruises rising beneath the skin already. Blood, pain and anger had always followed him like a storm and it had found him again.

Chapter Thirty

*T*he girls of the Gaiety dance across my mind. I hear the constant rustle of silk, yards of iridescent fabric, stockings that cling to curved legs, and the beautiful smells of spring hanging in the air around them. I wait as they pass and breathe in the scent that lingers in the air.

They move in flocks, like colourful birds and chatter excitedly, bright eyes darting around and taking everything in, even me. But unlike the vapid collections elsewhere, these birds sing and light up the stage with bright colours. I feel terror and excitement in equal measure and am a guardian of sorts if their fascination with the men at the stage door turns to something darker.

They belong to the Gaiety, and the Gaiety belongs to me.

Chapter Thirty-One

F anny dropped lightly from the cab, a booted foot hitting cobbles with a soft tap. The journey to the theatre along its normal route through the leafy boroughs of Kensington and past the monumental structure of the British Museum with its high black railings usually gave her time to prepare her mind, think about lines, improvisations and hum in order to warm up her voice. But this time, she felt the flutter of nerves above those of performance and as the unusually heavy traffic impeded them across the city, Fanny fell into a semi-dream state of watching the growler carriages with their distinctive snarl across the cobbles, the clatter of flatbed carts drawn by single rough-coated horses and the dodging forms of those on foot bouncing between them from pavement to pavement. As the traffic ebbed and flowed, the noises of the wheels, the jink of horse brass and the sharp crack of riding whips flowed in a rising tide until another stop returned the background noise to footsteps, the hubbub of conversation and the occasional shouts of a city easing its way from dawn towards mid-morning.

Fanny looked down at the paper in her hand, seeking for the hundredth time more meaning. Mr. Edwardes had summoned her by letter to the manager's office and the words of Pip Warde were arcing across her brain like electricity. It had been hand delivered by a boy to her dressing room after the close of last night's show and she had puzzled during the long hours of the night what the meeting may entail. The letter was polite and gave nothing other than a request to meet the following morning at nine.

Fanny recalled the name Violet Cameron from her meeting with Pip, but upon his return neither Mr. Edwardes nor the man usually lurking in the shadows beside him like a small worried dog at heel, Mr. Harris, had mentioned anything. New songs, costumes, scripts and effects were being run, edited, and blocked in positions across the stage, but she had not been affected unless it was a change specific to Florence and needed Young Faust by her side.

On the pavement Fanny drew her cape around her to fight off the cold which sought out vulnerable flesh. She took a moment to gather herself, rocking back on her heels and letting her body settle into its centre. Only the slight flutter of the two outer fingers of her left hand betrayed her anxiety. She was sure she had no reason to deserve pending catastrophe. Part of her wanted to postpone the meeting, pretending she was too busy and too industrious to have time to meet, but as she pushed a stray hair from her cheek, she swallowed hard and stepped forward. Uncertainty was a constant background noise in Fanny's life, enough to nearly be imperceptible and only noticed when it increased. It never went away. But this time, she had no sense of why a man like Mr. Edwardes wanted to see her privately.

At this time of day, the Catherine and Wellington Street doors were closed, so Fanny walked in through the restaurant entrance on the Strand. A few early lunchtime diners sat in quiet groups, the susurration of conversation punctuated by the sharp sound of crockery. Fanny made her way through the centre of the building towards the Manager's office, a sizable room straddling the place between audience and stage. A private staircase would lead Mr. Edwardes to the backstage or through an opposite door to the auditorium. From this vantage point, he acted as conductor and controller of all.

Reaching the office door, Fanny paused and drew in a deep breath. The air was thick with dust from heavy fabric despite the army of cleaners. She pressed her shaking left hand into the soft fabric of her dress, pressure and conscious thought ceasing the involuntary tremor. It was a performance. Fanny Cooper was not needed. This was time for Fanny Robina. An imperceptible change crossed her face, a relaxed smile replacing the tightness of a frown, and she knocked on the door.

Mr. Edwardes, a man chronologically in his early thirties but with the overall appearance of a man designed to be in his fifties, occupied the space behind his polished wood desk and professional throne. It would have been more impressive had it not been crammed with piles of paper arranged like the towers of a castle. The towering stacks made Fanny feel uncomfortable as if the slightest breath would fill the room with descending drifts. It was a working desk, busy, but there was an order to it, reflecting the mind of the figure behind as it peered over an untidy moustache. Paradoxically, George Edwardes' hair was the product of many products and Fanny found her eyes, not for the first time, being drawn to the dome as it shone almost unnaturally in the reflected light. The care given to his head, however, did not appear to meet his face, and the change in texture only highlighted the shiny pate above those piercing green eyes. Rumour from backstage was that he refused to wear glasses and his perpetual squint was to accommodate, stretching his eyes to slits on either side of an aquiline nose. It made his expression harder to read, and Fanny saw nothing to explain her summons. Neither a tall nor vast man, he radiated a presence. The head of a burgeoning Empire of theatres, George Edwardes, was a man with his finger firmly on the pulse of changing tastes, and Fanny was worried.

"Thank you for agreeing to come to see me, Miss Robina. I do appreciate that this is highly unusual."

"How was the voyage? I have not had an opportunity to ask," said Fanny quickly, clearing her throat. The tightness threatened to strangle her words, but she would be dammed if she gave him total control of the conversation from the first sentence.

Edwardes paused. The question seemed to have derailed him as she had intended. His mind was on a singular track, and this had been unexpected. Clearly realising in his rush to speak he had appeared rude, he pulled back slightly and let his face relax a little.

"Good. Yes, good. It's not the epic voyage to Australia, but pleasant enough."

Fanny knew 'pleasant enough' was a first-class cabin and fine dining. It was not ninety-eight days prowling the deck and battling seasickness as the horizon rose and fell to reach halfway around the world. This was a man who required the finest fuel for his engine. She smiled, easing a little at a small victory, and now she took control.

"Mr. Edwardes, I cannot thank you enough for this opportunity. It has been a pleasure to accept your invitation to join the Gaiety Company, and the reviews have been very positive. I look forward to launching the new production." She regarded his face, and she continued as he opened his mouth to speak. "But, I am aware Mr. Hawtrey's company have taken an unusual step and engaged Mr. Dan Leno to join the Atlanta cast. I understand this, of course, has prompted many changes for us Mr. Edwardes." Edwardes closed his mouth, a blank look on his face. That much was obvious, but she was glad to be confirmed correct in her surmise.

Fanny raised a gloved hand as he moved forward in his seat to speak. "Let me stop you. I have been in the business long enough to know what all this means. It means closure, changes to the show or cast changes. As changes are already afoot, we are clearly not closing." She stopped and waited for him to realise he had a voice.

Dropping his eyes as if studying the nearest pile on his desk, Edwardes nodded. He looked up. "I appreciate your directness, Miss Robina and your insight, and yes, we need to act now to prevent losing audiences to Mr. Hawtrey. I will lance the wound and say that you will cease playing young Faust and play Siebel."

Fanny felt her lips narrow as her heart gave a single, loud thump. She felt a rising heat from her chest, which climbed to the sides of her face unbidden. Her body stiffened, and she forced her breathing to a slow and deep rhythm, not breaking eye contact with Edwardes.

Seibel, she reeled, the slimy sidekick of Faust, who at first joined him in lechery and then later betrays him. A smaller part, a character part, a clear demotion from Young Faust. She would no longer be top-billing or star alongside Florence StJohn.

After what felt like an eternity, she spoke. "Why?"

"Your reviews are good. But it was always going to be hard for the London Company to step into the void left by the cast who went to America."

"You mean stepping into principal boy lead usually reserved for Nellie Farren." Said Fanny bluntly.

"Yes. Miss St John and you would always be subject to comparison to the usual company, and frankly, between the two of you Miss StJohn's reviews are better."

Fanny couldn't deny this, and she understood how careers rose and fell on the subjective wave of audience reaction and taste. But there was something there, something unsaid and rang out like the wrong note in an orchestra.

"So, please correct me if I am wrong, Mr. Edwardes. I am being demoted because my reviews are not as good as Miss StJohn's?"

He nodded, and Fanny paused. He leaned forward, pushing a neatly folded handkerchief towards her. She noticed intertwined letters GE embroidered on the corner.

Fanny pushed it back towards him using a single finger. "And?"

He looked up quizzically.

"Mr. Edwardes. I appreciate your kindness and," she motioned down, "the clearly expensive handkerchief, which I will not be needing. But I believe you are not being entirely honest with me." She felt the blood pulsing around her body, driving the mind which raced ahead of her, forming the sentences which came almost without conscious assembly. "To complete with an engagement such as Mr. Leno and of course replace me as Young Faust, you must also have engaged someone to spark the press. Who?"

"Miss Violet Cameron"

Fanny leaned back. It suddenly made sense. Pip was right. If a star like Mr. Leno couldn't be found, someone drawing scandal behind them like a comet would do. Pip had been right as always, and Fanny had not been idle since their afternoon tea. She had found out all she could about the woman. Mr. Edwardes was a traditional man with strict views on family and relationships. However, he was also a businessman with considerable skill in managing the press. Miss StJohn had come to the theatre with an undeniable talent, but also in the wake of a scandal which had drawn people to her from the moment she arrived at Waterloo Station.

Violet Cameron came from Operetta and, most importantly, had, until recently, been the Mistress of the 5th Earl of Lonsdale. This combination of the more respectable theatre tradition and the end of an affair with an Earl, who had left to explore the Arctic at the end of the relationship, had a romance she could never compete with.

Fanny ached to break eye contact and take a moment to absorb the news, but she pressed her hands into the fabric of her dress to still the turmoil inside.

"I see." She said. "When?"

"Miss Cameron has taken up residence in a suite of rooms in Kensington and has been rehearsing there ready to attend the theatre for final rehearsals and assuming the role in two weeks. Miss Jones, one of our chorus girls will depart for a role elsewhere for pantomime I believe, and Miss McNulty will be recast from Siebel into the vacant role." He drew a deep breath. "I am sorry, Miss Robina. Your contract will be adjusted, and your pay accordingly, for the less prominent role, but I will agree to an additional period of two weeks commencing from today, while Miss Cameron is costumed and rehearsed at the theatre."

"And the press?"

"We feel it best to announce Miss Cameron's arrival without drawing specific attention to the cast changes as soon as possible. In the wake of Mr. Leno, a change will be less remarked upon and should draw little attention to yourself and Miss McNulty." He paused and looked at her, Fanny also knowing the lie this was. She had been demoted, and comments would be made. Her options were limited; Christmas engagements had been secured, and her only option was to take the new role and give a performance which attracted good reviews if she could outshine Miss Cameron, all the better.

"As you say, Mr. Edwardes, I am pragmatic and have a distaste for games. I am disappointed, but I am professional. Thank you for the opportunity. I will endeavor to perform to the highest standards as always." Fanny rose to leave and proffered a hand to Mr. Edwardes. "Thank you"

As she turned to leave, her face pointing away from him, for a moment the cracks of emotion started to widen across her face, Mr. Edwardes' voice followed her.

"Please report to Mrs. Freeman to check costumes, and Mercy will help you clean your dressing room. Miss Cameron will be arriving at the theatre tomorrow, but has kindly agreed to let you remain in situ until she assumes the role."

"Of course." She said brightly, without turning towards him, her hand paused upon the door so he could not see her face.

Chapter Thirty-Two

I can feel it rising, and I am not certain I can control it. I feel as if it is tearing my muscles from my bones. I want this, but without control it becomes a mindless animal.

The shoes of pale silk, arched to a curved heel and sprinkled with tiny flowers, had called me. Delicate and small, one single shoe could fit in my hand as if designed to be held. It glows gently in the candlelight, and I feel that thrill.

But I also feel mounting horror. How could she be chosen? I begged, and I prayed all night for someone else, another choice, but I cannot deny she is perfect. My head is clear: she is the one, but my heart cannot sink a knife into someone who has smiled at me and seen me.

But I know it will be guided, so I place the shoes in the circle of light and wait in the darkness until my knees are bruised and my skin becomes so cold that it feels like it belongs to someone else.

Chapter Thirty-Three – December 1888

N apper Challen was back on the boat coming home from war, but instead of the gunmetal grey of the slick waves, they were awash with a deep red, crowned with pink foam. The deck was empty of the crowded bodies he remembered, except for one figure he knew would be behind him. Wherever he was, it would be there in its terrible, frozen stillness, and he didn't have to look directly to be able to describe in detail every inch of it.

And the smell, not the salt of the open sea and the sewage of the rivers and estuaries, but the sour smell of old drink, rotten violets and the metal of blood, so plentiful it carried on the air. It was the scent of betrayal, infidelity and death that burrowed through soft flesh in the heat of battle. He spat a wide, foaming globule of spit on the floor, trying to clean his mouth, and the result slowly widened, joining the others which coated the floor in stomach acid and bile.

That first time she had risen to accuse him, the rain had turned the sky dark, and it had beaten on his shoulders like tiny fists. He had found himself walking the street one night when sleep would not come, lost in every way possible. It had all seemed strange, and he had started to feel an unfamiliar panic, which grew into a rage that even his streets were betraying him now.

And then he saw her. She had walked past him as if she didn't know him; her face, like the street, had the sense of one he knew well but underneath a layer of confusion. She looked older, but it had been twenty years. He had followed her, in some way, to control his confusion, following something familiar like a beacon. Despite the rain and cloying darkness, the streets felt crowded with blurred faces and was strange and distorted.

On that night, he had lost her trail and felt his heart aching with pain and grief. He waited for weeks, searching for faces until he saw her again. This time, he had followed her in the shadows and saw her walking into a house. It had taken hours to gather the courage, almost fearing what he would see, but finally, he knocked on the door. The woman answering said she did not know him. He tried to speak to her and explain, but her face seemed to vibrate, and he found her eyes blended into a line as they moved from side to side with speed. He found her shouting through the confusion, and the word 'no' finally rose into his consciousness. He had pushed at the closing door and followed her into the house, begging, pleading, but when the realisation it was not her finally dawned, he felt the tears running rivulets down his face. It wasn't her, and another piece of his heart turned to ash.

The anger was always there, rolling around inside. He had done his duty through hell and beyond and the police badge held so tightly in his hand had driven deep grooves into his palm before it had been taken from him. Napper had brought the battle back with him and all this beneath St Mary Matfelon, who was watching, guiding and judging his worth. But for the first time, he had started to feel afraid. He no longer had his badge, but he had kept his uniform. He had no other clothes; he had never felt the need, and on the rare occasion he tried, it had felt wrong, alien. So he affixed his campaign medal to his chest on the darker fabric of his jacket where his shield had been. The green ribbon, wrapped in an oak leaf holding the silver disk with an image of the Queen. But on the reverse was another image, one of a warrior who had done his duty and was being crowned by an angel with a laurel wreath. It would be in heaven he would be rewarded.

He continued to patrol at night, rising out of the darkness and protecting his streets. He was needed now more than ever. A nightmare was haunting Whitechapel, his Chapel, and he would chase it down. During the day, he ached and tried to sleep, but his mind ran away like water, and he felt afraid. He couldn't remember eating or drinking anymore, and when he did, it rolled in his stomach, and he expelled it like poison.

She had returned again and again, and each time, he had demanded, pleaded, raged, and simply asked her to leave him. Sometimes she laughed, sometimes she looked afraid, but each time it was still the same familiar face, the ghost who would always find him.

The streets of Whitechapel had devolved into fear and, at night, had become emptier than he had ever seen. It was like fear had done what law could not, and the gangs of vigilantes and groups of concerned citizens had made an uneasy truce with him, two habitual enemies who now operated in an uneasy alliance against a monster.

Napper would catch this creature. He felt the solid presence of the knife in his boot, the one handed to him by a friend in the mud a lifetime ago. With this, he would do what the Police and no other could do, and he would kill the Ripper.

But the patrols had taken a toll, and he felt an exhaustion in his bones, which was in danger of playing with his mind. He had seen the sleep-starved and crazed in the army. Men who started seeing things that were not there, heard noises no one else could and began to leave reality. These men were a danger to themselves and others, believing they could walk on water, walk through a hail of bullets believing there was no war and they were simply crossing the street for bread. These men got themselves and others killed.

As he went to spit again, he saw boots on the floor and looked up to see a suit and a face gazing down at him in concern.

"Mr. Challen?" came the query.

The door was open, and the shaft of light blinded him, and he saw only this silhouette and what looked like two others in the door. He tensed. He had not heard their approach. How?

"Mr. Napper Challen?" came the voice again.

"Corporal Challen, sir." He said, standing and saluting. Still in his uniform, his jacket open. It flapped either side of his torso as he raised his arm and rolled back his shoulders to draw himself ramrod straight.

"Corporal. My apologies. I am Doctor McDowell, and it is a pleasure to meet you. I did knock, but I think you were preoccupied."

Napper didn't move. He remained still, waiting for orders.

"Corporal, do you know why I have come to see you?"

"No, sir."

"I would like you to come with me to visit some colleagues of mine."

Napper's face remained fixed, but his eyes were full of query.

"Oh please..." said the doctor. "You can stop...." And then he came to a conclusion: "At ease, soldier."

Napper dropped his salute and relaxed his stance a little. The two figures at the door were still standing motionless, but, he reasoned, officers often had escorts.

"Would you accompany me? I have a carriage."

Napper continued to stare ahead. "Sir, yes, sir. Sir, I have a patrol at sunset and must return by then. I'm needed."

The Doctor smiled.

Napper insisted on buttoning his coat and putting his hat back on. He needed to be smart to meet these people. They were clearly influential, and they had recognized his hard work, realising the mistake they had made. They wanted him back.

§

What Mr. Field saw from his balcony above was a stick-thin man, slightly wobbling as he was helped into a carriage. His uniform was loose around his skeletal shoulders and covered in stains and tears. Field felt guilty that he had called Robert again. The boy had been through enough with this man, but it was clear something needed to be done. He had been slowly unravelling for months. Dr. McDowell had agreed, and the black carriage had arrived quickly.

Inside the carriage, Napper had looked out and seen a flash of a familiar face, but he shook his head. It couldn't be.

§

At dusk, when the sun was falling from the sky, Napper started to become agitated and asked, then demanded, to leave. Dr. McDowell had kept him waiting for hours, and he needed to return to patrol the Chapel. No one seemed to want to understand him, and the clamour from the other rooms had started to climb until the place was full of screams. He put his hands over his ears, but he could feel his now bootless feet sinking into mud, and he cried out for his uniform, knife, and medal. Once words were exhausted, Napper roared, long and loud, until hands, so many hands, crawled all over him and pushed him into silence.

§

Robert had watched the carriage leave from across the street, his face impassive. His eyes raised until he could see the door to the place, which was never a home. It stood open and drew his gaze into the darkness beyond. He thought about his father, now a husk, and he felt nothing but the wish he could sever the ties that bound them completely. If he could scrub the resemblance from his face, he would. He saw Mr. Field walk back into his home. Robert would never return here. Mr. Field could have anything in there he wanted.

Chapter Thirty-Four

*T*he fury is rolling around inside my ribcage, and it rocks me back and forth with its energy. Bile is running in rivers behind my tongue and collecting in my throat. I want to vomit it all up and cleanse myself. And this is why I acted with such impulse. I had seen this girl earlier. She was younger than usual, but she had the well-scrubbed and healthy look of someone not yet ingrained with life. And I wanted, needed, something clean and she was the alternative I had prayed for.

When I first approached her, she smiled. Something inside me wanted to see her face, look in her eyes. And in her eyes, I saw the smile drop away when she saw my face—really saw my face—and took a step back.

I saw her eyes darting back and forth, realising it was only the two of us and the mounting terror. I couldn't and didn't understand what she had seen, and I felt the anger rising. I stepped forward and put out a hand to push her against the wall and demand what she saw, what was written on my face. I had to know.

And she punched me.

Chapter Thirty-Five

The following two weeks were some of the hardest of Fanny's professional life. She had continued to perform as Young Faust in front of the audiences, but in the wings, like a malevolent shadow, lurked the figure of Violet Cameron, watching her like a fish gasping on a block at the market. Violet's smooth face wore a flat smile that never showed her teeth and failed to reach her eyes. Each move was a carefully rehearsed pose as if she existed below a carefully curated outer shell.

In the corner of Fanny's eye, while she stood bathed in the light of another performance, Violet was always there, mimicking her moves with delicate grace in the wings. During the day, Fanny watched with detachment as the cast practiced the changes, were fitted for new costumes and swarmed around Violet, who blankly smiled, appearing to stare through them. Fanny was the same size as Jenny, who had played Seibel before and would be handed the costume unadjusted at her last performance as Young Faust. She was being pushed into the sidelines, and she couldn't bear the looks of pity. On the surface, she appeared stoic; inside, she was falling to dust.

Violet Cameron had arrived at the theatre the morning after the news of Fanny's change in role was officially released. She had only a few hours to absorb it all before the fuse was lit and explosions of "No!", "Poor Fanny!" and "How the mighty have fallen" were sotto voce whispers in darkened corridors backstage. The only constant had been Teddy, who had entered quietly into her room and hugged her. He said nothing, letting his gesture speak for him before he left.

According to Mr. Edwardes Violet had 'kindly' agreed to let Fanny continue in her room until she took over as Young Faust. But the next morning Fanny arrived at the theatre to find Miss Cameron ensconced at the mirror applying power to a pale cheek. Even as the door to her dressing room opened, and Fanny's arrival and gasped apology obvious, Violet continued to pat her face with the small silver handled brush. Violet judged the perfect interlude between engrossed and rude before she put down the brush, closed the lid and slowly turned in the seat to look at Fanny. Without speaking she rose to her feet and picked up a white fur stole which had been artfully draped over the back of the chair.

"Fanny, isn't it?" she asked and without waiting for a reply left the room.

Fanny took a deep breath and rolled her head until her chin rested briefly on her upper chest and stretched out her neck to lengthen out the muscles which had tensed like rock. It was the first time they had met and Fanny already knew all she needed about Violet Cameron. It was about the only time Violet spoke to Fanny, unless on stage in character. Fanny had seen actresses like this before, pretty little yapping dogs with personalities of pure evil. This was Violet Cameron marking her territory and Fanny wondered if, like a dog, she had urinated on the seat.

§

Rehearsals continued, with changes being hammered into the cast through repetition and liberal shouting from Mr. Harris on behalf of Mr. Edwardes, whose voice had started to suffer.

"I have no idea why we are doing this. This is ridiculous." huffed George, finally putting a white hand around one of the handlebars of a cycle when he noticed the less-than-jovial warning glare from Mr. Free. The idea to flood the stage with bicycles and the sound of bells during the Act 2 song "Up to Date" had clearly been intended as a visual spectacle, thus proving the point the show was throwing everything it had at the audience. What it had not considered was George and the chaos of seven cycles and two tandems setting off from the relatively small space of the wings on either side of the stage. The idea was the audience would see lazy cyclists' mid-ride, singing as they peddled in a figure of eight across the stage and then off into the wings. What they currently had was George and various chorus members loudly huffing themselves vertical and setting off from a dead stop only a foot from the stage. Errant wheels were getting tangled, and Mr. Free was putting serious thought into gagging George to muffle the swearing.

§

Fanny hadn't cried; she had been too angry and had held it inside her like a ball in her chest, forcing it down until she had the time and space to let it go safely. Part of her was afraid it would grow and engulf her, exploding at a time when she had no control. Of course, she had experienced rejection, disappointment, and the sense of injustice that comes with these, but this was more public than most, and there was a real risk of damage.

Fanny's agent, Mr. Fox, of Fox and Co, a dapper man of striped trousers and Youman's hat, the popular winter alternative to the derby, had, of course, made haste to speak to her as soon as he heard, accompanied by his headgear, which perched on his head in a state of permanence. The combination, almost shouting his American heritage before him, even confirmed it with the laconic music of his accent. A showman brought across the Atlantic in the wake of the likes of Barnham and his circus, he stood out amongst the clusters of dark suits of London. Fanny understood many people's first impression of him; she had felt the same, but her brother-in-law recommended him and trusted his judgment. Mr. Fox, as it had become apparent, was well-named.

As soon as was possible he swept up the pathway to Fanny's home, early frost crunching underfoot and leaving neat prints behind him. Sitting, one leg bent and one straight, as if he was dismounting a horse, Mr. Fox, elbows on the table, had spent a long moment looking at Fanny.

"You know what I want to say, so I will not waste time."

Fanny had smiled, knowing he would have swept into the meeting with Mr. Edwardes, and her presence may not have even been necessary for negotiation. But she also knew the chances were the outcome would have been the same with or without him.

Stan was working this morning, and the baby was tucked up into a pram under copious layers of thick blankets; the only parts visible were two large eyes and a red nose. She was being expertly steered through the park by Mary, who was likewise wrapped up, her breath leaving clouds of silver whose path indicated her speed and direction of travel.

"Yes," Fanny said frankly, "I appreciate your concern.... And", she continued as Mr. Fox's eyebrows rose, "your role, but I needed to do it myself." Equally, she also accepted, albeit only to herself, that she had not anticipated the turn of the conversation, and this rankled her.

"We have two options. The first is we fight your contract, and the second is you leave entirely. The problem with both is lengthy litigation and court. However, it also means press."

Fanny drew a deep breath. She had been unable to sit down and was pacing on the woolen rug, her shoes sinking into the thick fibre. Pausing by the mantle, she caught her face in the mirror and saw herself stripped bare of the layers of physical and emotional artifice and the wetness threatening her eyes. She placed her hand on the cold marble and borrowed the shock of the touch to drive down the emotion.

"And the third?"

Mr. Fox sat back, his head tilted and lips in a thin line.

"I said two options, Miss Robina."

"I know, but there are three."

He blew air between his lips and seemed to deflate a little. "Go on."

"I do nothing. I keep quiet, accept this, finish the show as Seibel and move on. I give the press nothing, and they quickly forget."

Mr. Fox looked at her for a long moment. "Is that what you want?"

"Mr. Fox, Charlie, I have thought about this, and I think I should finish the job, still giving my all, and slip away quietly at the end. I have future engagements and a family to think of." She paused and waited.

When he did not immediately respond, she added, "I know what this means for you as the payment will reduce, but..."

Charlie Fox stood and walked over to Fanny. She never asked him to remove his hat when visiting. She recognised, like Sampson, it seemed to be the seat of his genius. But he removed it now and held the brim. His exposed head looked smaller, and she noticed a line across his forehead where the hat habitually sat.

"Fanny, we know the business is brutal, but you are an extraordinarily talented performer. You shine on stage, and people love you. But the business is also a cruel mistress; sometimes, she demands an innocent sacrifice, and this time, it is you. But what is precious and shines is also hard and cannot be destroyed, so if this is what you wish to do, then we will do this. I think you are correct, and although this will be a difficult time, you will survive. And I will be with you at every step."

And Fanny knew she had made the only choice she could to preserve and protect her career and her family. Charlie Fox was a friend but a realist and a businessman. He had cards to play, and she was sure some well-timed stories would emerge over the next few weeks, which would draw attention from her.

"And if, in the meantime, Miss Cameron and her travelling scandal is overshadowed by real talent, it would be a dreadful shame." He winked, and a broad smile split his face and lit up his green eyes.

§

Fanny had felt relieved after her conversation with Mr. Fox, and even when cornered a few nights later in the hot air balloon at the end of act two by Florence, she felt her resilience slowly returning. In the wings was Miss Cameron, her thin and dead smile appearing to have no relationship with her mood or activity. It had started as an annoying affectation and had now become unsettling. It made her unreadable. This time, she was not deigning to look at Fanny; she was gazing out across the auditorium, her pale face bathed in reflected light and her eyes ablaze with ambition.

"It's such a shame about your role, dear," Florence had whispered as the basket under the balloon rose into the fly tower. The basket, as always, creaked under the strain, and Fanny felt the familiar lurch against each pull of the rope from the wings.

"After all, you do your best, and I hear this new 'you' is adequate but more famous for off-stage activities and busy popping out the Earl's bastards. I'm sure she thought enough little darlings dogging her heels and she'd be set for life, but it didn't stop him hopping on a boat into the wilds to get away from her." Florence continued to wave and resolutely face the audience, a broad smile plastered to her face, but her eyes slid to her left to Fanny, who continued to face front and smiled through the daggers.

When there was no response, Florence continued, "I shall refuse to work with her. After all, we are a pair, aren't we? During all this time, we have had a bond. She's got dead eyes, like a fish."

Fanny's smile only cracked slightly, but her eyes widened. "No need to do anything on my behalf."

As the basket soared into the darkness and left the brightness of the stage, Florence turned to Fanny.

"I mean it, Fanny. This isn't fair. It's shocking. I don't think anyone knows what to say to you." Strong hands grabbed the basket and guided Florence to the gantry, where she stepped lightly out. For a moment, shorn of the exuberant personality, Florence had seemed smaller and full of sincerity, which stunned Fanny. As they rushed onto the stage for the applause, Fanny walked out into the audience's roar and bowed. As the cast took their final group bow in a long line, Fanny next to Florence, and they took hands. As they bowed, Fanny whispered 'Thank you' and received the smallest of squeezes in response.

§

As the two weeks finally drew to an end, much of the dressing-room was now full of Violet's belongings, and Fanny's were thrown into a corner. Already a space full of the riot of heavy floral wallpaper, gilt, blown glass lights, and scroll-carved furniture, it was now bursting at the seams with flowers, cards and a selection of expensive dresses.

Fanny had taken to asking her driver to take her past the new Ravenscourt Park on the way to the Gaiety. She ached to get out and walk, using the time to stride in peace, her legs beating out her frustration and to be able to breathe in the sharp air by the ornamental lake. It wasn't visible from the cab, but she always imagined the frozen water, opaque and brittle behind the screen of trees, as the fish glided beneath the barrier in the silence. On the surface, ducks would be paddling around on splayed feet, looking for a small gap to slide in and swim or huddle in little piles of dark feathers on the banks. Fanny felt the aching gap of freedom curtailed. There had been five women now murdered in Whitechapel, two on the same night and the last only weeks ago, Mary Kelly, an Irish woman, had been emptied of all her organs, which had been thrown around in a seeming fury. The press had gone into sickening detail, but what stuck in Fanny's mind was the last sightings of Mary before her grizzly ending. She had been dancing in the street before returning home and was heard singing 'Violets From My Mother's Grave'. It was an old folk song and one Fanny's own mother had sung to her when she was a child in whatever makeshift home they had made on their perpetual touring lives. They were miles apart in circumstance, but this single thread of a song connected two women, one now beyond the hand of God and one too afraid to walk in a park.

Fanny hummed as the cab clattered past the bank of streets, towards the clustered stone of Westminster, and onto the Strand. The humming grew until she found her mouth rounding on the words which came from somewhere deep in the past.

'Only a violet I plucked when but a boy,
And oft' times when I'm sad at heart, this flow'r has given me joy,

But while life does remain in memoriam, I'll retain
This small violet I plucked from mother's grave.'

It was quiet, and the heat from her body seemed to glow against the cold. The air was crisp and still. Noises from outside the cab travelled in as notes, loud and sharp. Even with the door and windows closed, it felt like ice as she drew deep lungfuls and felt the familiar band of cold beneath her ribs before she exhaled its warm companion breath. Fanny looked out across London, realising for the first time that she was truly physically alone since she lost her role. It was almost overwhelming and broke over her in a wave which threatened to engulf her. She lived in perpetual noise, chaos and sensory stimulation. For the first time, Fanny was quiet enough to truly hear her body, thoughts, and that innermost world. And she knew it was time to let the grief, the anger and the hurt go. The silent cry erupted, animal, without articulation and not designed to amuse or please. It was raw, unfettered, and for the first time, Fanny let the tears flow.

Chapter Thirty-Six

*M*y ribs are on fire, and when I pull up my shirt, I can see the bruises rising up to the surface and know there will be more to come. She fought me until my vision blurred and narrowed, and so my fists rained down.

I pounded into soft flesh, and when her arms finally stopped flailing and clawing, I slid my knife out of my coat. Standing above her, I took a handful of hair and pulled her head back, drawing my knife from one ear towards the other. I felt the skin and sinew splitting in response to the blade, and in my fury, I pressed too hard and felt it bite into the bone and stop.

I pulled it away with what was left of my strength and heard the grind as it tore free.

Chapter Thirty-Seven

The two weeks had ended in a heartbeat, and before she knew it, Fanny was in a smaller dressing room, a floor above the rooms reserved for the stars and Violet Cameron was crammed amongst pillars of flowers, cards and admirers. Jenny McNulty, who had initially played Seibel and had been displaced by Violet Cameron and Fanny, moved up to the large chorus dressing room. She was subject to the largess of the girls who showered her with sisterly comfort and promised never to speak to Miss Cameron. Jenny seamlessly slotted into the dressing table and role of the girl who had left at Christmas. Fanny tried to talk to Jenny, but a defensive barrier of girls was in constant attendance, and Fanny felt tinges of resentment, which, while she understood, made her feel like an outsider.

Mercy had arrived at Fanny's new dressing room with armfuls of the Seibel costume, which she dropped on a chair without a word and walked out. The careful subservience much in evidence since Fanny's arrival was now gone and replaced by a thin veneer of civility and a total lack of interest. Fanny now had to fend for herself, and Mercy had made it clear her job was done, and she was now fawning over Miss Cameron and Miss StJohn with what appeared as conspicuous efficiency.

§

It was with relief and delight to arrive home that night to find Stan and Florrie both awake and in the parlour.

"She's grown again and why on earth is she awake!" Fanny laughed, pulling the girl into her arms and pressing her face into the soft hair.

"Our precious jewel has indeed grown to titanesque proportions and, I fear, has given up sleep entirely." He smiled and wrinkled his top lip playfully. "I think she needs new shoes, love, but I haven't the first idea, and Mary said that there are some waters only a mother should swim in."

Fanny held her daughter's foot in her hand and examined it. It still had the rounded softness of the newly minted baby, but she could see it starting to lengthen, and her heart gave a slight lurch at another change she had missed. She looked up and caught Stan's eye.

"Are you surviving my love?" he asked. His face was a mask of concern. Fanny knew she would worry him if he saw her distressed, but she also needed to share her world. She nodded in agreement and assurance. Stan rose and walked to her, his large arms encircling his family.

"I am grateful for what you did, and I know it has cost you dearly." Fanny shrugged.

"No, hear me. I must say this. You are my wife in every way which matters. My heart is and always will be with you here. And for Florrie and myself.... thank you."

Fanny felt Florrie squirm in her arms, knowing she was probably feeling her discomfort. Stan kissed her on the head, and she relaxed, knowing that this was now over and she could return to her happy domestic bubble. She hoped it would last.

§

The following morning, Fanny's boots felt heavy and reluctant to return to the theatre. After only a few hours' sleep, she had risen early and took a cab to the theatre, gazing out of the window. In Australia, she had seen the cathedral-like red mounds of the swarms of termites in the outback. They had equally fascinated and repulsed her, but that duality had come to her as she looked at London and its equivalent. Figures, almost funneled into lines along the pavements and roads, busy and full of purpose against tall buildings painted in shades of black and grey—they scurried in and out, full of a sense of importance.

Albert was at the stage door. He looked up and nodded, acknowledging her presence.

"Auditorium at ten. Full run." He paused and seemed to conclude: "She's already here in the dressing room."

Fanny nodded in thanks, noting the word 'the' substituted for 'her' dressing room. Violet had walked into a difficult situation but failed to attempt to address it and appeared to have a deft skill in alienating people she clearly felt beneath her. This starkly contrasted her behaviour with those she clearly deemed able to offer her an advantage. Those individuals bathed in the light of her, bright smile, full attention and apparent admiration.

Fanny made her way to her dressing room. As she turned the stairs to her old room and onwards to her new, she felt a slight pull in her chest but suppressed it with a deep breath and continued to climb.

Fanny had adjusted to the new dressing room and took time to arrange things to her satisfaction before making her way to the auditorium for Mr. Edwardes' speech and a show rehearsal. Her heart fluttered, and part of her hoped to melt into the corridor walls on her way to the main stage. Mercifully, costumes were not required, but she made sure she changed her shoes and wore the character's hat to help her find the sense of this new person. Siebel was a poisonous snake of a man, and part of her felt the familiar twinge of excitement at a new role, and her mind was already seeking ways to manifest this individual from the shoes up. Judge the walk correctly and the character would rise upwards from there. Fanny would share some stage time with the new Young Faust, Violet Cameron, but she was determined to dive into this character and give it everything she could, even if it meant acting against someone Florence had described as having the blank stare of a fish.

Fanny found a seat in the stalls. The chorus was already occupying at least two rows, with heavy shawls, bags, and hats strewn over empty seats, creating a buffer zone in which they laughed and joked. Fanny saw them notice her as she took her seat in what felt like a de-militarised area between the star turns in the front and the chorus further back, knowing the choice would secure her as someone unable to let go of her elevated status or now lost in the masses. She caught the eye of Jenny, who gave her a small smile and a nod, followed by greetings from the other girls, who appeared to take Jenny's nod as a cue for how Fanny would be received from now on. Fanny greeted them all, thankful that the hurdle had been successfully navigated.

"Dear Boy," came a familiar voice as Teddy navigated the row of seats in front of her. Harry and George followed him like ducklings. George took a sideways hopping gait between the seats as his girth failed to allow him to walk down the narrow gap.

Teddy leaned over the seat and patted Fanny's hand. He winked, and she smiled back. George and Harry slid into the seats, the springs opening with an audible 'thunk'. George squirmed his knees to the right and, accompanied by huffs, puffs and groans, finally found a semi-comfortable position. Harry sat on the seat across with knees astride the arching back of the chair in front and slid down into a slouch. Harry seemed to be able to melt into furniture in a way which always found the optimal position of comfort. He closed his eyes and let the world revolve around him.

"I don't know how he does it," said George. "This is purgatorial. I'd rather sit on Teddy, and he's practically a stick."

Teddy grinned. "You can always get a bicycle now, George."

"No!" said Harry, his eyes slamming open. "I've had to push that lazy swine on the stage for the last two weeks. The only way he would manage alone is to lay on the ground and cycle on the air."

George squirmed in his seat and produced an arm which he used to take a swing at Harry, who accepted the wafting arm on the chest with a laugh.

"Is that all you have? At least we'll never lose you. There are people in Hackney who can hear you huffing and puffing your way across the stage."

"Well, it's rude to leave a lady alone, and who on earth would want to sit next to these two bores."

Teddy vaulted the chair back easily and took the next seat to Fanny.

"Show off", muttered George and went back to trying to find a comfortable position.

Teddy said nothing but glanced sideways at Fanny and winked as the sound of heavy footsteps filled the auditorium and announced Mr. Edwardes's arrival. He was accompanied by the faster staccato of the spherical Mr. Harris and, behind him, Mr. Free, who made almost no sound at all.

"Good morning, ladies and gentlemen of the cast. I am here to firstly thank you for the triumphal tour of 'Faust Up to Date' and secondly to welcome you to our refreshed and reinvigorated show. We have undertaken some cast changes, of which I know you are aware. Maria has left us for new pastures. Miss Jenny McNulty is now playing Martha and Miss Fanny Robina, Siebel. I am sure you join me in thanking them for their hard work and wishing them well in their new roles."

After a pause, Mr. Harris applauded, flapping his hands together and making meaningful looks at the cast, who unenthusiastically joined suit. Mr. Edwardes pursed his lips and looked at Harris, who stopped and smiled. He missed the brief flash of irritation on Mr. Edwardes' face.

"Yes.... Ehm... I am delighted to welcome our new star, Miss Violet Cameron, who....." He stopped and peered into the auditorium. From the side of his mouth, he hissed, "Mr. Harris, where is Miss Cameron? And..." He looked out again. "And we also appear to be lacking Miss StJohn."

A look of panic rose in Mr. Harris's pinhole eyes. He looked around until they alighted on Mr. Free, who was already striding off the stage and up to the dressing rooms.

Deep in the wings, Tosher was perched on a large basket next to Ida, her hand in his. Between his knees perched Mouse, grubby Penny Dreadful clutched in a bony hand, the paper frayed and creased. They watched the situation playing out on stage as Mr. Edwardes spoke animatedly with Mr. Harris, his shiny hair catching the light from above and reflecting it to the wings. The little party said nothing and watched as other pairs of eyes from the gantry, high above the crew, smiled and gestured between them in the silent language of the darkness.

Eventually, Mr. Free, accompanied by a red-faced Mrs. Freeman, rushed across the stage.

"Well?" said Mr. Harris. "Mr. Edwardes is waiting."

Mr. Free looked to his wife, who looked at Mr. Harris but wisely directed her response to the rapidly heating Mr. Edwardes.

"She won't come down until Miss St John does, sir."

Mr. Edwardes paused for a moment, letting the information settle. "And...?"

"Miss St John won't come down until Miss Cameron does." She finished.

"But... eh.... Mr. Free, help me." Mr. Edwardes finally stuttered.

"It appears Mr. Edwardes and Mr. Harris that both ladies feel, being the star turn......"

Mr. Edwardes raised his hand, stopping her. "I think I understand.

A voice from the auditorium called, "They could come down together......."

"Mr. Lonnen," cried Harris, "I don't think that is appropriate."

"So," came Teddy's response, "it's a case of the last woman standing, and we wait here until kingdom comes or George needs another cigarette."

"Good call, old boy," said George, standing.

"Sit down!" came the exasperated cry from Edwardes. I will speak to them and try to broker a truce, and Mr. Harris, please run anything you can that does not include either lady."

Edwardes strode towards the dressing room and high-level negotiation. Mr. Harris flapped his hands as if shooing a flock of pigeons. "Up, up, up......"

Reluctantly, the cast rose to their feet and made their way to the stage.

"Mr. Parker, we will start with your entrance. Mr. Lonnen, standby. Act One Beginners!"

Chapter Thirty-Eight

I *see it all, the conversations, trysts, things hidden so deeply people thought they were invisible: Miss St John and her creeping maid with the sharp face, who changes shape to suit her audience. Mr. Stone scuttles from the scene dock door to avoid the men in suits who politely but firmly wait to speak to him at the stage door and Mr. Free who hides himself behind the walls of misfits and his nosy wife. I see them all, even the ones who think they step lightly.*

Miss Robina had been a mystery, but a little conversation, a real name, and the right ears, and he found Fanny Cooper's extended East End origins. For example, a bastard father, the butcher and poultry thief uncle who had been boated to Australia in chains for theft. That would take the shine off her if everyone knew she was from a piss-poor East End family of thieves.

It is so easy. I am always pleasant and courteous enough not to be a threat. People live in little bubbles with themselves at the centre looking out. Still, they never realise the crumbs of information they drop, the weakness they broadcast, and that someone willing to patiently wait and watch can eventually own them.

It always amazes me how willingly these sheep seem to lead themselves to slaughter.

Chapter Thirty-Nine – January 1889

The sense of levity accompanying Christmas and New Year was now replaced by exhaustion. In the chorus room tired feet were rubbed with aching hands, faces pinched to try to bring the appearance of health back to sallow cheeks, and the usual bubble of conversation had withered away to the passing of necessary instruction only. Alice cast a weak smile on Emma, who puffed out her cheeks and placed her forehead on the cold dressing table. Everything was like ice up here. The place appeared made of holes, and she wondered if dressing out on the street would be warmer. A cold theatre always seems to settle into conditions below those of the outdoors, and any measures, such as the deployment of hot water bottles, just seemed to make the areas not immediately around the source of the warmth even colder.

In the corner across from Alice, Mabel had tried to wring out the cloth she used to wipe the remains of liberal applications of cold cream off her face, but it was almost rigid with crystals. She placed it down next to her brush, and the fabric seemed to maintain the shape of her hand. Mabel was exhausted, felt ignored and was wondering why she was even here instead of at home in the warm. She had danced until her fleet erupted in blisters, making her silk stockings stick to her and she painfully peeled them off. Her muscles ached and prevented her from sleeping and, on some occasions, locked so hard she was unable to move and only whimper until the pain passed.

Christmas, only a few days ago, had been rounds of parties, events and special shows for the Prince and his endless entourage. A large man, made of soft curves upon stick-thin legs, his neat, angular beard already showed some grey. His hooded eyes gave him the appearance of one who was barely awake, but when he insisted on meeting the cast after the show, he walked from person to person, greeting them by name and pausing to share words based on keen observance. The Prince had insisted on meeting the chorus and had held Mabel's pale hand, muttering "Thirteen? So young..." and moved on. Mrs. Love had questioned her in minute detail afterwards and appeared disappointed at the outcome.

§

Fred and Earnest, still semi-inhabiting their onstage characters of Fan-Fan and Estella, were sprawled on the floor, propped up against the side of the dressing table and covered in a nest of blankets. Frank produced a small, pewter hip flask and took a small sip before passing it to Earnest. Both wore a mix of plaid trousers, vests and braces, but their faces remained heavily made up in the white powder of the simulation of a female. Black liner cracked at the edges of painted eyes, which had lifted with the sweat of exertion. The bold line would have met their wigs, but currently, they were lying on the floor in a pile a few feet away.

Jenny frowned as Earnest took a drink, and then she pointedly handed it to her. She took a large mouthful.

"Ah!" said Frank in dismay.

Jenny smiled, wiped the top of the flask, and handed it back to Earnest, who handled it with two fingers like a dead mouse.

"The Frenchman has been trying to worm his way back in again." Said Frank, peering into the flask and shaking it to ascertain what was left.

"He offered me money to smuggle him in," said Emma.

"How much?" demanded Alice.

"A pound," Emma announced.

"That's a handsome sum. Then he hasn't got it, has he? Paid on St Never's Day, I'd imagine," laughed Jenny. "He's broke. Trying to get in to have a go at the great Miss StJohn's jewel box."

There was a snort from Frank and Earnest.

"Anyway." Warned Jenny. "There's enough going missing as it is."

"What with all the moving about, things are bound to disappear Jenny. It doesn't mean anything is going on," said Alice with a sigh.

"Jenny's too late to lock up her jewel box anyway. I think the key is broken." Laughed Emma.

Jenny grinned as the laughter rolled around her. "At least mine aren't covered in dust."

Frank took a last gulp of the flask's contents and went to stand. He swayed.

"Go easy on that," said Jenny. "We can't roll you home."

"The night is young ladies. I am going out to play," he responded, waving the flask in the air in a salute.

§

In the fly tower, William was raising the final backcloth back into position to be ready for the next show. He tied off the ropes and rubbed his sore hands. His breath left clouds in the air. Even up here, it was perishing, and the rising heat of the lights usually warmed the space by the show's end. But it was something to do on his day off, and he would never admit it to anyone, least of all Robert, but the Gaiety had cast a spell on him, and he ached to be here.

He swung himself onto the ladder, and accompanied by the sound of metal vibrating, he placed a practised foot on the side rails and slid down to the stage floor. Despite his size, he was agile and quick, a legacy of another life.

Mrs. Freeman jumped as the figure landed behind her.

"Oh my stars, you scared the life out of me." She paused, fanning herself with a hand. "William, isn't it?"

"Yes, ma'am", he responded, taking off his hat and nodding.

As his face caught the light, he saw her startle again. It was instinctual, and she covered it well, but he saw it because he was looking for it.

"I have to go," he said. "Working tomorrow, so I need to get to bed."

"Thank you for your help William."

He smiled and walked away, his face dropping as he turned away from the small woman.

Mrs. Freeman scolded herself. Of course, he had noticed, and she felt terrible. Robert had brought his friend here to help, and she had just insulted him. She knew he was a police officer, but he looked incongruous. It was abundantly clear in the daylight that he was a product of the street and, from the look of it, the ones akin to hell. He looked like the devil himself in the semi-darkness of a steady theatre light.

As William replaced the hat on his head and went to the door, he passed Albert, who was guarding the door from the crowds outside.

"Goodnight, sir" William called.

Albert nodded. "Robert'll be along soon."

§

As William walked back between pools of darkness and the street lights, hands thrust deep into his pockets, he huddled his shoulders against the cold. He couldn't afford a good coat yet but had survived worse. He was getting soft, but he was also looking forward to some time alone at home without the presence of Robert. Albert would undoubtedly take his protégé to the pub as a thank-you for helping this evening.

Chapter Forty

The hunt is only ever a part of the process, and tonight, I have unexpected time. It is only a tiny slice of the whole thing, but it is the moment in which my heart beats the loudest. I am always amazed that it isn't audible above the sounds of the streets, even on the quietest nights.

She sung out to me like a siren, drawing me behind in her wake as she lightly stepped across slick cobbles, delicate steps with a slight click as the heel touched down. The need was overwhelming, and I could feel the familiar and satisfying tingle of hairs rising on my neck. She was perfect. I looked down; yes, I had my knife thrust into my boot. I reached down and felt it slide into my hand like an old friend.

I carefully kept her on the edge of my vision, not near enough for her to identify my presence but near enough for her to fully enjoy the moment. As she started to leave the main street and enter the rookery of narrow back alleys, I drew closer, already feeling the warm wetness of fresh blood.

And now, I am near enough to go back to the theatre and collect a sack, and by the time it is finished, the space would be empty and belong to me. No one will miss me this evening. I have all the time in the world.

Chapter Forty-One – February 1889

Jenny and Earnest's joint effort finally managed to push the door to the dressing room open, and the chair blocking it had fallen aside. On her way up the stairs, Jenny had seen a pale Earnest knocking on his dressing room door on the middle landing; his pleading entreaties for Frank to let him in were eliciting no response. Though not an abnormal occurrence there was something in Earnest's tone which made her stop and take in the scene in more detail. It was then she noticed small spots of blood in front of the door and a smear of red finger marks around the doorknob. A heavy feeling spread through her gut, and she joined an increasingly frantic Earnest at the door.

"We have to get in, Jenny." Earnest turned to Jenny, his round face drained of colour and clearly on the verge of panic.

"I'll get Albert", she started to say, but a voice cut across her, and a hand gripped her arm as she turned to leave.

"No!" Earnest hissed, "Please, just help me get the door open." and he applied his shoulder to the splintered wood. Jenny, despite her confusion, joined him.

The locks were old, and the wood around them chipped and dented from years of abuse, so a shoulder applied to the beleaguered door took little real effort. The sight that greeted them left Earnest frozen in the doorway, eyes wide with horror. A trail of blood led across the ancient and balding rug into a corner where Frank was curled, his hands a mass of red, and his clothes torn.

"Go away! Please, just leave me. Please," his hand waved at them, palm up, and his face streaked with gore and snot was swollen and disfigured.

"Oh God" Jenny gasped, her face paled.

"Please, go away, please. It's.... It's...... I can..." Frank put bloodied hands to the floor and, as he tried to rise, jolted like he had been shocked, and his arm gave way, dropping him into a heap. He cried out involuntarily and started to sob. His body rocked with the strength of it. Earnest ran forward into the room and pulled the door closed behind him.

"Jenny, get some hot water and clean towels."

Jenny looked at Earnest in shock.

"Now, Jenny. And don't you tell anyone. "He looked away, the request made and pushed back Frank's hair.

"They really got you this time didn't they love."

Frank nodded, the corners of his mouth downturned in a grimace of physical and emotional bewilderment.

"I'm so sorry, I only...... they.... they,.... they wouldn't stop." Frank gasped in pain as he tried to say the words "I begged them..... And they wouldn't stop."

"Oh, love," said Earnest, stroking his head. "You're safe now, and we will clean all this up."

Frank nodded, and slowly, like a child learning to walk, Earnest guided him on unsteady legs to the battered couch. Frank looked down at his torn shirt and the trail of blood on the rug. "I will clean it up. I promise."

"Damn the bloody rug. I don't care about the bloody rug. It can catch fire. We'll sling it out the window."

Frank regarded Earnest in shock. The usually mild, steady, dependable foil to his exuberance was angrier than he had ever seen, and he felt a sliver of shock stab past the dull aching of his broken body.

"I don't care," said Earnest quietly, searching Frank's face for understanding.

The door opened, and both heads quickly turned, relaxing at Jenny's face. She was carrying a large bowl with towels slung over an arm. She closed the door with a foot and placed the bowl on the floor before them.

"What happened?" she said, kneeling by the bowl as Earnest started to wet and wring out a towel before placing a hand on Frank's chin to raise it.

"You know the drill," he said, and Frank winced as the water touched his bruised and lacerated skin.

Jenny sat back on her haunches and regarded the scene. Frank's slight and usually joyful figure seemed so small and fragile, and Earnest, quiet and often fading into the background off-stage, appeared to fill the couch.

She reached into her pocket and took out a small tin and bandages. "I have these," she said, proffering the items to Earnest. Albert keeps them behind his desk for emergencies."

Earnest's head shot around, words framing a protest.

"No", Jenny interrupted. "He never saw me. I can put it back when we're finished and I've wiped round the door. I'll say I borrowed these for my feet...... Lots of dancing in the chorus." She looked down, her smile brittle.

Earnest regarded her. "Thank you." He looked round at Frank, eyes narrowing. "And you?"

"I'm careful, I always am. I only go to meet .... "He winced, not finishing the sentence "...at Molly Houses only, but no, this was those bloody vigilantes."

Earnest nodded in realisation. "Oh."

"I was on my way back....from a Molly......" he looked at Earnest's disapproving face. "Where else can I go? It's not like you see men walking around carrying signs, is it?" he paused. "Well, one of those bloody vigilante groups that have spilt out of Whitechapel started to hassle me about being a man out late. 'Concerned Citizens and Local Business Owners' keeping the streets safe and hunting for that bloody .... Leather Apron, Ripper, whatever the bastard is called now. Bloody ironic if I was him! I'm the last person out looking to do anything to a woman." He looked down at Jenny, and red flashed in the spaces between bruises.

"I know about Molly Houses."

"They thought you were the Ripper?" said Earnest.

"Of course not! They're gangs of men who'll tell the Coppers they're trying to keep the streets safe from bloody murder, but maybe along the way, they can clean up a few of the least desirables, shut down a few unwanted rivals, settle old personal scores and maybe help themselves to a few things gratis."

Earnest put the used cloth into the bowl, and red bloomed through the water.

"Hand," he commanded, and Frank placed it on Earnest's proffered one. Dark jelly gathered around a perfect line of sliced flesh, exposing white and pink layers. On the other side of the hand was a smaller wound, just as ragged. "A knife?" he almost shouted. He looked up and around Frank, exploring for any more cuts.

"Well, once they'd stuck me in the hand, they couldn't get it back out to do more damage." He motioned to a bloody knife by the door. "I managed to pull it out when I got back here. It feels a bit strange."

Earnest looked at the damaged hand and back up at Frank. Tears were flowing freely down his face. "You fool."

Frank ran a hand across a running nose. "I'll survive."

"And next time?" demanded Earnest. "The next time when they bring more than one knife, big fists and no brains?" Saying nothing, Earnest wrapped the hand and picked up the bowl. He left the room in silence.

"He'll deny it, but he loves me," Frank said.

"Then why?"

"You wouldn't understand."

Jenny frowned.

"Like you and your sisters upstairs, we are birds in a gilded cage. We flock together to keep safe and are tolerated for our talent and beauty. Outside of the cage, we are ... A problem, vulnerable to anyone who hates us or wishes we would disappear. Freedom is an illusion my lovely girl."

Chapter Forty-Two

*T*here is a legend. To possess someone's boots is to hobble their spirit from roaming.

And I crouch, my whole body balanced on my flexed toes, as I watch the light shimmer and cast shadows across the remains of a woman.

The boots are like the first, solid and brown. Mud and wear have darkened the toes, but the heels and ankles remain lighter with patches of the original soft fawn brown. The soles are soft arched towards the heel and worn smooth but even, and the heels show a crescent of five small nail holes where the head of the nail glistens with wear. When she walked, they had a distinctive click that called to me, cutting across the mundane noises of the night.

There is a slight imperfection on the ankle of the right heel, and I pick it up, turning it gently in my hands. The leather is thin, and I can run my hands over cracks and dents where it has molded to her foot like a glove. My fingers run across the boot in the half-light, using my senses to explore, memorising the texture and shapes. I hold it up to my face and breathe deeply.

I am the red boy, naked and baptised in blood, and I listen to the tale the boots tell me before I pick up a soft cloth and start to work.

Chapter Forty-Three

Mercy straightened her skirt and smoothed her hair. Caesar was all hands, but that was one of the attractions. The hands making a mess of her clothing during stolen moments in borrowed corners, usually behind the lounge gallery, were smooth and not unpleasant. Caesar could slide away from the restaurant from the front of the theatre and Mercy across from the backstage area to this place in the middle, out of the gaze of others. It was convenient. She had time to indulge his wish for a short fumble and could ensure he didn't start to become creative and deviate from the plan.

Mercy! She had liked that name. Caesar had suggested it as they strolled along the Thames on the way to find work. This time, they hadn't gone far, only a few miles, but she had learned people never really look at an individual and even less at domestic staff. It was a cloak of invisibility and access to all areas. Working in the big houses had been a good start, rambling estates where staff could be let go on Tuesday and turn up a few miles away, on the same estate, with a new name on Thursday and get a job. She had started in service at thirteen, farmed out by a family with too many children and sending all her money home to support the arrival of even more. Her life had started before dawn and consisted of dirty grates, a hard wooden floor, and hands that were so raw they were constantly swollen and cracked. Mercy decided early on that hard work or constant pregnancy was not going to be her fate, and she felt nothing but revulsion at the whole process. The expectation had been that she would find a boy, marry and become like her mother. Mercy packed her bags, filled her pockets with whatever she could find and left. She never looked back.

Those early weeks had been an interesting lesson in humanity. She was young and relatively nondescript. On the rare occasions she had enough to eat, she never seemed to put on weight, but she was driven by force, a fire, which seemed to eat everything and lit a flame behind her eyes. When she was old, she would have time to rest and grow fat, and she looked forward to it and to the maids who would bustle around her.

It had been easy to secure another job in a neighbouring town. She had travelled far enough for her old name and the familial features of her face to blend into obscurity, but she had spent time watching the place and the people and learned. By the time 'Annie' arrived at the door, neat, scrubbed, and meek, she knew the names of all the staff and those small pieces of information that opened an individual up like a clam. Mrs. Burbidge, the housekeeper, was a woman with a love of the Lord and a sincere drive to save lost souls. It had been easy, a cross, subtly worn and a suitable sprinkling of verses from the bible, and she had been welcomed without the need even for references. Annie had accompanied Mrs. Burbidge to church twice weekly and tried not to fall asleep in the unforgiving pews. Once the spring arrived and a bed in the warm was no longer needed, Annie helped herself to the smaller, easily transportable pieces of silver and some choice pieces of jewelry which could be taken apart and sold. Mrs. Burbidge's cross was cheap, and as she left, Annie let it drop from her fingers on the garden path. Annie became Josephine, Ada, and Bessie before she struck on virtue names, and these had the dual benefit of suggesting her piety, which amused her immensely.

Caesar needed careful steering; he was handsome, which helped, but he tended to be reckless and act too soon. Indeed, on many occasions, she needed to cool him off to prevent trouble in many guises. Caesar had provided opportunities from the restaurant for low-grade cheque fraud—the subtle addition of zeros and minor tweaks to amended amounts brought in a small but regular amount. Mercy had also solicited his help with placing bets for chosen clients, such as Mr. Stone. It was more convenient and also circumvented any unhelpful bans or scrutiny. Her commission was significant, and she had started to purchase debts, which gave her power and even more opportunity for revenue. By the time she was ready to make her big move, she would have the nineteen pounds for a one-way ticket for the seven-and-a-half-day voyage to New York and enough stored chaos and dead ends to leave the Police chasing the unfortunate Caesar for months. She would miss him, but it was like replacing a shoe; you eventually wore it down to fit, but while you might be sad to throw the old one away, it was just a useful shoe for a time. What Mercy had on her mind was a prize of a different nature, which would secure her future.

It, or they, had been the main reasons for seeking the job at The Gaiety. Mercy enjoyed the energy and the chaos of this bubble. She had worked at the Whitechapel Theatre briefly. No,' Prudence' had worked there and had a fortunate and narrow escape from the Lloyd sisters, who appeared far savvier than their brash exteriors suggested. Part of Mercy had respected how quickly they had seen through her performance, but she had learned and treated it as a dress rehearsal for the main show. The main event as her new identity Mercy, was Miss Florence StJohn, or rather, her famous box of jewels.

Mercy had studied her pigeon, read papers, watched shows, and joined the crowds of the adoring public outside the theatre and on one occasion, given the star flowers. But the most helpful information came from the staff, maids, and crew who knew her without the glamour of the show. Mercy had discovered that theatre people liked nothing better than a late night out after a show, with liberal amounts of alcohol and gossip. As long as Mercy was present and willing to keep glasses filled, she was fully supplied with the latter. So she had discovered that Miss StJohn's discarded French husband, who dogged Miss StJohn's steps, was a fellow actor and on-stage romance Claude Duplany, someone whom Miss StJohn would willingly cut loose. She had tried to leave him taking their baby son, and he was following her. The man was a drunk and a leach, with no genuine interest in his progeny but a keen interest in money due to his constant debt. It took about a week and nearly all her money to discover that he was also often eager to pawn Miss StJohn's famous jewels and was not above helping himself to them in order to settle his debts. Mercy eventually had first-hand experience of this, and the real reason 'Faust Up to Date' was delayed in opening. Miss StJohn had been assaulted by Duplany on one of his visits to borrow a necklace to pawn, and she was left too shaken to perform. Duplany was ejected from the theatre, and several gentleman admirers, including a Mr. Cohen, often attended the theatre to cluck around her like overgrown fowl.

Mercy had to be careful; the unforeseen complication had been the Crushers. Two of the bastards flapping around the theatre whenever they were not patrolling around in their blue capes, heavy soled boots and silver whistles. She had thought them to be stagehands, and the first time she had seen them arriving through the stage door in uniform, she had thought for a fleeting second of running. Had she given anything away? No, she realised she needed to stand firm and shot them a bright smile. One had smiled back and greeted her. The other, the one with the face full of scars, lingered behind him like a shadow. Mercy knew a dangerous Leg when she saw one, particularly one who looked like he could take care of himself. She would have to be careful. But despite the inconvenience of uniforms lurking around the stage, she had noticed that one was definitely interested in one of the Molly's, Frank. Each time they left the theatre, a recognisable figure would detach itself from the shadows and follow him into the darkness. Mercy put her money on the little one fixing to tap him up for a quick screw. Knowledge was currency, but she had to focus on her prize.

Miss StJohn appeared constantly in malady, and much of Mercy's day was facilitated with hot water, salts, tinctures and balms. People thought the woman was talented and were happy to indulge her. She dressed like a Duchess but guarded her possessions like a street hawker. Mercy often ended the day exhausted, with barely enough energy to think, but it all paled into nothing when the box opened. Miss StJohn always kept the key on her and ensured the box remained in the room locked. She had seen enough to keep her from leaving and would take an opportunity to look at the lock, hinges and how she could remove the contents without causing an immediate hue and cry leading to her. She would need to be shrewd to give herself time. Mercy had quickly made herself indispensable to Miss StJohn and her fragile health, and she rarely had to add small amounts of crushed tulip bulb to the tinctures to maintain that dependency.

The jewels sang to Mercy. The delicate pendant of circled silver cradled a string of diamonds under which hung a single sapphire that trembled with movement and the entwined gold of a choker from which were suspended pearls like teardrops. Mercy dreamed of them, and she would keep one when she arrived in America. In America, she would never be anyone's servant again.

Chapter Forty-Four

I have lost track of time, that motion of the hands of a clock that arbitrarily slices up the day. I am in a timeless space deep in the earth and am unseen, unheeded, suspended in glass. My only company comes in the form of the waves of rats who emerge from tiny cracks with questing noses and root and steal. But light drives them away to a safe distance, and they will continue to be my secret keepers.

Around me is the dark, sucking void of dead space, which sings to me with its silence. Down here, I am safe, I am real, and I am at peace.

The boots are neatly perched on a shelf out of harm's way, and I start to navigate the clips and ties to remove the clothes from the body. I fold the fabric carefully and place it on one side. I regard my canvas, starting to calculate quadrants and examining joints. I start to unroll the well-worn oil skin package, and the knives catch the light.

I lay out paper, twine and a pot of lime and began.

Chapter Forty-Five – March 1889

"Where the hell is she?" came the urgent whisper rising from the clustered figures in the wings. The music had started, and the house was full, but someone was missing.

The sense of annoyance aimed at the missing chair that Saturday in a grey spring had slowly evolved into concern and a rising sense of panic when the call came for Alice to attempt to cram herself into the petite costume for the maid Totchen and assume the role. Emma was given the Pas De Quartre dance costume from Act Two and was in the wings practicing with Lily in order to play the next vacated role. Against the slowly increasing sense of anxiety, Alice found a quiet corner and started to pace out the role of Totchen, reminding her body of the placement of steps and melody. She had practiced for this occasion as the understudy. Still, it had always been for a planned reason, illness, or accident, but it was as if Mabel had ceased to exist.

The empty space in the corner of the dressing room had a gravity of its own and seemed to suck the energy out of the room. It pierced the usual chaos, and each woman felt a brief stab in their core. The small void in the room had started to expand and was drawing others up the winding stairs. Questions had been scattered by worried management at each cast member, trying to gather information and reassurance as if the right question would reveal Mabel.

There was a sense of barely suppressed panic by the time a boy had been sent out to number thirty-three, The Strand, to inquire of Mabel's mother if she knew where her daughter was. She had arrived back at the stage door with the boy rocking in her wake, boots clattering up the street, skirts hoisted to her knees framing her black-clad legs as they pumped like pistons. Despite the physical activity, her face was drawn and devoid of colour. Mrs. Love came to a halt in front of Mr. Free at the Wellington Street door, her breathing ragged, and her questions came out in short gasps.

"Where is she? Have you found her?" the words seemed to spill out of her like a torrent as she looked from face to face as if trying to draw the information from them physically.

Albert waved the boy inside. "Mr. Edwardes, now!"

"Please!" she cried. "He... he..... The Ripper."

It was as if the name was a knife, the same knife which had sliced the flesh of women, butchering them until all that remained were disarticulated lumps of horror. Mrs. Love's eyes were wide, her voice elevating in pitch as her panic rose, and silver streaks of tears rolled unbidden down her face. She fell upon the chest of Mr. Free, who sharply pushed her away. A look of confusion briefly crossed her face; for a second, it pierced the panic and rolling emotion.

"Oh, thank you, sir," she responded to the proffered handkerchief from Albert, who stiffly patted her on the shoulder.

Mr. Free breathed and cleared his throat. "Mrs. Love, we cannot give ourselves to panic and wild speculation. Do you have any idea where she might have gone?"

Mrs. Love loudly blew her nose and shook her head. She took a deep breath and wailed. The noise caused an explosion of birds from the pavement and startled passers-by to look on with bewilderment at the display of high emotion.

"I think we should go inside, Mrs. Love." Mr. Free looked up at Albert. "Please take Mrs. Love to Mr. Edwardes' office."

§

In his office, Mr. Edwardes was already barking orders into his phone, sending runners to search the streets surrounding the theatre. Instructions were to walk and not run. As the performance continued and crew members were temporarily released from duties, they left in shifts from the theatre. They hunted amongst the foreigners milling about Charing Cross, confused tourists, suited gentlemen strolling to dinner at the club, and early prostitutes jostling for favourable positions. The night had already drawn in before the show started, but even punctuated with pools of lights from the lamps, it seemed to deepen.

The usual energy on stage continued, but in the wings, it was unusually silent and thick with trepidation. Heavily made-up faces were flat and grim. As he hung in the Fly Tower from his red silken parachute, waiting to descend into the light of the stage, Teddy dabbed a tear which threatened to carve a pink trail through his red makeup. She was only just fourteen. Not much older than his daughter. He knew the Ripper was unlikely, there had been nothing in months, but other, real demons stalked the streets. However, the Ripper still blazed like wildfire across the city, and the name meant grizzly death.

He shook his head to clear it from the cloying feeling of dread and melancholy and drew a breath as he heard his queue.

Panic was contagious and had already started to ripple through the cast and crew. It felt like, finally, the rolling threat from the East had crashed into the Gaiety.

§

Saturday passed in a tide of activity and barely suppressed panic, and Monday brought no relief. No sign of Mabel was found, and Robert and William joined in the search. It was impossible to suppress the news as it bled out and came to the attention of the press. The stage door became a rallying point for men in oversized coats and hats, jostling to speak to those leaving and arriving. Albert, leaving his usual position, placed a stool in the doorway and pointedly whittled at a piece of wood with his knife.

Mr. Edwardes appeared at the Strand entrance attempting to draw fire away from the stage door to make brief statements of information, pleading for help from the public and describing Mabel. The small, blond girl would be hard to ignore, he had said. She was much admired and photographed. Her face would be familiar, and her dress fashionable and worth noting.

Despite the careful descriptions and management of the press, the tales of horrible murders and lurid speculation blazed across the newspapers. The mixture of innocent youth devoured by the vice and evil of a city still in the grip of ongoing horror stoked a fever which also drew thrill seekers to the show and the stage door.

§

By Tuesday, the pieces of Mabel's disappearance slowly started to coalesce. Mabel had apparently arrived at the Gaiety the morning she disappeared, as she would normally do, to collect her pay of £3, 2 shillings and 4 pence. Mr. Edwardes paid well, and it was a significant sum. While typically, she would return home immediately to place the sum in safety, she failed to do so. Mrs. Love had eventually wrung her hands between moans and whimpers of distress and admitted the night before they had quarreled.

"It was only a small thing, Mr. Edwardes. Nothing of significance," she had said between wracking sobs. "I'd scolded her about something small, and now she's been taken!"

Mr. Edwardes had plied her with tissues and made sure she was accompanied home, both for her safety and to exert some control over outgoing information. On his desk was a copy of *The Telegraph* titled "Disappearance of Young Actress" in thick black ink. He sighed. Of course, it would bring audiences, but they were balancing on the edge of a knife. If Mabel Love were dead, the effects on the show and the jobs depending on it would be profound.

§

Behind the stage, the routine and rhythm of the days continued, but the sense of pressure escalated. Mabel's dressing table continued to loom in the corner, but now it had filled with flowers left at the stage door by well-wishers and, Jenny suspected, her mother. Initially, Mrs. Love had vacillated between perching on a rough wooden chair in the corner of the room, staring at the table and on her feet, arranging flowers by stalk and then petal, framing the mirror like a shrine. Eventually, Mr. Free had to gently propel her to the wardrobe, where Mrs. Freeman plied her with tea, tissues and lent an ear. The girls, while sympathetic, had found her presence difficult to manage and needed time in peace to prepare for the performances, which continued without abatement.

"Where do you think she is?" said Frank, slumped in Mabel's vacant chair, idly running his fingers across a rose.

"If she's got any sense, she's found herself an Earl and is shacked up." Said Jenny.

"I hope so", said Alice, applying scarlet lipstick with a practiced hand. She pressed her lips together and regarded the painted O in the mirror solemnly. "I hope so", she repeated to herself.

Frank leaned forward, elbows propped on the table and hands cupping his temples. He rubbed his palms in circles as if trying to massage answers from his mind.

"Look," he said ", Edwardes has engaged that Private Detective... ..err. Tall cove." he made circular motions around his head. "Bowler hat"

"Moser" supplied Alice.

"Moser, yes." He said, referring to the Private Detective engaged by Mr. Edwardes as soon as Mabel had gone.

The Police had arrived on Tuesday to start to search, but Robert and William had taken the responsibility on Sunday and had spent long hours into the night peering into dark corners with safety lamps in hand. Despite Robert and William's efforts, there seemed to be minor official appetite at that stage, and official activity only escalated once the press speculation reached a fever pitch. There was no doubt the recent spate of high-profile Whitechapel murders had damaged reputations and stretched resources past the breaking point, but the situation and now engagement of an ex-member of the Criminal Investigation Team had pressed a nerve, particularly since his progress had been rapid and decisive.

"Surely he will find the silly bint," said Frank.

"Course he will", said Jenny, patting him on the shoulder and squeezing the fragile frame. "She's a silly girl."

"Jack only goes after prostitutes," said Emma unthinkingly and was greeted by disapproving glances. "I'm only saying," she defended. "She's a good girl. Good girls don't end up in pieces in alleyways."

Jenny caught the eyes of Frank. A little older and wiser than the rest, they had a clearer view of the precarious nature of things. Frank rubbed a thumb unthinkingly across the still-livid red wound on his hand and stood with a sigh. "I'd better get back to Earnest; he's been down with Mrs. Love for the last hour trying to stem the tide of water. Better get to him before he starts to drown."

With a fragile smile, he affectionately squeezed Jenny's hand. The bruises and cuts had been explained away by an 'accident' no one really believed. Hidden by a glove and thick bandage at first, his hand had started to heal, but the stiffness remained. One finger was frozen, and he doubted it would return to movement. Earnest also refused to thaw, and there was stiltedness between them. Whereas they would still walk home to their lodgings together, Earnest was markedly more absent the rest of the time, and Frank felt a corresponding gap in his heart. He had sometimes heard the sound of boots behind them when walking home and glimpsed the shadow of a policeman's hat. Frank suspected Jenny had spoken to Robert and he had nodded his thanks in a quiet moment to Robert one evening at the theatre. Robert had firstly given him a blank stare and then smiled thinly. Frank thought he had embarrassed the man, so he had mumbled a brief salutation and made sure he acknowledged him when he saw him.

§

In his office, Mr. Edwardes was on the telephone when Robert knocked. Waved in and motioned to a chair, he declined and stood quietly to attention, patiently waiting for the call to end.

"Robert," said Mr. Edwardes. "How are you?"

"Mr. Edwardes. I came to ask if there is anything else I can do. I've come off duty and straight here. Give me a task, sir. I know she's out there. We searched the theatre top to bottom sir. William thoroughly looked in the traps, and I did the rest, sir, every inch."

"I don't..."

"Sir, let me search the traps again. William's a good lad, but he's still learning. I might find something he missed."

"Maybe you should get some rest, Robert."

"No, not while she's still out there." Robert saluted, and Mr. Edwardes felt his hand rising to do the same.

§

Fanny was in her dressing room while the chaos continued around her. The usual activity of the show and the panic which had now hardened to a leaden dread that pressed down on the company.

Violet Cameron had cried continually, without, it appeared any moisture leaving her eyes. There were only brief periods of remission for her audience and nods of thanks with a hand pressed to her heart when she accepted their applause. In public, she wore elegant tilt hats with a veil strategically angled across her red-rimmed eyes, ostensibly to hide them but not quite doing so. Fanny felt the pressure herself but wondered how much of the red rims around Violet's eyes washed off with her makeup at the show's end.

Florence, however, had been subdued and without her usual bonhomie and vivacity. In the last few days, instead of leaving for a party or social engagement, she had quietly taken a carriage home. George appeared to continue his routine unaffected, with only a slight increase in the empty bottles removed from his room at night's end. But it was Teddy and Harry who had most noticeably changed. Harry's courts during the show ceased, and his door remained firmly closed. This morning Teddy had been found by Fanny staring into space, powdered puff halfway between pot and face, suspended in the air as if frozen.

As time bled on and still no word, by midweek, rumour had started to echo through the corridors that Mabel had been seen at a ticket office on the Great Northern Railway and had then taken an Omnibus to Euston. It appeared she had seemed perfectly composed and was unaccompanied. Where was she going, and what was the girl thinking? The questions increased, with it a rising sense of anger that Mabel had duped everyone.

Chapter Forty-Six

I had never planned to deviate and do something other than offer my gifts to the river, but that day, my path had taken me past the site where the new police building would be at Scotland Yard. Something inexplicable made me change my mind as I saw the cutting into the earth of the new foundations.

The parcel in my hands seemed to pulse, and I found myself on my knees, scraping the mud and clay over the oiled paper package, adding it to the bricks and mortar of the roots of the building. It would be my gift.

I realise now I was guided by her hand and my gift to her, the flesh, blanched white with the loss of blood and wrapped in brown paper and twine had another destiny. It would appear in the foundations of the temple of law, anonymous, but the meaning would be clear. London would be built upon the bones of the sacrificed souls tethered to me. Now I listen and let go, hearing the voice which guides my feet to places, significant places, some of which I understand and some I must trust have a reason known only to her. I will listen to the story of blood.

This is my masterpiece, my rite of passage, and I cannot be denied any longer. I have spoken to her directly now, and I know now that she hears and guides me. It is a considerable risk and a powerful statement.

But it is eloquent and a masterpiece should be admired.

Chapter Forty-Seven

"What were you thinking?! Two weeks!" came the shout which bled out from the Manager's office and into the auditorium. Figures paused in their work, curiosity and flushed embarrassment for overhearing tingled everyone's ears.

"Dublin?!" came the subsequent explosion—a question, accusation and expression of utter disbelief. As the volume emanating from the office decreased, the activity back on stage commenced, but with a palpable reduction in sound as if to squeeze the most out of the opportunity to overhear what was being discussed behind closed doors.

Mr. Edwardes was prowling around behind the desk, the already worn patch of carpet testifying to years of the physical expression of pent-up emotion, but this time, his wrath overflowed and poured over the desk like the fires of hell.

The figure of Mabel, small and doll-like, perched on the end of the proffered chair, wide eyes downcast towards a swirl in the pattern of the carpet. The pale fingers on her right hand interlaced with the black glove of her left. Somewhere on the return, she had misplaced

her glove, and she sent her mind back to the silent journey home
and wondered if she had left it at the train station. She should have
returned home to change and fetch her best before she ventured to the
theatre.

A pause in the tirade and the side of her mother's boot impacting
on her own brought her back to the musty room, and the question
that was suspended in the air like a noose. Mabel's face slowly rose to
meet that of the scarlet visage of Mr. Edwardes, and she brushed away
a loose blond curl from her temple, carefully tucking it into her slouch
hat. She took a deep breath and, in a low whisper, responded, "I don't
know Mr. Edwardes. I am sorry for the inconvenience."

Mr. Edwardes opened his mouth and was cut across by the rapid
fire of Mrs. Love. "She was overwhelmed in her efforts to please you,
Mr. Edwardes. I see her practicing at all hours. Her singing, sir, she
sings until she is hoarse - on her day off, of course. She dances until
she fairly wears the floorboards smooth. She is dedicated to you, Mr.
Edwardes, and as her mother, I should have come to you earlier and
told you. I blame myself, sir. She is a good and talented girl."

Mr. Edwardes realised he had been staring with an open mouth and
felt the clack of teeth as he consciously closed his jaw. "Nevertheless,
Mrs. Love, your daughter vanished without a trace, failed to attend
the theatre for her engagements, worried her friends half to death and
wasted police time. This is not something I can take lightly."

Mabel cast her eyes down, and as the tear hit the black and white
of her skirt, doming briefly on the fabric before soaking down and
widening into a perfect circle. She made no effort to stop the flow
as they trickled down her dimpled cheeks, causing wet dots to grow
across the striped skirt. As she took the proffered handkerchief from
her mother, she raised her head to look at Mr. Edwardes with a wan
smile and then dabbed her face with an almost inaudible apology.

Mr. Edwardes paused in the face of the tears. At fourteen, she was barely an adult, and he felt an intense protectiveness towards his cast and crew. Despite the sensational reports and press speculation about her disappearance, he was finding it hard to quell the panic he had felt when Mabel had gone missing, those days in purgatory being some of the longest of his life.

"Why Mabel? Why did you just leave us? Us, your family?"

Still in the clothes she had been wearing on her return to London, Mabel sat next to her mother, a frequent figure backstage. Mrs. Love had insisted on remaining at the theatre and not their home on the Strand during that time between her daughter's disappearance and the moment of her return. Making journeys during the day back to their Guest House home, she had passed the mounting numbers of the press, handkerchief to mouth and shaking her head when approached. As she had slowly mounted the step to the carriage, laid on by Mr. Edwardes, to allow her to make the journey unmolested, she would lower the handkerchief and mutter a "Thank you for your concern, gentlemen".

At Mabel's return, she had run into the street with a loud cry, enveloping her daughter in her arms and as the press swarmed in, alerted by the cry, they ran towards the stage door in an increasing clamor of questions. Press speculation had been rife, plentiful and lurid. But the Police who escorted Mabel home had confirmed a physician had seen Mabel, and she was untouched. Reputation assured, speculation as to the reason for her vanishing did not dissipate.

"Mr. Edwardes, you know I am aware of how things are," Mrs. Love said. He nodded, knowing Mrs. Kate Love had walked the stage of the Gaiety before her daughter. A father before her with equal talent had fallen on hard times, and the Theatrical community had held a benefit performance which helped the family buy number thirty-three, which eventually became a theatrical guest house that she now ran.

Kate Love had experienced some success, but with a father unable to push and support his daughter, she had fallen short of her own expectations, and even an iron will could not bend others to her benefit. When she had recognised the same talent in Mabel, she didn't hesitate and spent every moment molding her daughter into a star. Mabel was beautiful and talented but young and under a significant amount of pressure.

Mr. Edwardes, realising he was unlikely to obtain an answer now, sat down behind his desk like a collapsing balloon.

"Miss Love, Mrs. Love, I believe it is time to rest, and so I propose a hiatus where you may recover from your ordeal."

"How long?" shot Mrs. Love, almost without thinking. She smiled sheepishly. "My apologies, Mr. Edwardes. Mabel is keen to return and put this whole episode behind her. The press will be keen to know she is safe and unharmed, and what better way than to return to the stage?"

Mr. Edwardes smiled and looked at the small, blond figure before him. He rose from his seat and rounded the desk, perching on the end directly in front of Mabel.

"Mabel." He said quietly. He paused for her to look up, her milky blue eyes still brimming with tears. Expecting Mrs. Love to prompt her daughter, he put up a preemptive hand to quell her as he heard her intake of breath.

"Mabel"

"Mr. Edwardes, sir."

"I want you to go home, rest, have some good meals and stop rehearsing. You know your role; you have skill, but you have been through an ordeal, and I need to protect you now you are home. The press is sometimes to be courted, but like animals at the zoo, they need handling with skill and often a large stick. They can and will turn on you if you are not careful and not guided by someone like me. Do you understand?"

He paused for the benefit of Mabel as much as her mother.

"Before we even think about your return, I will also require a full explanation of why you chose to do this. I recognise you want to succeed, but you are also very young. You have been lucky this time, but I cannot save you from folly."

He looked up at Mrs. Love to see if she also understood. "Mrs. Love, I will not tolerate folly and cannot tolerate it if it damages this theatre. I will protect people under my roof. I want to continue to care about you, Mabel, but I cannot if you will not let me."

§

At the stage door, a chastened Mabel stepped down worn stairs into the waiting carriage, her mother following behind.

Inside the cocoon of black fabric and dimpled leather, Mrs. Love looked down at Mabel's hem, where a small tear in the fabric poked out from the neat line.

"I think that's for burning. You can't be seen out in that again, and I won't be seen using it for rags." She sat back against the rigid backrest and sighed. "How much?"

"I used it all. I had to change hotel."

"Well, girl, I hope it was worth it. We can't do that again. You'll have to practice your set piece when we get home. It was almost perfect, and yet you blunder an audition." She bumped her back against the backrest with frustration and drew air through pursed teeth making a sucking sound as she gazed out of the window for inspiration.

"Listen to me. You will practice until you are flawless, day and night. You will convince Edwardes you are ready to come back. We'll stick with you being overwhelmed or something." She paused. "No, not overwhelmed, or he might think you're too fragile. You're...." She waved her hand, inventing wildly, "You are such a perfectionist, and you were exhausted from giving your best each night. You were... In a fugue."

"A fugue?"

"Trust me, and it might go some ways to explaining the audition." she sniffed. "It's what leading ladies get when they catch a hangover. You don't think this show opened late in the first place because a hat wasn't ready? Miss StJohn had been out on the town with that Frenchman of hers."

Mabel's eyes widened.

"Edwardes has warned us off from the press, so we keep quiet. But it would be best to be back on that stage before everyone forgets your name. Hear me?" she paused, and a smile crossed her face. She reached into her bag and produced a black glove, handing it to an astonished Mabel.

"Officer gave it to me. Mabel, you were so keen, so distracted in your need to get back to the theatre, to return to the bosom of your employer, you lost an expensive glove—such dedication. And your distraught mother forgot to give it to you. The tears were very nice. Miss Farren herself couldn't have done better."

"And what about the police? They're furious. Everyone thought I'd been murdered."

"I can manage the Beetle Crushers. If they were that smart, they'd have caught the Ripper by now, and we'd all be safe in our beds. We took a chance, Mabel and we have to make the most of it. Do you want to rot away in the background until you have nothing left?"

Mabel looked into her mother's bright, staring eyes, the unsaid end to that sentence punctuating the air. Enough alike to see a glimpse of herself in the future, in her mother's drawn face, she saw what unrealised ambition could bring and shuddered, pulling her fur-trimmed cape around her shoulders.

"I love you." She whispered to her mother.

Mrs. Love continued to look out of the window. "I know."

Chapter Forty-Eight

*T*he rain has been relentless, filling the spaces below with mud and brown water, which hits the back of my throat like acid and steals my breath. It must have happened during the night. The ceiling to the tunnels has partially collapsed, sending a wave of stone and mud across the entrance, blocking the passage. Everything smells of unfamiliar dampness, but I can still squeeze through the hole in the wall from beneath the traps and the theatre above.

I have built stones up around the entrance to damn the water, which is rising below the traps and can no longer be absorbed by the sodden earth. It is climbing up the walls, and I need to keep it out, keep it away. I know I am unlikely to be disturbed yet as they try to stem the tide of water falling from above as it runs along the beams of the roof. From now on, the only way in and out of my sanctuary will be through the theatre, but it will be temporary, and I can easily steal a key to come and go as I please.

But this time, I have been able to plan and take my time with my offering and immerse myself in the ritual. I am doing something that *will imbue itself into the very core of the theatre and the earth beneath. I can see the lights of the stage; they blind and fill my vision, my soul, with the dazzle of heat and illumination as the audience roars before me like a pulsing beast. I bathe in blood, light and sound, the visceral pleasure of the moment, and I rise to meet them as they wrap me in sound. I raise my arms high to gather in their adulation, and I bow deep and low.*

Thank you. Thank you all.

Chapter Forty-Nine – May 1889

Spring had continued to be damp and May became a month of torrential rain. It had been relentless and battered the roof of the theatre, seeking out and finding cracks. It flowed into the recesses and dripped down beams, flowing downhill and through piles of dust, causing them to merge and flow down soot-darkened walls. The Gaiety had faced onslaughts of relentless rain before and heavy snow the last year, but as the cold gave way to the spring thaw, gaps and weaknesses warped and opened to the air. The cracking of the skin of the theatre started with hidden drips, then buckets in the attic rooms, where the chorus danced between the accompanying patters of rapidly filling porcelain. When the ceiling finally gave way and a river flowed down the stairs towards the wardrobe, any measures to move cast around to share rooms and passages would no longer work. Even with an army of builders on the roof trying to cover and patch with oilskins, water was running out of the stage door and building up against the sandbags Albert had put against the stairs down to the wardrobe. Mr. Free had called Mr. Harris at three in the morning, who in turn called Mr. Edwardes. While Mr. Free and Albert continued to deposit the bags of sand Tosher was handing them through the stage door, Mr. Edwardes and Harris stood in shock as water eddies danced around their shoes, staining the leather in patches and splashes.

"Can't we stop it?" muttered Harris, in desperation rather than sense.

"No sir," said Mr. Free. "It's been raining for days, and no sign of stopping." Mr. Edwardes, even propelled from his bed before dawn in response to the worsening situation, still appeared to have had time to assemble a three-piece suit and slick his hair. His moustache, as always, stood out in a dim comparison, but Mr. Free marveled that despite his immaculate attention to grooming at detail, there was something always fresh about Mr. Edwardes. Mr. Harris, however, looked exactly like a man who had been dragged from bed and only nominally past a bathroom.

Mr. Edwardes ran a hand across his forehead. "I suppose", he said, "We are now without options here."

Mr. Free stopped stacking bags and, for a moment, stood. "I think so, sir. There is no telling when the rain will stop, and when it does, we have a lot of work backstage to repair everything. We have a wardrobe full of expensive costumes and millinery, and even if it doesn't get wet, it will get damp and spoil. We need to empty it all, sir. Mrs. Freeman is doing what she can with the girls, but we cannot go on with water everywhere."

"And the rest of the theatre?" asked Harris.

"Cold and damp, but nothing which can't be fixed with a good airing. Which," he paused, knowing this would be bad news, "could take about two weeks if the rain does stop."

Harris opened his mouth to speak, and Edwardes raised a hand, his eyes wrinkled in deep thought. A brilliant impresario all present recognised this expression and knew Edwardes was working his way through the problem and forming a solution. They waited.

Finally, Edwardes appeared to return to the room. He barked a string of orders without seeming to draw breath. Mr. Harris waited; his skill was to make Mr. Edwardes' plans a reality, and he knew his cues.

"Mr. Harris, please find a company and engage them to clear the show from the theatre and transport it to the Newcastle Street Theatre. Mr. Free, please ask your wife to empty all costumes and dressing rooms ready to transport. Mr. Free, I also need you to arrange for sets and special lights to be packed. Mr. Lightly, please engage the boys to inform all the cast to report to Newcastle Street tomorrow at ten am. I will speak to Sir Charles Hawtrey at the New Globe Theatre Newcastle Street and tell him we will be moving to his theatre for the foreseeable future."

Harris's eyes widened, "The Globe?"

"Yes!" exclaimed Edwardes, his face lighting up with the enthusiasm of a new plan. "Mr. Hawtrey's play has closed, and his theatre, which is very similar to ours, is dark. We will arrange a transfer, and I will alert the press that against almost unassailable, no, insurmountable obstacles that would crush a more mundane organisation, we will rise above and the show will go on."

Mr. Free smiled; it was likely it would be a long day, and Mr. Edwardes had failed to mention he would need to visit both Miss StJohn and Miss Cameron at home. An uneasy truce had descended, but the misstep of sending a boy to either and, god forbid, knowing he had visited one before the other could reignite hostilities. As it was, the ascending balloon at the end of the show, when the lovers fly away, was the only time the 'lovers' willingly stood within arm's length of each other, and even then, they were as far apart as was safely possible. Several crew members had started to place wagers on the basket catching fire, if one would jump out to get away from the other, or if one would finally shove the other out. It had recently become close when a tussle had broken out between the ladies regarding who was helped out of the basket first and down the ladder to the stage. Fingers had been trampled, hair dislodged, and resentment steamed from ears red with fury.

Mr. Free had stood outside the stage door after the furor later that night with Albert, who offered him a pipe. He had accepted it gratefully. They sat in silence, exhaling clouds into the air, Albert producing perfect circles that grew larger and thinner until they gently disappeared, framing the sky. Mr. Free always enjoyed time with Albert; he asked for nothing, and his silence wrapped around him like a cloak. He felt at peace in these moments and looked up at the soft blackness above.

But the present was not one of those moments, and for now, it was moving a show and as fast as possible. Revenue would be lost, and a new theatre needed to be hired, but Sir Charles would, of course, agree to a show ready to start and be paid nominal rent to give him time to recoup his current losses and think again. There was also the delicious irony that although the Gaiety was temporarily out of action, Sir Charles was in a worse situation. "Atlanta" with Dan Leno had done well, but his other theatre, The Globe, seemed to be having significant problems. These appeared again to be associated with his brother, Mr. Hawtrey's insistence he would continue to write plays for the theatres. As far as Mr. Free had heard, they weren't terrible, but they were too plentiful, and audiences had become bored of what had once been a novelty. Once audiences started to slack, stars failed to sign, and a cycle of decay started. Pip, Fanny's friend and font of gossip, had already flown away once Atlanta closed and when that bird left, it was a good indication the rest of the flock would soon be following. The Globe was dying, and she would not last long.

§

It took all day, all night and most of the following day with crews from both the Gaiety and Globe moving the show into its new home. The layout was, like most theatres, similar, but backcloths were raised, ropes marked for position, floors chalked, and props laid out. Rumour spread quickly that the traps were to be avoided. A giant had taken up residence and was operating all the pulleys independently. Helping but unhelpful hands had been firmly ejected and sent up into the fly tower to move the forest of ropes on cue. The only ones to descend without fear into his domain were the stage manager, a limping girl with red hair and a boy who looked and moved like a wisp.

By the time the cast arrived and the show started, it was as if nothing had changed. There was a frisson of anxiety that the unfamiliar equipment would do as required, but once each hurdle was made successfully, the company started to relax. It had been the latest in a catalogue of upheaval, but better than bicycles and cast changes. So, for two weeks, the Gaiety would be dark while the backstage was repaired and aired. The stage, the tower, the auditorium and the traps, for the time being, would be silent.

Chapter Fifty

*T*he offering was laid out before me, and in the chaos above, they do not hear my screams.

Winter seemed to be hanging on. The cold clings on and the nights bite at my bare hands. I had found her dressed in layers of fabric, knitted garments and a shawl that softened her silhouette, so I did not see it. She had fallen to her knees without a sound, her hands not clutching at her throat as her silent scream erupted in blood but around her waist, and she had fallen to her side, her hands still holding on tightly. I watched the movement slow and rolled her onto her back, and then I saw it, the rounded belly containing a child old enough to kick in protest as its mother died.

I felt the impact of the pavement as my legs gave out from under me. I was suspended in time and space during the lifetime it took to cease to move. For a while, I imagined it continuing to fight for life as the blood around the body turned from liquid to jelly. She was heavy and I was almost bent double with the weight, but mercifully I had little distance to travel.

In the space below, I peeled aside the sodden and rotting fabric from the form and screamed my frustration and horror to the dark as the rounded belly was laid bare. Sitting there all night as the body rapidly stiffened in the damp, I kept imagining the flutter of movement, and it was only the pressure of time which forced me to action, so I began to cut. I left the torso as long as I could and carefully placed the detached head in the recess I had prepared for her. I did not take her boots this time; they will go in the river with her clothes and 'it'.

Time has come back to me like the rising of a sun, but my hands are shaking more than usual and the cold is clinging to me, drying and cracking the blood that clothes me into a thin dust which falls away as I start to work. I cannot look at it and push the corpse onto its side removing the liver and sawing the pelvis from behind, placing it onto the oiled paper. I have to continue and dispose of it, so I try to wrap it up so I do not have to see, but I do, I see...him.

I will leave now and scatter the parts further this time. The show is moving back to the Gaiety soon and I need to act now. It was supposed to have been my moment. The time the Gaiety was entirely mine, where I could possess her entirely.

I need to distance myself from this now, from the boy.

Chapter Fifty-One – June 1889

It had only been a few short weeks since the flood at the Gaiety. The skeleton crew left behind to air the theatre had ejected the worst of the damp while the roof bristled with workmen from the weak light of dawn to the fading of the day. From the street, the Gaiety had become an anthill of activity. Mr. Edwards was never far behind chivvying them on, acutely aware of the cost trifecta associated with hiring a theatre, having repairs on his existing one, and that one also being without an income. The torrential rain of late May had given way to an unseasonably warm June and this had done much to draw the majority of the moisture from the building.

Albert had remained at the Gaiety. Doors and windows open in London on a hot day were an invitation to burglary and mayhem. Between shifts Robert and William had also continued to help. Both were acquiring the policeman's tan on their face and hands from long patrols in full uniform, but beneath that they both looked tired and drawn.

Slouched on the ground, back against the wall, Robert drew a last deep lungful of his cigarette before stubbing it out on the cobbles which abutted the wall by the Wellington Street stage door. He shielded his eyes against the sun which was starting to rise over the bulk of the Lyceum opposite. On his customary stool Albert sat, face turned up towards the sun, for once his hands free of knife or pipe. His breathing was slow and steady, but Robert could see the customary lines in his face seemed to have become deeper even in a few short weeks. It had been a strain on everyone and Mr. Edwards' pace towards getting the roof even semi-watertight and the company back, had been relentless.

"I don't think I could have gone on much longer. "Albert nodded as Robert got to his feet and stretched his legs.

"Back to it. William and I'll lock up. You go home, have an early night and be ready for tomorrow."

Albert looked about to reject the proposal, but Robert urged him "You are exhausted. William and I will manage."

Finally nodding in ascent Albert stood.

§

George Edwards, seemingly recognising his flagging company needed a break had graciously allowed one day for the company to move back to the Gaiety. The patchwork repairs on the roof were nearly complete and as far as he was concerned 'good enough for a sunny June'.

But, rest did not feature and they had all been unpacking all day. The theatre was a riot of boxes, people squeezing between moving sets and the cries of those who failed to move fast enough. There was still a faint smell of damp in the air, but the company were too consumed in activity to notice and finally around one in the morning they had all made their way home. It was good to be back at the Gaiety.

Tosher, being strong and willing to help had finished with the boxes for the wardrobe and was mounting the stairs back up towards the stage. He didn't need much sleep, and so had made his way back before dawn the following day. He had just left the soft, feminine warmth of the Wardrobe beneath the dressing rooms. When full of busy seamstresses, the beat and hum of delicate machines in the wardrobe were soothing as they cut, stitched and seemed to magic exquisite garments into existence. Across the floor, scattered pins covered every surface and lay like man traps across the wooden floor. Tosher always found pins, however well they had been cleaned away and would silently curse at the needle pricks which always managed to bore through his thick-soled boots. A nail or plank could drop on his feet and produce nothing but a dent in his boot at worse and maybe dull sensation in his foot beneath, but a needle would burrow and bore through to his sock-clad feet and find a fleshy point to bite at each time he moved. He sat on the step to the Traps and sought out the one which today had bitten his right foot like a wasp and drew it from his boot with the knife he kept in his belt. He smiled as he liberated and then regarded the shining sliver of metal; he would walk across a thousand for Ida.

Tosher had hoped to have the theatre to himself and, with his knife, sat at Ida's tiny workbench and, with great care, carved a small daisy into the stained wood. Tosher was still a novice at woodwork compared to Albert, who, in the watches of the night, had taught him how to carve, sand, and feel the grain of the wood. Under his tutoring, Tosher had improved, but his efforts had always paled against the beautiful, vivid and almost sinuous shapes which emerged from discarded offcuts. Albert would pause, look and somehow see what the wood wanted to be, what it was and help it appear with deft strokes of his knife. Tosher felt he sawed and gouged away with thick fingers. But now, with the image of Ida in his mind, a thread of silver in the wood seemed to appear, and the image's shadow was set free. Now, he understood. When he finally sat back, satisfied with his work, he placed a real daisy that he had picked from the park on the way to the theatre in the early dawn hours. It had been closed and sleeping when picked, and by the time he finished and placed it on the bench, it was awake, open and perfect in its round dial-like face. He had sanded the wooden facsimile smooth so a gentle hand stroking the carving would find no splinters—a permanent daisy which would last forever. On top, he placed the fresh flower, and for a moment, the carving looked like a perfect shadow. He smiled with pleasure at her imagined face when she discovered his gift.

The night before last, he and Ida had walked along the bridge again, across the river as it played and frothed around the bridge supports, and they silently held hands as they leaned on the parapet and looked into the distance. It had become their afternoon ritual before the evening performance, and these few weeks had been the happiest he could remember. But yesterday, Tosher had wanted to ask her, then and there, but to break that precious moment seemed the worst sacrilege, so he waited and planned. It was too important a question to get wrong.

Tosher was not a religious man, but he felt something inexplicable moved the water below, moved the clouds above and caused the sun and moon to rise in the sky. It was supposed to be the age of reason, where everything could be rationalised just by applied thought, but people still went to church, and he never understood. He had no name for his feelings when he was with Ida, but it was real, and the churches and rituals made him uncomfortable. But, under the open sky with Ida, he was sure of the existence of something. He was wrapped up in the thought, the feel and the smell of another human being, and she had laid on his mind like a soft snow.

§

He didn't know how long he had been sitting there, but it would be some time before anyone else started to arrive. The air outside would still be cold and damp, and the sun would not be high enough to reach between tall buildings and burn off the frost. The theatre always had a strong feeling of expectation when empty, as if it breathed softly while it waited to be fed with colour, light and sound. He treasured those moments when he could walk in from the bustle, crowds and noise of the city into this unexpected cavern of silence, if only for a while.

Tosher stood up, he had a pulley change to make. He'd inspected them when they had returned to the Gaiety and noticed one had started to show stress fractures. He knew it needed to be changed before it split and failed. It would mean dropping the screen it supported and rethreading the rope. Usually, a two-man job, Tosher was often seen raising and lowering back cloths alone, his muscles barely seeming to strain. Ida had said in a rare moment of nostalgia that Tosher was stronger than the circus Strong Man, Hercules, whose act involved holding an axe in one outstretched arm, perilously balancing the blade down over his head for impossible lengths of time. Just as the axe looked like it would drop towards his face and a tragic outcome, he would stop it mid-fall and hold it again, dropping it once more and again, arresting the fall until it was the breadth of a cobweb from his face. Hercules, Tosher, thought, the name of a circus star, and as Ida told him, an ancient hero, felt a world away from 'The Best Tosher in London'.

Tosher pulled at the heavy rope and started to lower the backcloth. His arms steady, and his concentration entirely on the task at hand. But as he leaned back to angle the rope, his foot slipped from beneath him and although it was the task of a second to pause and reset his feet, his knife, which he had absently put back in the top of his boot and not secured in his belt, dropped and fell between the boards. When he lost sight of it, he heard the clatter of it hitting the boards down below in the traps.

"Damn," he muttered, securing the backcloth rope and running a calloused hand through his wiry curls. He made his way down the steps to the traps. A quick search with a lantern revealed the knife had landed on the floor as expected, but as he bent to pick it up, a noise in the unusual quiet made him pause. It came from beneath his feet.

Tosher sighed. For some reason, the Gaiety was plagued with rats. Down below the Traps, on the infrequent occasions anyone ventured down there, detritus and rubble had dropped down through the boards and landed amongst what seemed like thousands of beady eyes and sharp teeth. That night in the sewers, when he had earned his name, had given him a healthy respect and maybe even gratitude towards them. So, often, he left well enough alone. But there were so many scurrying rats now they were starting to become bold, particularly since the company had been absent. The last thing Tosher needed was nibbled ropes and perhaps furry visitors in the auditorium during a show. Maybe it was time to do something or at least take a look.

Tosher hitched up his lamp and started down the stairs. The Gaiety was his home, he knew each brick, each rope and the darkness felt like an old friend, but with the sense of an old friend he knew when something felt wrong. As his foot landed on the compacted earth beyond the final step, he was certain. The hairs on his neck rose, and the skin started to prickle with animal terror. Tosher's nose was hit with a thick smell with an edge while felt chemical and it landed on his stomach with a lurch. There was a hole in the opposite wall, loose bricks and the sense of space beyond. Putting his hand to his mouth, he stepped forward towards the space and slipped. He pointed the lamp down and caught a glitter of something thick and black coating the mixed mud and stones on the floor below. Tosher regarded it uncomprehendingly and stepped forward to get a better look at the floor. Was someone feeding them? His questing foot hit loose rubble between the spaces, and he lost his footing again, his head pitching forward and his hand landing on the wall just inside the space heavily and dislodging old bricks to arrest his momentum.

But Tosher's hand didn't stop as expected at the old rough brick. It pushed through the crumbling surface into a void, landing on some-thing yielding, sticky and cold. He quickly pulled back his hand from the engulfing darkness and felt moisture collected in jellied lumps on his thick fingers. The smell was overwhelming and punched out into his face with physical force. It clawed at the soft palette behind his tongue and nose. With senses now screaming and stomach lurching, he slowly raised the lamp.

It couldn't be a rat, it was too big. He steadied himself and removed more bricks. At first his brain was unable to piece together what his eyes saw by the flickering light. But the rolling realisation fed by his senses finally provided the identity of what he was looking at.

"Oh my go......"

Tosher's body froze, but he had no time. There was a sensation of movement behind him, breath in his ear, seconds before the sharp, hot pain that flashed across his throat and a warm gush of wetness down his chest. In that moment of shock, he pulled his head backwards and out of the hole, becoming aware of the minutiae of the bricks in front of him, their colours and the dips and pits and spray that covered everything. He gasped, mouth wide and soundless in shock. Tosher's knees gave with a sudden finality, and he folded to the floor. The lamp fell alongside him, marking the remaining seconds of his life, before it also hit the floor and went out. And the unseeing, milky eye behind the dripping bricks watched him descend from view before it returned to the dark.

§

The theatre was waking up as people started to arrive. Albert was first and noticed the stage door was wide open. He had knocked for Tosher but had no response. Increasingly, Tosher had been in the company of Ida and sometimes did not come to the door of his room if she was there. Albert smiled and remembered times when night didn't involve sleep.

Albert always liked to arrive early, and his long-established routine involved collecting a paper and, with ritual care, reading it from the front page to the end. Long ago, a younger Mr. Free, who had once a streak of waggishness, had placed an advertisement for "Moustache for Sale, large and immaculately kept. Bring scissors. Call at the Gaiety" and waited in the wings with the other stagehands for the roar of tonsorial fury from the small man as he completed his scan of that issue.

Putting down his worn hat, Albert mounted the stairs and cried out backstage, "Holla!" And a voice came back from the wardrobe

"It's us, Albert, we just got in. Mr. Freeman has just gone to turn on the house lights."

Albert walked out onto the stage. He had done it thousands of times but never felt comfortable. He preferred the shadows and for others to be in the light. The transfer between light and dark lost your advantage, and even now, his guard was never down.

"Mr. Free?" He called

"Holla", came the answering call from the back of the auditorium, where a familiar shape was walking back to the stage from the stalls.

"Jamie, was the door open when you came in?"

The use of his first name made Mr. Free pause.

"I think so. Why? What's wrong?"

Albert sucked air through his teeth. "Don't know. Maybe nothing."

Mr. Free jumped athletically onto the stage and walked up to Albert. "I know you old man. Something's adrift."

"Funny feeling is all."

"Well, I trust your funny feelings. So let's do a walk-round and check all's well."

As both men turned towards the stage door, they heard a creak. Mr. Free looked around and caught movement by the steps to the traps just as a massive set of shoulders dragged itself up the final step. Tosher was awash with blood, his hands red and his eyes rolling so the whites were glowing in the half-light. He tried to speak, but his voice gurgled, and white foam gathered at the sides of his mouth.

Mr. Free screamed, "Dora! Dora! Get a doctor. Now!"

Albert ran to the mountain that was Tosher as he crashed to a stop on the top of the blood-stained stairs. Feet ran from the dressing room, and a gasp heralded the arrival of Dora. "Oh God, Jamie." And without a further word, she ran on fleet feet, pulling her shawl around her and sped from the theatre, one end dangling behind her.

Albert and Mr. Free rolled the heavy form of Tosher onto his back and gasped. His face was blanched. Blood, almost black, stained his white shirt, and his mouth opened and closed wordlessly.

"Alright, lad, I'm here," said Albert, shifting Tosher's head into his lap. He took a handkerchief from his pocket and pressed it to the ragged wound, which opened and closed with each breath, the livid pink flesh of the wound in stark contrast to his darker skin. In his heart, Albert knew it was futile, but for Mr. Free and others who would at the moment still have hope, he would go through the motions before death.

Tosher gurgled, his eyes darting between faces and the ceiling. "D ......D...."

Mr. Free looked at Albert with incomprehension.

"What is it, boy?" Said Albert

"Dead..... down......" Tosher's body was wracked with coughs, and a gout of blood rose from his throat, coloring the handkerchief and rolling down the sides of his neck, soaking the back of his hair. Tears spilt from under brown lashes and rolled down the creases of his eyes into his hair as his body rocked, trying to fight as he drowned in his own blood.

"Mu.... Sorry.......sorry........" his eyes moved, locking on a figure frozen in the doorway. "I....."

§

Ida had run up to the stage with Mrs. Freeman, ready to help. She had frozen as if preserved in aspic when she saw him. A bloom of cold had rushed through her body, and the fingers which had just finished exploring the small carving on her bench were numb. The world had stopped, and all that filled it was him, lying there.

In the moment Tosher's eyes had locked on her, Ida saw the light dim and his lids settle half open, framing pupils that slowly fixed into the distance, One moment, the man behind the sad brown eyes was looking at her, only her, and then they were just eyes, vacant and staring. Tosher had gone.

Ida felt terror descend on her like a heavy rain. It beat on her head like tiny fists. She watched as Albert slowly bent and planted a kiss on the forehead of the dead man, closing his eyes and then sitting back on his heels, looking up at the heavens. Mr. Free bent over Tosher, taking a blood-soaked hand he placed across the man's chest. And Ida, on light feet, stepped forward and knelt beside him; a tentative hand reached out to touch his hair. She felt the familiar spring of compacted curls under her fingers, so soft and dry, and her hand lightly touched the still-warm skin around his temples and felt the path of a tear. But his extremities had become pale as he had bled, like life was a liquid that could drain away. He had slipped away from her, and as she touched his hand, which for the first time failed to respond to touch, she knew. At that moment, the millions of possibilities of the different lives she had planned with him vanished.

§

A sheet was brought from somewhere, and Tosher disappeared beneath it. It wasn't long before it was soaked with patches of drying blood, and by the time the doctor arrived, he was cold to the touch. Ida had willed the heat from her hands to keep him warm, but eventually, the chill started to travel up her arm and drain her of feeling as his brown eyes slowly faded to the pale sheen of death.

As the world's noise buzzed around her and kind hands steered her to the wardrobe, putting a blanket around her shoulders, she felt slow and miles away. People flew around her like moths, fast and unintelligible, and she stared into space, a creature of pure numbness. For a brief period, she heard low voices outside, maybe familiar; she couldn't tell, and for that moment, she had been left alone. Ida rose and walked to the bench and the daisy nestled in the carving. She lifted the flower and regarded it as if seeing it for the first time; it was almost translucent, with white petals in perfect formation around the yellow centre. Tosher had said daisies were supposed to symbolise innocence and purity. Carefully, she placed it back on its wooden shadow and let the blanket fall to the floor. Ida drifted like a ghost through the frantic activity of the theatre, vacant faces streaked with tears and out of the stage door.

In their grief and shock, only one person noticed the tiny figure limp away. Mercy leaned against the wall to the stairs up to the dressing rooms, arms crossed and head on one side. The sides of her mouth twitched in a smile.

Crouched under the props table, a small boy sat alone, staring at nothing, his hands covered in blood.

Chapter Fifty-Two

No, no, no. The fool wandered in and nearly ruined everything; he forced me to kill him. I had no choice. I didn't want to, but I had to. He left me no choice.

I didn't think. I had to act, and from the dark, I stood motionless behind him, my lungs filling with the oily smell of his hair and skin. I drew my blade across his thick neck, releasing the sharp smell of metal, watching the eruption of crimson hitting the wall and soaking the stones. It was as if my hand acted on its own, and I was there as a watcher. As I tried to sink back into the shadows, I saw him look down in confusion, hand instinctively going to his throat, and the shock of seeing blood flowing like an unstoppable tide, rolling down his shirt and turning the fabric dark. He made no sound, just the crack and grind of broken bricks sliding under his feet as he lurched backwards, but a foot slipped on blood and loose stone, and he crashed face down on the floor; his fingers grasped the step and then became still.

I felt the knife in my hand, both familiar and alien as the bricks pressed against my back as I tried to distance myself. The invasion had *tainted something and the softly lit world of my sanctuary felt harsh and brittle. It wasn't supposed to be like this.*

He didn't move, and it took all my might to push his whole body out of my sanctuary and into the space below the traps. I needed to close up the hole and eradicate any trace. There was no other way out for me; the damage from the collapse had been extensive and my other exit was gone. My time was limited. I needed to brick up the wall, hide it with stones and the detritus thrown down here and forgotten and leave before he was found.

I was buttoning my jacket and running up the stairs clutching my last packages when I heard a sigh, and my blood froze. The sound of movement from below and the dawning realisation he was not dead. I had no time, and I paused, not knowing if I should go back or if my blade had gone deep enough to make death inevitable. Had he seen me? But the sound of movement above told me the early risers had arrived, and the time to leave was now. I would hide in the shadows as they opened doors and slid away into the dawn.

I had to think.

Chapter Fifty-Three

Ida's face was cold, the tears had dried in the night air, her hair had stuck to the wetness and she ignored it. Her body, feeling as if it belonged to another, had forced her mind away, and she looked on at the small, limping figure with numbness. She had felt the physical pain after her fall, the sharp pain which calls forth involuntary cries and then the dull pain which rolled in waves and dogged her steps. But this, this was beyond that. With pinhole sharpness, she could recall every detail as it wormed into her brain. She hadn't cried; the tears had nothing to do with weeping. Something was overflowing and leaving her.

He was gone. She forced herself to frame the words silently. If she could think of the words and put them in a box and bury them down deep, she might be able to survive. But she was drowning in the night air, and she couldn't breathe.

Ida gulped as she felt a howl escaping her body and soar into the night, bouncing off walls, roofs and miles into the cold night. Maybe the Ripper would hear her and come and claim her. She did not care.

Her mind full of the dried blood on her hands, and she never wanted to wash off because it was all she had left of him. A sob erupted from her throat, and she fell awkwardly to her knees.

Time passed; it must have done, but she couldn't feel it. A thread of gold on the horizon told her the dawn was coming and the peace of the night would be broken by noise and more horror. She slowly climbed to her feet and looked around as if for the first time. Then she realised she had circled to the south of Waterloo Bridge and back towards the Gaiety. On ice-cold feet, she slowly returned. She had nowhere else to go, and her heart withered.

Ida's feet had carried her unthinkingly as they had all night. She had let the muted colours of night wash over her and the darkening blues and greys give way to the approaching dawn. She had felt separate to her body, like an observer , sounds, sensations and smells travelling from miles away, each slowly rolling into her mind and flowing away like water. Nothing elicited a reaction, an emotion, not even fear of a knife in the dark.

Ida turned to look at the city as it crowded along the side of the solid expanse of dark water which travelled out to the sea and the open sky. The thread was cut, and she was flying around in the breeze. She wanted to break free, run, fly away; yes, she remembered flying. Ida started to quicken her pace, her leg was painful, but she pushed the feeling down and increased her pace.

Ida felt a surge of energy, and her legs, which had failed her for so long, suddenly felt solid and sure. Her feet started to speed up under her. She almost laughed with the marvel of it and the sense of escape as she started running, full speed, towards the Gaiety. As she broke out from between the shield of the buildings on either side of the river, the wind hit her. The push, counter to her direction, seemed to ignite something in her, and she doubled her efforts, reveling in the battle.

Her feet slapped a counter rhythm to her pounding heart. In her ears, she felt the rushing of air and the rippling of her hair as it broke free from the barrage of pins and fell out in a comet tale behind her.

Images flickered through her mind, and she saw Tosher, giant and gentle, with large brown eyes always so unsure. She felt freedom when she looked down at an audience from the roof of the big top and the sensation of that first step into the air. Tosher and his big, calloused hands swamped her small ones as they walked along the bridges, lost in conversation with each other. The snap of a catch on a swing's arc defied the gravity that pulled at her.

Yellow and white daisies, which sprouted in plentiful clusters in parks and by the water, seemed innocent and jewel-like as small, perfect gifts...

Tosher, his sweet curved face, so kind......

Tosher......

§

The woman with the small shivering dog said the girl hadn't slowed down. She had run north across Waterloo Bridge, towards The Strand, diving between the people and looking almost mad with increasing speed. It had nearly been like a ballet as, without warning, she leapt onto a parapet and flung out her arms. Without hesitation, she had arched her back and had flown out from the bridge into the air. It was as if she had hung there like a firebird, her dress and flaming hair flowing out behind her in the rising sun as it lit her petite form. There was no fear, no cry, and no ripple once her arc brought her down. The dark water closed around her, and the morning sun turned the river to fire.

Chapter Fifty-Four

I felt it all leaving my body as the spray of yellow vomit driving up from my body arced into the river. It was bitter, and my ribs felt sore as I pressed into the stone of the Embankment to borrow stability and still my shaking body. It has been building since I slipped out of the theatre, but I know I have come far enough away now, even though each step has felt like my bones have shattered with each footfall. The cold stone is soothing, and I press my forehead down onto the flat surface as if I am greeting the dawn with a bow.

This mess, which started with the ... boy, is deviating me from the plan, and I feel uncertain and without control. Do I return once the body is discovered under the traps and wait for calm to return? Will they find my sanctuary? Is it over?

Do I run?

But I know I cannot stop. I must not stop, and if she smiles on me, my place will remain secret and inviolate. But what if? The grip of panic is something I have not felt for a long time, and the old paralysis is shocking. My heart is still so loud, I am sure it is enough to be heard across the darkness, but I still it and close my eyes, forcing it into the steady thump of a predator.

I had only wanted her, never her child. It had been a boy and I look down at the shapeless package at my feet. There is no hint of what is inside or of the curse which has been placed on me by this nameless child, born into death and the man who even now waits to be found.

I put down my hand to pick up the last package and throw it into the dark water, but I can't. This last one won't let me, so I step around it and leave it to the dawn.

Chapter Fifty-Five

The news reached the company just after dawn had taken Ida away. Search parties had been out all night and a stagehand taking a last sweep of the embankment to turn to the Strand heard a shocked cry and saw a woman leaping into the water. Word had passed on fleet feet from fellow stagehands to lodgings, to homes and as far as Fanny in Hammersmith, where a bleary-eyed Stan had heard hammering at the door and had shaken his sleeping wife awake. Of course, he had said she must go, and she had sped to the theatre, leaving him with a kiss and again knowing how lucky she was to have this man in her life.

But when she arrived, Fanny stopped, not knowing what to do. The momentum which had carried her to the theatre had drained away, and she felt paralysed. Pushing her numb body to respond, she passed the empty stage door office and, without conscious thought, found herself at her dressing room. It was still bare by the standards of most of the cast, but having brought the single article from her previous dressing room, which had decorated her mirror, she had not been able to bring herself to put it back up. Maybe hubris had dammed her and the production. It had felt triumphant and now people she knew were dead and the world was falling apart. A fat tear rose and rolled down a cheek, but she brushed it away and took a deep breath. Tosher and Ida were gone.

Fanny knew the rest of the cast would be gathering in the auditorium, but she instinctively needed to hide. On the day her mother died, she had crawled under the bed into the darkness and solitude where she lay, wide eyes watching the never-ending parade of feet and the sound of muffled sobs.

The past melted as a movement at the door brought her back to the present moment, and Fanny saw the figure of Mercy as she walked silently past a cigarette in her hand and a trail of smoke flowing out behind her.

"Mercy?" Fanny called out.

"You should be in the auditorium, ma'am." She bounced a neat courtesy, face pinched. She made no motion to hide the cigarette and took a deep pull before blowing a jet of grey smoke from between pursed lips. Emotions were raw, and surely even Mercy would be in a state of shock.

"Were you and Ida friends?" asked Fanny.

Mercy snorted and coughed. "No" she replied. No, it wasn't a cough; it was a laugh. "You're wanted downstairs. You should go."

The air was still, and everything became cut glass sharp. The sparkling dust motes hung in the air, frozen in the pinpricks of light which made it through the high, smeared windows downwards into the dressing room.

"They're dead. Ida is dead." Said Fanny, feeling that maybe Mercy had misunderstood.

"That tends to happen when you take a swan dive in the old Thames. If the fall doesn't kill you, the shit will."

Fanny rose to her feet and felt them take the weight, stockinged legs shifting in her soft leather boots so they stood squarely under her—a woman containing the rising fury of a Valkyrie posing for a fight. "That girl and that young man are dead, one murdered. How can you be so... so....?"

"What?" whispered Mercy quietly.

Fanny recoiled. Mercy took a few steps into the room, her steps slow and deliberate as if each were drawing energy from the deep in the ground. She paused a few feet from Fanny in a fury of stillness that felt worse than waving hands, flushed cheeks and prowling like a caged animal. This was something of diamond hardness which had been forged for years.

"You don't get to speak now, Miss High and Mighty." Her lips curled in a sneer, and her eyes flashed with malice. "You, always the one with the airs and graces, like that pathetic StJohn bitch. I see it all, you know. You waltz in here, into my theatre and all I can hear everywhere I go is your voice, you singing, you dancing, you taking the applause, and where am I? Picking up your shit. I'm forced to service vain, stupid women who aren't even fit to scrape my boots."

Fanny bridled and opened her mouth but was interrupted by Mercy, who started to speak with what seemed like a rising sense of enjoyment at this moment of freedom.

"I know what you are. You're just a jumped-up hall girl. The only thing you had was you'd been in Australia, so you're a bit exotic, but that shine wears off pretty damn fast when everyone realises you're from London scum and criminals. The only difference between you and your uncle going to Australia is that he got his passage free because he went in chains." Mercy smiled, relishing the moment like a taste.

"I'm glad the lazy little bitch and her ogre are dead, means more for the rest of us. If you can't survive, you die."

Mercy stood back and looked Fanny up and down. "What you going to do, Miss Robina, tell them all about it? No one'll believe you. I'll deny it, and I know enough about you to make things very hard if I want, and at the moment, that's the last thing you need." She flicked ash on the rug and ground it under the sole of her boot. "Fanny Robina, King of the Boys. Your majesty," she made a florid theatrical bow, her forehead nearly brushing her knees. "Fuck you" she whispered and left.

Fanny sat down and rocked back on her seat like her knees had been scythed out from under her. In her rage, Mercy had expertly assessed her weakness, weaponised it and struck. But she was right, this world required you wore a shell, protected yourself knowing if you were really seen, or let someone in they could use it against you. Even tragedy and death were no off limits if they served a use.

Scandal propelled Florence and Violet into starring roles, and Fanny had been a casualty of this for the first time. As men, Teddy, George, and Harry could do what they liked, and their opportunity was about their talent. A woman, well, she had to be something more. Fanny felt her head reeling, and it was as if the earth under her feet, under the theatre, had shaken. But, Tosher, Ida, had done nothing and paid the highest price of all.

Fanny looked up and saw her adult face in the mirror, which she only vaguely recognised as her own. There were more lines, and the bloom of her cheeks was less pink. Every detail was seared into her memory, and she saw the imperfections in the mirror's surface, creating a pattern of dots like a falling blossom. Around the mirror, most would stick postcards, dried flowers, and souvenirs, but for the first time, Fanny was struck with the bare mirror in front of her. For what felt like hours, Fanny stared at this woman reflected in front of her. The contours of a face she thought she knew better than most. A vague appraisal of a life caught in visual form. The blank canvas she would put on before a performance and scrape away afterwards, leaving what, who? She wanted to close her eyes, reach out and find a friendly hand, but back in the dark, it concentrated her mind on thought and feel, and the feelings threatened to overwhelm her. So she stared, eyes wide open, letting the light in to chase history away and visualising the shell around her, searching for cracks which needed repair. Slowly, she started to return to herself and with deft hands, she corrected the hastily applied makeup and slowly stood. Fanny fixed her face into a neutral expression and brushed imaginary dust from her skirts. Hiding under a bed in the dark wouldn't be possible anymore. She would never fit.

And she felt herself stop.

A silver image flashed across her mind. It was there, elusive and small, like the end of a thread, and any movement would lose it. Darkness? Why darkness?

Slowly sinking to her seat, Fanny thought about Tosher. He worked in darkness in the traps. He was attacked in the traps. The Police had been clear. He had surprised a thief who had killed him. But why was a thief in the traps? Valuable items were in the dressing rooms and the manager's office. There were plenty of places to hide and slip out past Tosher. What was down there in the dark which was worth killing for?

Fanny stood slowly, knowing her feet had already made the decision, and she found herself in the stage's wings at the top of the stairs. A glimpse of the auditorium showed her figures huddled together. The sound of muted crying and whispering filled the space like whispers. Wrapped in their own world, no one saw her as she took a lamp from a hook. The trail of blood and Tosher's final effort to emerge from the cellar coated the centre of the stairs. Fanny gulped and raised the hem of her dress and carefully placed her feet to avoid the drying stains.

She had been in the traps hundreds of times, but now it felt cold, forbidding and alien. Fanny tried to concentrate on placing her feet and avoided looking at the ghost of bloody fingers on the stairs below her. Her boots found the wooden planks at the first level. They felt hollow, rocking almost imperceptibly on their joists. Lifting the lamp, she looked around, searching for something, anything and saw the trail led further down into the darkness beneath her feet.

Without warning, one hand slid around her waist and another over her mouth as it started to frame the O of a scream. She felt the warmth of a body against her back, and she went rigid. "Don't scream, Miss Robina, please. I beg you," Hot breath in her ear whispered, and she felt the heart behind her thudding against her back. "It's me, William. Please don't scream. Hear me out. I promise I'm not going to hurt you." Fanny felt the hand loosen. It must have been out of sheer instinct, but she turned and swung the lamp out at head height in an unstoppable arc of terror, and as she felt it connect against bone, she turned to run.

"It was Robert!" Came a cry.

Fanny stopped as if hitting a wall. She paused, panting, foot on the bottom stair.

"You're lying."

"No!" William put his hand to his head. The blood was running trails down the left side of his face, matting his hair in shiny clumps. "I'm not." And he paused. The energy seemed to drain from him, and Fanny saw a young man in despair.

"I don't care what happens to me, Miss. I lied about who I am. But Robert, Miss, he...... he has to be stopped."

Fanny paused. "Tell me. And if you take one step forward, I will scream so loudly it'll raise the roof."

William sat back on his haunches. Briefly looking at the blood on his hand, he drew a deep breath.

"He calls me his Guardian Angel, you know. It's his clever joke. It's a little dig, a reminder in plain sight that he owns me. I'm his puppet and, I think now, his scapegoat. I've been a fool. He's been planning this all along, and I...." he paused. "I am the perfect villain and'll probably hang anyway." He breathed deeply as if dredging the truth from a deep well.

"William Pennett is a name from a gravestone I found. Little gravestone, must have been a small kid. I liked the name. It was like my own name, Bill, but complete. I'd fallen asleep in a graveyard against it. It was pissing with rain, and I traced my fingers around the etching on the stone and wondered if one day there would be something, somewhere, with my name on it. Maybe I was William, too. I only just had my letters, but I read his name and the shape of it. He had a family who cared enough to remember him. No one would remember a dead gang member with half a name."

"So you've been lying about who you are? Why should I believe anything you say then?" Fanny paused. "Why were you running?"

William looked up, sole full eyes full of resignation. "Because I killed someone, Miss."

Fanny started, "Tosher?!"

"No, I would never!"

"Tell me. Tell me everything." Fanny lowered herself to perch on a crate. To occupy her shaking hands, she brushed the dust from her skirt.

William moved from his haunches to sit.

"I grew up in Manchester. I don't know where I was born. I don't remember my parents. I don't know if I was lost or thrown out. But a street kid in Manchester makes sure they get adopted by a gang, or they get used one way or another, and none of it's good. I became an Angel. See? Robert's favourite little dig.

"It's about survival. You join up, get a room, food, and protection, and in turn, you fight and steal for each other. We did it all.

"But the streets are full of gangs, and there isn't much around, so we fought. Some used knives and coshes, but them that does, don't end up around long. They get stuck, arrested, boated out somewhere, or worse. So you use what you have on you." He looked down.

"Like a belt. You get searched, and all it's doing is holding up your trousers. But it can be wrapped around a wrist or swung, and, "he laughed, looking at the blood on his hand. "...it has a nasty bite."

"Who did you kill?" Fanny responded slowly.

"Don't know his name—another rat like me. We called ourselves the Angel Meadows, and he was a Bengal Tiger—gangs that stalked the streets, named after places like Hope Street, Angel Meadows or Bengal Street. A gang gave you safety, security and power. You walked tall and were full of piss and wind. But the price was to fight when another gang stepped on your turf. And in a clash, it's claw and belt fighting, and it was joy. We owned the street.

But one day, we were in the thick of it with the Tigers. Blood and snot flew around, and I swung at this big lad. I reached back and brought my belt around in an arc. It was the perfect wide swing. It hummed through the air, and as it sang, it hit the sweet spot, and the kid went down. I knew he was dead before he hit the ground. Eyes went blank. You hear stories about those who went down in a clash. Everyone knows someone who did. But no one sees it."

"Did you mean to?" Fanny asked.

"He was the enemy. He would've killed me without a blink. Like looking in a mirror it was. I knew it was run or see a noose. Too many people saw it happen to keep quiet. The Tigers would have peached on me for a fee even if the Angels said nothing. I'd have been hunted, so I ran. I ran for days, resting for a short time and then having it away before anyone saw me. I ended up in that graveyard. I figured I'd fall asleep and not wake up. I was colder than I've ever been, hadn't 'et in days, and I kept seeing him fall. And I thought, what's the point? What was the bloody point? All that fighting and crowing and ends in a dead kid bleeding all over the stones. Like the stone I was leaning on, only I doubt if the boy I killed got one.

"But the light came, and I was still alive, so I looked at the stone, and the last thing I stole was a name. I didn't know where I was going, but my feet carried me to London. And I thought, 'Why not?' so I worked a bit and made some connections. Slept in gutters, avoided the gangs, perverts and made the odd mistake. But I made myself useful and learned to read and write better from a friendly shopkeeper I protected from little swine like me. It took two years, and I'd forged my way into a uniform.

"Bloody funny, me in a uniform, but it's better than dead in lavender because not many street kids grow up, do they? But I felt pride for the first time in my life. I saw those who used the law as a weapon, and I thought maybe after a few months, looking about and finding a big score, I could get on a boat to New York and live like a king. But I changed. I wasn't looking for the edge anymore. I can do something here. Something good. And maybe, maybe, I can scrub my soul clean at the same time. I kept the belt to remind me."

"Like a trophy?"

"NO!" He almost shouted. But then William lapsed into silence.

"No, I suppose not. "Fanny sighed. "So, did the leopard change his spots, or are you still Bill?"

"No, Miss, he died. I'm William. But Robert found the belt. Dug through my stuff. He was always prying and looking for things. Ways to get something on you, like power. He loved it, made him the big man. And part of being the big man was being the 'golden boy'. He wanted to look good and did everything he could. Not a crack on his face, unlike mine. I look like the villain; I can't change that. He's got scars, though, covered in 'em. His old man went at him with a belt daily. But put on a shirt, and no one knows."

"Say I believed you." Said Fanny, her mind working at speed, trying to find somewhere to start to make sense of this and knowing if she was wrong, she might not leave alive. But something in his face, beneath the network of scars felt sincere. "Why are you down here?"

"Something was off. Robert came back agitated this morning. He shouted at me to go out, so I went for a walk. It doesn't pay to be around him when he's like that. He's unpredictable.

"So I waited for him to leave and went back. The floor was dripping with water, his clothes strung up on the line, sopping. I went to put a bucket under 'em and saw some spots of blood. He's not so good at washing if he can't get someone else to do it for him.

"It wasn't the first time he's been like that, but this was worse. He looked mad. Madder'n his old man, but cold, like ice. And I heard about what happened so I came to look. My belt was gone from my trunk, and I knew something was in the air.

"I came here and saw where Tosher came from. So I came down to look and then saw you........Tosher died down there Miss. He crawled up those stairs. He saw something which meant he couldn't live."

Fanny jumped to her feet, looking at the stairs. Bile rose in her throat, and she turned to William, fury erupting.

"You will show me now. No more stories, no more lies, no more half-truths."

William opened his mouth to protest but saw her face and slowly got to his feet.

§

Fanny's fury took her as far as the bottom step and on to the rubble of the basement, at which point it drained from her and she realised she was in the semi-darkness, standing in blood and with a man she did not know.

"Now what?" she asked as she took in the slime encrusted walls and debris.

"We look." said William simply as he started to run his fingers across the brickwork.

"Do you know what we are looking for?" she said casting the lantern light around the space.

William paused and turned to her, the light of the lamp catching his eyes. Fanny felt the shock of fear. "Blood"

She looked down "There is so much, and the police have trampled it everywhere."

"Not on the floor."

Fanny's curiosity got the better of her. "What do you mean?"

William waved his arms around at the walls. "Look", he motioned to a section of wall cluttered with debris and rotting planks.

Fanny's nose wrinkled in confusion. "I..."

"No blood on the planks, but a spray on the wall. See?" he motioned, and Fanny saw an arc of red splatter surrounding a section of clean brickwork. "The blood goes outwards when you cut deep enough. It sort of explodes, so why is that bit clean?"

Fanny swallowed back bile and nodded.

"He was facing the wall, and the first cut was here. Why would he be looking at a wall?"

As if convinced by his own words William set to pulling aside the planks and pulled at a loose brick. The waft of fetid air hit them both, and Fanny bent double as she was noisily sick.

William pulled at the surrounding bricks, exposing a hole. He looked back at Fanny "I'll go. Can I have the light?"

She wiped her mouth with the back of her hand. "No. We'll go."

Chapter Fifty-Six

The auditorium was blanched, stark and slightly shabby in the absence of the magic of a live show, and it gaped like a maw ready to be fed. Clusters of people sat in the worn seating in the stalls, and stagehands sat, legs hanging from rigging or over the side of the stage. No one spoke, and an eerie stillness lay thick over the auditorium.

Mouse sat with legs drawn up and encircled in thin arms. He had remained under the props table since yesterday and throughout the previous night's show. No manner of coaxing or cajoling would persuade him to move, so he had slowly become surrounded by blankets, apples and things to drink. Mr. Free had kept a close eye on the boy. No one would force him, and Mr. Free had made up a bed with Mrs. Freeman in the wardrobe so they could check on him if it took another night for him to emerge. Mouse's head lay on his knees, resting in an oversized cap, Penny Dreadful clamped in his hand. Not a sound rose from him, but gently shaking shoulders stood testament to his grief.

As soon as they realised Ida had slipped away, search parties were sent out. But no one had found her, and by 2 a.m., some of the more exhausted had reluctantly been sent home to bed.

Mr. Edwardes had cancelled the two shows of the day without comment, managed the search and the terrified company with the skill and deftness of touch of a magician. Instructions had been issued to Mr. Harris, who had passed them on to others in hurried whispers before each group exploded in different directions like blowing on a dandelion. Mr. Edwardes' face was drawn, and deep lines had appeared in the usually soft cheeks. The usual bombast and spark of excitement was absent, and his energy was now tinged with profound exhaustion. Initially, Miss Cameron had refused to come to the stage with the others to help and could be heard in her room, her voice rising above the eerie silence. It had been Florence who had quietly walked in there, softly closing the door behind her. The conversation had been low and lasted only a few moments before Florence emerged, followed by a chastened Miss Cameron, who could barely make eye contact with the rest of the cast. She quietly disappeared into her carriage and departed for the evening. Florence had left not long after in a hired carriage; her own had been left at the stage door with instruction to be available to Mr. Edwardes all night if needed.

The River Police had launched, looking for a sign of the red-headed girl. Stagehands had run to the river, ready to dive in, but the police had turned them away. The Thames was polluted and had a treacherous undertow that belied its calm exterior. And with sinking hearts, they knew this was a kind way to say Ida was unlikely to be found alive.

It was as if she had faded into nothing. Not a trace was there, only the unspeakable void left by the figures of a giant of a man and the small bird who flew away. The echoing silence felt deafening. Mr. Edwardes stood on the stage speaking quietly to Mr. Free and Mr.

Harris. All looked haggard and defeated. Mr. Edwardes thought, and not for the first time, how immaculate Mr. Free was; even now, after a sleepless night, he was clean-shaven. He scratched his stubble and looked at Mr. Harris, who was equally disheveled. It was odd how, in one short night, everything had broken apart so quickly. Perhaps this would be the end of the show, the theatre and the tragedy that had touched every one of them would continue to send ripples out into their lives. For the first time, after a night of managing a crisis, it was now over, and he felt the void of inactivity and helplessness. He would have given it all up in that moment to be with Julia in the safety of their home.

"Charles." Said Mr. Edwardes, patting Harris on the shoulder. "Sit down, old boy. Rest."

Mr. Harris nodded and retired to one of the many chairs littered on stage amongst the set.

A figure in a white shirt and dark blue uniform trousers flecked in dust walked up the steps from the traps and on to the stage, followed by a visibly shaken Fanny. Both looked at the figures on the stage and littering the auditorium and drew deep breaths.

"Miss Robina?" said Mr. Edwardes, his face etched in worry.

"William hasn't got long," she said

"Murphy will cover my beat. I told him I had an emergency. But, if I'm not at the cross-section to meet the next shift, someone might come looking."

William paused, looking around the auditorium. "I'm so sorry", he whispered, and the sound rolled and travelled like a sigh around the space.

"It's not your fault," said Fanny. "I had you all wrong, William. Police said they found nothing down there. It's full of rubbish. They think Tosher was in early and stumbled on a thief who was hiding and is gone now. As far as they are concerned, it was a robbery that went wrong."

William caught his breath. "I should have known. If I couldn't see what he was doing, what kind of copper am I?"

"He's an actor", said Fanny. "Finest I've seen."

"Miss Robina....?" Mr. Edwardes's question hung in the air. "Please", he finished quietly.

Fanny looked into the questioning faces. She knew, just as the subconscious twinge of a cue line, that this was the moment she had to speak. Her corset was pricking against her skin with the sweat and grime of that place. She felt a thousand washes would never clean it from her body or mind. But, those people, faces usually obscured in paint, looked raw and diminished in reality and behind the shine, she now saw them, frightened. She glanced at Alice who had her legs curled up in front of her in a red auditorium chair, almost protectively. She returned Fanny's gaze expectantly and Fanny took a slow breath.

"It is true; something terrible has been happening here," she said, her voice wavering. She stopped, swallowed and tried again. "Tosher was murdered. But not by a stranger, a thief, but by someone we know. Someone who is not who they appeared to be." She glanced at Teddy, "Like the deal with the demon who takes your soul."

William saw her falter and stepped forward, but she waved him away.

"NO!" She paused in shock at her sudden ferocity. "No," she said, quieter. He nodded. "Tosher found something. Something dreadful under the stage. Under our feet. He found a space full of candles and remains, human remains hidden in the walls. Women...."

Mr. Free's hand flew to his mouth, his face grey.

"There is a space, like a chapel. And.... in the walls, shoes. Behind the bricks. Women's shoes....... And ..... A head." Fanny continued, her mouth dry. She could feel her whole body trembling and clear in her mind the images.

Gasps and cries erupted around the auditorium. Cries of "No" and "I have to see" mingled with inarticulate wails. William nodded to the gazes which landed on him in silent confirmation.

"Oh my god", whispered Mr. Free as his wife moved swiftly to his side, and both unconsciously clutched hands. Tears were running rivulets down Mrs. Freeman's face. "Who?"

"The Ripper!" came a shout from the front row as Harry jumped up in a fury.

"No!" called Fanny, raising her voice against the shouting and crying. "Listen! No", she repeated, "It's different. Candles, stains..... It is not the same. This one, he plans, takes his time but hides in plain sight. It's like a ritual. He's a hunter like the Ripper, but he keeps trophies. I think this is someone different."

Harry started to stride up to the stage—Teddy behind him. "Harry, listen, she's not finished." But Harry ignored him and strode to the Police Officer standing beside a stupefied Mr. Edwardes. "Well?" He blustered. "Aren't you going to do anything?" He paused and threw his hands up in conclusion. "So that's it. They arrest him, and he's hanged." Said Harry, "The Ripper is dead."

"But there's no proof! All we have are some remains, hair and some shoes. It's nothing. It proves nothing. Half a dozen police will turn up, tramp around, and he's gone. He'll vanish, and there'll never be justice." said William. His breaths came out hard and sharp. Eyes locking on Fanny's, he exhaled and seemed to deflate into misery.

"I'm as scared as you all are," Fanny whispered. But her voice caught the space around her and traveled across the auditorium like a sigh.

"So, who is it, Fanny?" Said Teddy. His usually large eyes seemed wider and mirrored her fear.

She turned to the company tears pricking the corner of her eyes and lanced the wound. "It's Robert. Robert is the demon."

She had expected it, but the roar of denial, demands, and shouts of horror hit her like a wall. The tremor in her body increased and she felt for a moment as if it would overwhelm her.

In the front row of the auditorium, Florence StJohn sat, her face drained of colour and motionless like a statue. The accustomed seat usually occupied by Miss Cameron, equidistant to the front, was empty. Mr. Free drew a hand across his forehead. Mr. Harris slowly rose to his feet, his mouth open, framing words he could not find. In the back of the stage was a lone figure holding a whittling knife in one hand, which dropped to the floor. The bright clatter of the metal hitting the floor pierced the clamor.

"I have to see" stammered Edwardes "It can't be." Without waiting for others he grabbed the lamp from William and made for the traps, followed by Albert. No one moved. All were frozen in the moment of terrible realisation, as if stillness would somehow hide them from the horror. It felt like hours before Edwardes re-emerged, handkerchief pressed to his face, what remained visible was grey.

"Dear god, how many?" Said Mr. Edwardes, eyes wide in horror.

"I don't know sir. Can't tell without making more of a mess." Replied William.

A sob rose from the auditorium as Jenny put her face in her hands and her shoulders shook.

"And Tosher...found it", started Fanny. "He must have disturbed him or something and..... Well, he's scared now, probably more dangerous. But I think he'll be back to collect his possessions."

"Possessions?" Mr. Free queried.

"Oilcloth with ... knives........ "said William. "His dad's old butcher knives.....and a pouch full of teeth," Albert added and Mr. Edwards recoiled in horror.

Fanny shuddered at the thought of such barbarity just below their feet, down in the dark. Had he been there when they were on stage? Had he stared up through the boards, watching them through the traps and did their voices travel down there, comic songs played to the butcher as he sliced at flesh? How many women were trapped down there by this monster, and had any been alive when he started to .. She shuddered to end the thought. It would drive her mad.

Albert felt a falling sensation in his gut. Robert was the son of a fellow soldier who was a survivor of the carnage of Sevastopol, where the broken came home and passed their madness to their family. William may blame himself for not seeing the demon in his fellow police officer, but Albert would never forgive himself for not seeing the seed of evil planted in the boy. He had felt sorry for him, treated him like a son, encouraged him unquestioningly, forgiven, and explained things away.

§

In the darkness, a small figure watched with interest. She had raised long skirts and run up the stairs to the dressing rooms. At the door, she had listened for any sounds coming from the stage and let herself in. This was a gift, the perfect time, and she would take it. The box was still on the table, and she pulled out lock-picks from her apron and got to work. Caesar had been helpful with many things, and she had been a quick study. Before long, the box was open, and she was plunging her hand into the top tray and removing the contents. Miss StJohn trusted her to look after the box but never the key. It would be easy to run, box in hand, but why become hunted, run the risk of Police waiting in New York for her? She had chosen two pieces because Mercy now knew Miss St John's secret and this secret meant she could never go to the Police. Carefully closing the box and hearing the click, which indicated she had managed to keep the lock intact, she carefully left the room. The whole backstage was empty, and as she passed the door, she opened a basket and removed her coat. Removing the apron and screwing it into a ball which she dropped to the floor, she turned the necklaces over in her hand and smiled.

"Goodbye, Mercy." she curtsied and left.

§

"So what do we do?" said Mr. Harris. "The Police will never believe it is one of their own. I ..." He looked to Mr. Edwardes, who shrugged.

"Well, we think he is coming back, yes?" said Fanny to William, who nodded in response. "So we lay a trap."

Fanny was shocked by her own words. It sounded infantile, foolish and naive.

"Are you insane?" roared Harry.

"This has nothing to do with us! It's the Police's job." Agreed George.

"To arrest one of our own? The son of one of our own? With no real evidence?" Shouted William, cutting across the rising clamour. "It wasn't so long ago that murdering a copper was called 'justifiable' because we were hated so much. Officers held down so a cart could run over them, and the crushed badge hammered out and given to the next poor sod. It has taken years for people to trust us, and even now, the Ripper has made us look like fools. There are coppers out there, ones better than me, who are out there daily, running into danger against... God knows what, armed with a stick and a bloody whistle. They, we, are dying out there. Robert has done unspeakable things and could bring us all down with him, but we have nothing but suspicion and no idea where he is. I... I...don't know what to do." Tears were running freely down William's face.

"We have to find him and stop him, or he will continue, if not here, somewhere else," said Mr. Edwardes quietly. "I think this is the best chance we have. William is correct; the city is on a knife edge. It could topple everything."

"So we herd him and catch him." Came a voice from the back. Albert stepped forward, the light catching the hollows of his face. Hand, empty of his whittling knife, still hanging frozen by his side. "He's frightened, more dangerous than ever. He'll lash out at any weakness, so we have to catch him, confuse him and scare him in front of enough witnesses. We already have a bated trap, and we know where he is going to go."

"This is crazy!" George exploded, raising his hands in appeal to the company. I cannot believe I am hearing this insanity. You!" he pointed at William, striding towards him. "Let the law deal with it."

"And do what?" said Fanny quietly. "They'll investigate, pull the theatre apart and close us down, for what? If he knows we're onto him, he could be halfway to France. At best, the police will arrest one of us because we're always here, George, at all hours. At worst, the theatre will be closed. Either way, lives will be ruined, reputations destroyed, and maybe one of us will be hanged. Because there is no more evidence against him than there is us, and they can't be seen to let another murderer get away." She placed a gentle hand on George's arm. "We have families, he will walk away and keep killing women. Do you have any idea George, how frightening it is to be a woman at the moment? We are being hunted by more than one person, like prey. We are not prey George, we are your sisters, your wives and your daughters."

George's shoulders momentarily sagged, and he looked appealingly at Mr. Edwardes. "Sir, please, this is madness."

Mr. Edwardes stepped into the centre of the stage. He scanned the company sitting in the audience and spoke. His low and clear voice carried across the auditorium. He did not need to shout or raise his voice; the acoustics were perfect, and Mr. Edwardes was still a showman.

"I cannot make any guarantee, but we must do something. Albert, you know him best."

Albert's eyes were blank "Thought I did."

"Will he come back?" He paused, taking in the faces staring intently at him.

"For the knives, yes," was the reply.

There was nothing more to say. The die was cast, and the stakes were more than evident. Words, so often sprinkled liberally across the stage to conjure, embellish and entertain, were not needed at this moment. The question was simple. How do they set a snare to catch a murderer?

§

In the silence, the air seemed to hum without sound and bluster, and the moment felt raw and painful. A soft step to his right drew Edwardes' attention.

"I'll help." Said Fanny.

A creak of the seating in the auditorium sounded, and Jenny rose to her feet and nodded. Around her, one by one, rose Emma, Alice, Jenny, Lily and the other girls of the chorus.

"They're girls!" exploded George. "You cannot let this continue! Mr. Harris?! Mr. Free?"

Mr. Free looked at Mrs. Freeman, and they both clasped hands, stepping forward. He nodded to Mr. Edwardes, and as if prompted by this, Mr. Harris also stepped forward.

George almost ran down the stairs into the auditorium towards Teddy. "Teddy, be the voice of reason here. Please!"

"I have a daughter," he said simply and stood. Behind him, Frank, Earnest, and Harry rose to their feet, faces set.

"Jenny?" George demanded, looking at Mabel, who remained seated, looking small and uncomfortable. "She's just a child." Jenny nodded and took Mabel's hand, taking her to the bewildered man. "You are right." George sagged with relief. "She is too young for this. Take her home, Mr. Stone."

"George, I ask of you one thing." George looked up towards Mr. Edwardes, who had walked to the front of the stage. Leaning down to look at him, his face became shadowed as it left the pool of light. "Give us until tomorrow. I ask, for all the times I have helped you in the past that you give us one day before you do anything. Take Mabel home and then go to your home. Please."

George looked up at the man, usually so full of energy and show, and saw a spark of flint but also ... fear. George nodded slowly. He owed this man a great deal, and to ask for one day was a small dent in the overwhelming debt he offered him. He nodded and gently guided Mabel out of the auditorium and out of the theatre. Mabel felt his hand shaking as it tightly held hers, and she squeezed it, knowing there were no more words.

From above came the sound of metal being struck in a regular beat. It was loud and incessant and sent shivers down the spine. Slowly, it increased in volume, and the pace remained steady. From above, the crew looked down from their gantries and eyries. Feet dangled from those seated into thin air, oily forearms leaned on rails, but all held pipes and poles and were beating them on walls, metals and calloused hands. Those who watched from the dark and were the beating heart of the theatre looked down on the stage. Feet joined the rhythm, and the vibration drove through walls, lifted frayed curtains, sent small piles of dust down onto the stage and shook the lights. It grew, evolved, and fractured into a wall of noise and shouts. It was raw, incessant and spoke of loss, pain, stolen lives and anger so deep it rose up from the earth itself.

The Gaiety herself had stirred.

Chapter Fifty-Seven

It was that bitch and her bastard baby. They had cursed him. His heart had made what he felt was an audible lurch when he had arrived back from the Embankment and slid back into the darkness of the theatre. He had seen William and then Miss Robina disappearing into the basement, and he knew he had to leave again and hide until his way became clear to return.

He had descended back into the tunnels by a hidden entrance at the Embankment and found his way back to the now-blocked second exit to his precious chapel. He could hear movement in there, the unintelligible hubbub of voices and the sharp cry of discovery, but then it went quiet, and he slid down to the floor, his back against the detritus hiding him from the invaders in his once sacred space. The cold chill of rage and panic ran down his wet back and froze his bones. He struck at his thigh with a furious fist, again and again, the pain bringing him back and clearing his mind. He had lost track of time, but he felt the sense of it slipping through his fingers towards a decision. No, this must not, would not happen. He was only now finding his power and would not let it go. All this time, he had been operating, hidden within a city of chaos, fear, and murder. He had been invisible. How could he be so stupid?

His body felt tense, on edge and ready to shrivel into nothing, but he steadied himself and took a lungful of fetid air. This time, he would not hide or beg. He would lash out and fight. Robert found his feet taking him back up the tunnel to emerge back by the river, the place where it all started, and he gazed out across the water as it snaked into the distance. It had been so clear as if he had been following a path which had risen to meet his feet. There had been something preordained about it all, and ever since that day the dead child had polluted his sanctuary, it had all unraveled, and he had found himself clutching at threads.

The sense of betrayal from William, Miss Robina, all of them, was a wave of heat which ran through his veins, burning his skin and threatening to burst out in thin white cracks, making him luminous and deadly. They were not following his script, his plan, his control. He was raw, like a nerve, and he felt his knuckles sheering on the stone of the embankment wall. He looked down impassively to see the pink under the white flesh and the darker dots of deeper wounds which were oozing blood. He licked his hand and tasted the metal and a faint taste of foul water, sharp on his tongue. It had always been about blood and had started that night with the blood of his mother and the throat sliced open into a beatific smile which vomited a baptism of blood over him. It had soaked his face, entered his mouth and dripped down his face in red tears.

His father, the man whose fury always rolled off him in waves, had seemed to act like an automaton, and even as he heard the thump of her body hitting the floor with sickening finality, he had removed the oilcloth from the dresser. There was no hesitation, no emotion, something had shut down in his eyes and the bundle was unrolled across the table by deliberate and steady hands. Robert had seen the gleam of the tools of the butcher.

Robert had learned all he needed to know at his father's knee, and he had watched impassively as she had been disarticulated, turning from soft, warm flesh to packets of meat. He had felt the blood drying in his skin and the now familiar sense of it cracking, turning to ash and falling away. He had been left alone as his father shuttled packages from the room and into the outside. He heard the creak of the steps as journey after journey was made. There were no footsteps, only the sound of the stairs shifting with his weight. Even then, he had attached old tyres to his boots to dull the sound of his feet. Even then, he was a hunter.

In the early hours, his father had started to scrub, first, the table and walls, working his way down to the floor and sending waves of dirty water and suds out of the door and down the Stairs. The whole house had been awash, drowned in water which went from red to pink to grey, and with that, all trace of his mother was gone.

Robert hadn't moved in hours. His limbs had frozen, and he couldn't break out. He stirred only when the bath was hauled to the fire and filled with water from the black range that steamed and boiled. His father had stepped in, fully clothed and started to scrub. He'd clawed at the blood-soaked fabric until he was naked and continued to scrub, first with soap, then with something caustic and acrid, which sent the smell of hot flesh into his nose. The man's skin was raw and bleeding, but he still scrubbed.

Robert remembered only impressions as he was lifted into the bath. The water was so hot his senses shut down and only slowly evolved into signals of excruciating pain in his brain. He tried to move his feet, but his father held his hair in a balled fist and started to scrub him first with the soap, then sand and finally, the burning came. It was the mortifying of his flesh, which scarred, cracked and then peeled. The pain was so intense he slid into a place beyond screaming, where all he could do was pant. His father's hand was holding his hair so tightly that he felt clumps dragging from his scalp as the blood being cleaned from his body became his own, and the water around his knees became red again. Blood of the mother and then blood of the son.

"Out," Robert heard the command, but it came from a distance, and he turned unseeing eyes to the naked, raw figure in front of him.

"OUT!" it roared. Placing bleeding fingers on the side of the bath, he put a small foot on the wet floor. Not fast enough, his father grabbed a stick-thin arm and dragged him out. He had fallen to the floor and crawled into a corner by the grate and pulled his limbs into his bleeding body as his father got back in the bath. Robert watched as his father took more of the powder and slowly poured it over his legs and genitals and scrubbed as tears rolled down ruddy cheeks.

Robert shook his head to dislodge the memory threatening to draw him away from the present. He felt, again, a sense of injustice. Bloody William, why couldn't he keep quiet? He had been so useful, but still could be. He patted the belt rolled up in his pocket. It had always been his assurance, and so he would use it now, put it in the basement with an old knife judicially covered in blood. When asked, Robert would sadly recount his misjudged attempt to help his colleague. The assumed identity, the murder, and all the sordid details would emerge, and William would hang for all of it. No one would believe him. He would hang anyway; there was no sense in two men going to the gallows when it could be wrapped up in a neat package. And who would believe hysterical actors with no proof? They make up stories for a living, after all.

Robert would wait and return to the theatre once everyone had left and set the scene in time for discovery early tomorrow morning. He would regret the loss of his space, his chapel, but that woman and baby had polluted it for him. It was time to leave. London was vast, and indeed, so was the world. Robert had always wanted to see Paris. Maybe it was time.

§

He had waited in the shadows of the theatre and seen the cast leaving through the stage door. The last to leave was Albert. Robert looked impassively at the man as he turned the key on the rough wooden door. Robert knew that he had been the only blind spot in the psyche of the shrewd old soldier. He knew he was unlikely to be able to talk his way out of anything with Albert now, so from now on, the man was his enemy.

Robert waited for an hour, watching the streets empty and the sounds of London start to become the sharper shouts of nighttime activity. Satisfied he was unseen, he crept towards the door and slid into the theatre.

Using his father's knives and punctuating the wordless conversation with the old monster had been so poetic. The father who crushed him in body and soul and used those knives to disarticulate his mother. But he couldn't leave them down there, he needed them if he was to start again. He took a small breath of relief and quickly glanced around again to check he remained unobserved. His dark widened eye saw nothing to cause him concern.

Robert started towards the stairs of the traps, not needing a light as he knew the way by heart. He counted to twenty in the darkness and felt his way along the brick wall, bumping his fingers with cleats, pulleys, and ropes, which marked the progress of his route. But something caused him to pause. In an ear, fear-tuned to subtle noises, he felt nothing, not even the building subtly shifting and moving in its dance between heat and cold. It was the silence of anticipation where the theatre and all the souls inside held their breath before the first note sounded. The first note was a subtle footfall above.

He looked up, his head snapping like a gunshot, sharp and precise, triangulating on his audible prey. Below the sound, he stopped, stock still, breath held, and lungs burning, ready to draw in what he needed to power his limbs to act. The pause felt like an eternity. When no repetition of the sound followed, the certainty hit him. Someone was there. He turned round in a slow circle searching above and saw nothing but deeper shadows.

A sigh rose in the dark. It bounced around the space, dividing as it hit walls and returning from each direction, confusing his senses and chilling his soul. He rocketed back as if scalded and collided with the wall, dislodging a fire bucket which hit the floor with a clang, filling the theatre with noise and then the sound of the gentle rocking until it came to rest.

Robert acted instinctively, no longer caring he had given away his location. The boy baptised in blood, remembered the threat rising in dark rooms during the endless hours of the night, and in the back of his mind, a child curled up in a corner and tried not to make a sound. The tide of threat made the dark tangible, and his actions were slow pauses between moments of crystal-sharp punctuation where the world sped up to eye-watering speed. The noise again. A sigh. He bolted, arms and legs like the pistons of a train, pulling him forward in a flat run towards the door across the stage.

A white light slammed on, surrounding him and reducing his vision to a few feet from his face. Night vision destroyed and lights blinding, he lost his footing and slid to a stop on his front. Rolling onto his back to fend off any attack, he tried to shield his eyes. There was no sound above the deafening pounding of the blood as it sped around his fear-accelerated body, but the second sigh caused his system to freeze as, this time, he saw the figure who had made it. Above him on the gantry, the sudden burst of light from a dark lantern framed a familiar figure in a cloak and domed helmet. A police whistle blew out, sharp and piercing.

Scrabbling back on his hands and feet in panic, Robert exhaled an involuntary cry of alarm and terror.

"NO!" He cried, more to himself, to shake the image from his mind.

When he started to stand, the light turned off, plunging him into darkness and confusion. In the auditorium, a light shone from the gallery, and a second whistle broke the silence. He shrieked again as the familiar image of his nightmares stood framed against the blinding light.

The light blinked off and then on again, and now two shone upon him as he struggled. His knees were buckling below him and he fought to remain upright. In the stalls were two more figures, framed by lights and in familiar silhouette. Two whistles sounded, the notes gathering more whistles until the layers of sound built higher and higher as more figures stepped out of the shadows, in front of him, below him, in boxes, in the tower above... Everywhere.

The figures started to move towards him in an indistinguishable moving wall of blue and silver, heavy boots thumping on the floor in unison. He could feel the sensation through the thin flooring of the stage, and it rose into his tight chest.

"No!" he screamed, looking around desperately for an escape from the noise and figures.

He reached into his pocket, drew out a shiny object, and unrolled the belt with the heavy buckle. He whirled it around his head wildly until it took on an arc of his own, but his fingers slipped, and it flew away into the darkness. Small, incomprehensible noises of pure terror escaped him. He was beyond speech and coherence.

The auditorium exploded into action and noise. A figure dropped on a rope from the tower, cloak flying out around him like dark wings. Robert uttered a guttural shriek, seeking an escape but only finding more terror. As more lights turned on, he started to see the figures around him in more detail, but the faces were hidden in the shadow of the hats. Police uniforms broke out of the formation and surrounded him in a circle, but Robert only saw his father, repeated again and again around him. The same face in unison, holding up a hand, starting to speak. His terror was a wave which flattened his mind into a silver arrow with one purpose: to get away. He raised a placatory hand and pointed it at one, at all of them and stepped back to try and escape to somewhere, anywhere.

And the floor vanished.

For a moment, Robert hung suspended like a man in the second before the noose pulled taut. Confusion and disbelief briefly coloured his face, and he fell backwards through the trap.

The trap alone had opened, but the standing board was not there, so nothing was in place to prevent his fall. As he struck the aged timbers of the floor below, they gave in to the force of his impact and shattered out around him like a corona. Picking up speed, he continued to fall as impact after impact shattered his spine limbs, and finally, in the darkness by the door to his blood shrine, far from the light, his skull hit stone.

The world had paused for Robert Challen, and the imagined death of his victims poured into his mind as his senses flashed in small explosions of colour. The crimson petals that had closed around the lives of those he had collected in that place closed around the boy, again in red, as his blood seeped through the fabric of his clothes into the mud and stone. It crept over and covered the existing stains of the nameless and lost women who had involuntarily travelled into the dark before him.

Chapter Fifty-Eight

It was still. No one breathed, and not a muscle moved. Each person was trying to absorb and make sense of what had assaulted their senses.

Slowly reaching up a trembling hand, Fanny took the helmet from her head as time started to speed up again. Around her, the identical figures removed helmets and moustaches. Alice, Emma, Frank, Earnest and the girls of the cast; a Greek chorus of vengeance encircled the dark void of the open trap door. Above them, in the darkness, the shadows of the crew stood, bearing witness. From the the wings, the light caught the shocked faces of Mr. Edwardes, Mr. Harris, Teddy and Harry.

A small silver whistle dropped from Jenny's fingers to the floor. The sudden noise bounced around the auditorium like another gunshot.

"Shit" she muttered brokenly.

Emma put her hand to her mouth in an involuntary gasp, and sob escaped her. Eyes wide with shock, they scanned each other.

It was a small sigh that broke the silence, a brief movement in the air of escaping breath that reverberated around the auditorium like the whisper of wings. In the wings of the stage, Mr. Free, eyes wide, put his hand to the side of his head. It came away, bright with blood which ribboned down his shirt, finally blooming on his waistcoat like a flower. The belt and heavy buckle whirled out in Robert's wild desperation had flown into the darkness of the wings and struck James Freeman.

Fanny's feet beat the hollow stage floor as she broke into a run punctuated by a simple thud as Mr. Free fell to his knees. Frozen, in a moment, as if praying, looked at his hand, bewildered, and then up at Fanny, who caught him as he started to fall forward.

A scream erupted from Jenny, who was silenced by Emma's arms as she pulled her close.

"Mr. Free," said Fanny, a ball of panic starting to grow in her chest. She put her hand to his smooth skin and held up his face. "James?" She held onto him, trying to keep him upright because, at that moment, laying him down felt like giving up. With a shaking hand, she started to undo his cravat, fingers fumbling and mind slow with apprehension. The knot was tight, wet and hard to undo, but finally, she felt easement, and it fell apart, exposing a pale, smooth throat.

Mr. Free's hand grasped her forearm, and a faint word "Please" escaped white lips, and as she locked gazes, Fanny felt the thin sliver of realisation. It had no form and swum in front of her mind, like the edges of a cloud before they merged into something recognisable, but in that moment, Fanny had the sense of something unseen, something she had missed every day.

The belt buckle had left a ragged mess of broken skin, which frilled around the edge and exposed the bright red flesh. It looked livid, and the blood which rose from beneath was horrifying, but it didn't pump or drive its way out in ecstatic escape. She took the cravat and bundled it into a fist before holding it down hard on the wound.

"It's bleeding like the devil, but I think......"

A figure dropped into the side of her vision, and frantic hands explored Mr. Free's face, neck and chest. Fanny, hand still firmly clamped over the sodden cravat, caught the anguished face of Mrs. Freeman. Her eyes were fixed, her face white, and small sobs rose like bubbles from her chest as she continued to explore Mr. Free. Her mouth formed a thin line, and her jaw started to wobble as words refused arrive. Fanny nodded.

"Dora, I think it clipped him.....Dora..... Dora?"

The repeated use of her name seemed to pierce her consciousness, and an unintelligible cry of relief finally escaped in an explosion of emotion. Wet rivulets ran down freckled cheeks and rolled along her angular jaw before dropping.

Mrs. Freeman reached out to her husband. "I'll take him, Miss. Give him to me." As her arms started to envelop Mr. Free, Fanny saw the unmistakable look of panic, which remained despite her reassurances that he would live. Mrs. Freeman was almost flat with anxiety and concern.

Fanny allowed Mrs. Freeman to settle onto the floor and position herself, holding her husband in a protective circle. Her hand, nails worn short and fingers calloused from stitching, gently took and pressed the cravat down. The bleeding was beginning to stop, but her hand moved to a position which obscured his face as much as she could. Gazing down at him in their private world, Mrs. Freeman kissed his head. At this moment, Fanny felt like an intruder.

William's hand lightly touched her shoulder, and Fanny turned to a face of speechless terror.

"He'll live. William, he will live. Go and get the belt, hide it and then throw it in the river." she said. Looking towards the open mouth of the trapdoor, the one she had risen through many times, she swallowed. "And then we go and check that the monster in the basement is really dead."

William knelt beside her, running a hand across a sweat-drenched brow with shaking hands. "Albert went down there as soon as he fell. He must be dead." William rose to his feet and held a hand to Fanny, who grasped it. She had worn men's clothes almost every day, but these felt awkward and strange, and she longed to put on a dress and vanish back into the ranks of invisible women, if only for a moment. She wanted to hide back under the bed from her childhood and not be seen. But the faces around her were blanched, shocked and stricken.

"The trap? Why wasn't the standing board there?" Fanny asked, bewildered.

A voice rang out across the stage. "Everyone, we need to clean up." Shouted Mr. Edwardes. The original plan was in tatters, and he fell into familiar command. "It has to be as if this never happened. No one can know, and we return to normal. One person speaks, and we all fall. Whatever he was, whatever he became, no one here deserves to be his last victim. It's over."

Fanny looked at William. "He's right; if anyone speaks, we all lose." William nodded. She had seen his expression, caught between relief and dread of secrets coming to light. "That man lying down there in the dark did terrible things, horrible things and Bill Cutter was a boy heading down a dark path. What are you going to do now, and who are you going to be? Bill Cutter can also die tonight so Constable William Pennett can have that new beginning he's worked so hard for. Robert Challen can disappear, and no one else gets hurt."

William looked up at her. It wasn't a smile on his face but some form of acceptance and the acknowledgement of something finished. Maybe it was not a neat ending, but in the only way which made sense. What could the law do now? The monster was dead. The women, those poor women, would never be claimed. There was no telling how many had died at the hands of Robert Challen, no telling how many he had tortured by degrees. If they exposed everything, the circle of fire surrounding the man would continue to burn, and many more people could be destroyed. Was he being selfish or a coward? Maybe. He looked up at the people around him. People who relied on this place, people whose livelihoods could end tonight. This way, the only thing left would be smoke, which would vanish from sight and leave nothing but a memory and a clear day. He looked at Fanny. "Let's give those we can peace and let the living move on".

Fanny looked down at Mr. Free, who was starting to stir amidst the rising clatter of activity around them. She knelt next to him and saw in the eyes of Mrs. Freeman, the lioness who was ready to spring. Mr. Free drew his legs up and motioned to stand, but Fanny's hand on his knee gently pushed him back down and into the arms of his wife. She took a strip of fabric from her shirt and tied it around his neck like a new cravat.

"I remember a story, a long time ago, about a surgeon, James Barry. Argued with Nightingale in Crimea, delivered the most difficult babies and was, by all accounts, a hard bastard. But when he died, it turns out he'd had to be. All that time, he had been a woman. When you put on a dress, the world only sees the dress and not the person underneath. It protects but can also be a prison. It hides what you are really capable of, particularly if you aren't blessed with money. I would say it is you, above all of us, who is the greatest actor, but I think I'd be wrong, what you are is........ Free. I didn't get it until now, but I promise, no one will ever know from me."

Mr. Free took Fanny's hand and squeezed it. "Thank you"

§

Robert lost track of time, lying there, broken. Above, he heard footsteps and movement. His hoarse voice dried in his throat as he tried to call for help, to let them know he was clinging to life. They would help him; he knew them all, and they didn't have it in them to leave a man to die. And when Albert's figure finally swam into view, which seemed like a lifetime later, he turned his remaining working eye up to that familiar face and its grey-streaked moustache.

"Help...me", he croaked, trying to raise his arm but only managed to lift a blood-soaked crooked finger.

Albert crouched down next to the boy. He took off his cap and wiped his forehead with a hairy forearm. A man of few words, he silently took in the scene and spoke with a deep sigh. "I fought with your dad, boy. It made us brothers. We looked out for each other. It was the only way we got out of Crimea alive. Do you know why they called him 'Knocker Challen'? 'Cos he preferred to use a big stick and knock on the Russki's head with a swift tap, spilling their brains. I used to send them off to lavender in short order as well. But I liked to be up, close and personal in the melee. He liked to knock, and I... well, I sent 'em off up close and personal in my way. When you hear the bugger's heart stop, you know they ain't going to get up and have another go at your back.

It was war, you see, and I did a fair bit of knocking myself. After a while, you give up counting who you kill. And you learned new ways to send 'em off. Your dad taught me a lot, and I did the same. But I dare say if I hadn't put 'em to rest, sum would've done the same for me.

I never told you this, but when we came back, everyone expected us to pick up where we left off as if nothing happened. But we got the taste, you see, and it's a hard one to let go of. War allows something loose, and not everyone can cage it when the last bullet flies.

I can see you've got it now. Maybe a gift from your dad. I don't know. But I go to the fighting pits and get it out legitimately. I won't say I don't have to pull up hard to stop myself from finishing them, but I do. But something is broken in you, lad, and I can see it's far beyond fixing. And then you killed Tosher—a good man. I liked him. So I'm going to give you a choice you don't deserve, and I'll be the father I guess your old man wasn't able to be.

You can go out quickly on this blade, or I leave you to the rat or hangman. But either way, it ends now."

Robert took a rattling breath, and blood-soaked phlegm collected at the side of his mouth. "Help me..." He looked at Albert, and for the first time, the boy saw the echo of the soldier. He saw the veil, which dropped and turned familiar eyes to a reflective black which bore through your head and ended miles behind. He knew now there was no hope, and he was going to die. They were only deciding how.

"You know what they called me, boy? Your dad remembered. He'd call it out often enough in the thick of battle." He said, taking out a small blade and running his hand through the mattered boy's hair, ruffling it affectionately. Then his fingers tightened into a firm grip, tilting the head backwards.

"Ripper", and he made a swift cut ear to ear.

Blood didn't gush; Robert had already lost too much, but it rolled in a dark wave down his chest and onto the stone. It was more of a mercy than Albert suspected the boy deserved, but he couldn't turn the clock back. He could only stop it from ticking. Albert carefully wiped his knife on the fabric of the boy's coat and stood back. Without a word, he turned to the light.

Small questing eyes that had, until now, been driven off by light edged forward across the rubble and drying blood. They sniffed, whiskers twitching and rolling across angular cheeks as they caught the scent. Tiny paws explored safe passages towards the silent body and heralded the arrival of the rolling wave of boiling rats. By the time anyone else came looking, Robert Challen, murderer and victim, would be quickly divided and carried away into the earth.

Albert had made sure he had been first into the traps, and when he emerged, maybe he didn't see a small mousey boy who had followed him and then appeared seconds after on silent feet. Perhaps he did. The monster had killed Mouse's friend, haunted his waking moments since and caused nightmares which froze him. Albert had heard the cries which had rocked the boy awake. The boy needed to see the monster defeated and know it would not return. He knew the traps better than Tosher himself; he had taught him everything. Albert returned to the open trap and re-secured it, replacing the metal safety pins from his pocket on the rising floor. The plan to trap the boy and call the Police would have worked, but what then? It was cleaner this way and a fitting ending to it all.

§

Mouse had seen the dying man, the flash of silver cut as blood rolled down his chest in a thick, dark wave and had crept from the shadows when Albert left, taking the last of the light. He had stood over the corpse as the shadows reached out and started to swamp him. As Albert's lantern was carried upwards, the blood became black in the growing dark. It rolled towards Mouse's oversized shoes. He reached down and touched a finger into the rapidly congealing liquid. Around him, he heard the shuffle and crawl of clawed feet, and he knew they were coming. Clutched in the boy's hand was a blood-stained cap, which he carefully placed on his head. It dwarfed him and was only kept out of his eyes by his protruding ears. He would grow into it in time. Carefully, he placed the dog-eared remains of a once cherished Penny Dreadful on the corpse. The dancing figure capered on the front under the title 'Spring Heeled Jack'. The grey paper became damp and soft as it soaked up the blood. The cheap print started to warp and flow across the now crimson paper.

"You know what they call me, boy." He said "Rat" and ascended to the light and air as the wave of dark bodies descended on their feast and took the monster away.

Chapter Fifty-Nine – August 1889

There was a party at the end. The lights from the Gaiety restaurant had spilt across the cobbles of the Strand in an invitation, illuminating the faces of those passing along the crowded pavement. By the early hours of dawn, when the rising sun had crept up behind St Mary's on the Strand, climbing the tower and on into the sky, the party-goers had started to disperse with embraces, kisses and promises of forever friendship which would vanish before dusk.

That was the scene in the front of the theatre. Florence StJohn shone and only occasionally adjusted her necklace with trembling fingers, for the first time declining those who wished to admire them more closely with a generous sweep of the room and assurance she did not want to outshine her fellow cast. Within a month, the box would be reported stolen at Manchester Station by thieves unknown. Across the room, she caught the eye of a man, sitting, legs crossed. She smiled as his eyes caught hers, and for a moment, she felt a brief flutter. Maybe happiness was not entirely out of reach.

Fanny had attended in purple satin. She had carefully selected this months ago. The new purples and fuchsias had widened the colour palette of dresses, and she determined to be remembered when she had arranged her wardrobe for this engagement. Her departure costume was as important a part of her performance as what was worn on stage. It was an opportunity to meet, be seen, and, when new opportunities arose, be remembered. But it was different, and for the first time, she found her smile brittle and the lights, sounds and colour surrounding her somehow wrong. She felt conspicuous and uncomfortable. Searching around the room, she saw the door to the auditorium and started to pick her way past the revellers towards it.

As she headed away, Fanny saw the tall figure and shiny domed hair of Mr. Edwardes. Violet Cameron was actively competing for his attention against Mabel and her mother, who had all but pinned him against the flock wallpaper. The look of consternation on Violet's heavily made-up face was one that Fanny would treasure for some time. It appeared Mabel had failed to learn the lessons Mr. Edwardes had tried to teach her about the press. Six weeks before, Mabel had left thirty-three The Strand, walked to the Victoria Embankment, down the stairs and launched herself into the river. Miraculously, a passing Police Officer and now lauded hero had seen her, blowing his whistle, and colleagues collected her from the water. Fanny recalled Mabel's recent interest in William's job, his patrol routes and how flattered he had been by this beautiful woman's interest. Fanny smiled. Love may be blind, but William was far from stupid. Mabel's enthusiasm for swimming prior to the event had not gone unnoticed by him, so he had quietly faded into the background without much notice from the suddenly famous woman. After an appearance at Bow Street and stern rebuke from a judge, Mabel had returned to the Gaiety, apparently repentant and apologetic to 'Dear Mr. Edwardes'. But others had remembered Ida, and forgiveness and understanding from many would be in short supply. Maybe she had considered this and thought it worth the chance; perhaps she was as self-absorbed as many thought, and it simply did not occur to her other than an idea to be used.

Fanny had seen the photograph Mabel kept in her pocket and how she would gaze at it when she thought she was alone. Fanny had no doubt Mabel Love would always be someone in love with the subject of that photograph and would be unlikely to have space for anyone but the familiar face beaming up from the paper, herself.

While appearing thoroughly uncomfortable, Mr. Edwardes, the subject of the three women's attention, would always be a man with an eye for the show surrounding the show. Even while Fanny seemed to have drifted out of his sphere of interest, Mabel would ensure she remained within his gravitational field.

Sometimes, Fanny would see a look in the eyes of someone who had been there that night as the memory flickered for a moment. The looks, sometimes solitary, sometimes silently shared, had started to happen less often in the months since, as if they were fading from memory. As the company concluded the show and started to leave the Gaiety, it would eventually evaporate like a half-remembered nightmare.

§

Departing from Southampton to New York, the newly minted Grace Van Holden settled into the arms of Antonio (her idea) and felt the warmth and feel of the bank notes lining her corset and the remaining pendant of diamonds and solitary sapphire stitched underneath her chemise. It had been quite the surprise, but Miss St John was more of a performer than she had given her credit for. Not many women could market a whole box of paste jewels as real. She had taken the only two that were genuine and expected Miss StJohn was unlikely to make a fuss and draw attention. Divorce was clearly expensive. It was a perfect moment, and she would find it hard to find another man like Caesar who was willing to indulge her and hold all the keys to their – her – future. Grace had changed her mind and decided to keep him a while longer. There was no sense in being bored on a long voyage.

§

For the last time, Fanny walked down the illuminated corridor and into the expansive space of the auditorium as it rose above her, with its vibrant colours and the faint smell of warmth from the lights. She stepped onto the stage, boots softly tapping a staccato beat, but as she stopped dead centre, the echo of the steps stopped, and the auditorium, hungry enough to amplify any sound, however subtle, waited for more.

Without the spotlights and bank of stage lights, Fanny could see up into the vibrant blue of the domed ceiling, the bright gold edging, sinuous shapes and decorations and the soft, opulent fabric. It stood revealed now the blinding reflection that always prevented her from clearly seeing the sea of faces against undulating rows of chairs had gone. The sense of hundreds of eyes always watching crept over her, and she held her breath. She felt the familiar pause in the air before the stamping of feet, the sharp pounding of hand against hand and cries of voices raised in song, joy or even disapproval. She spun around, feeling the swell of the sounds that were not there but a moment away from breaking like a wave against the stage. Fanny felt the voices of the last year raising and lowering around her. Snatches of dialogue, fragments of songs, lost conversations in dark corners, secrets, lies, the sounds of souls torn from the living and imprisoned in the darkness beneath the bright lights of the Gaiety. In one loud crescendo, they became a singular performance of sound and memory.

And all was silent.

Noone would never know how many souls were tied to the theatre, willing and unwilling, but she knew hers was also tied here now. William had taken a last exposed piece of remains, part of a torso, far away from the theatre and into Pinchin Street, Whitechapel, where he could discover it on patrol and ensure she had some kind of burial. William said the bricks were loose all around that awful place, and it would be impossible to know how much was hidden. Albert, William, and Mr. Free had mixed mortar, filling the gaps in the wall, closing up the hole to that chapel of horror. Mrs. Free and Fanny had collected flowers from the market and left them in front of the fresh mortar, saying a silent prayer for the nameless.

Fanny walked to the stage door; her few possessions had been taken home, and all she had to do was hail a cab. She stood at the door to Wellington Street and breathed in the air, the smog, the life of London. It.... She was always moving, evolving, changing. But she was resilient; no, she was resilience. Fire, flood, death and mayhem and she adapted and continued to cling on. London thrived, and so would Fanny. She would never sink if she kept fighting.

It was very late. Fanny decided to walk down the Strand and take a cab from the rank by the bridge. The night was clear, and she felt the warm breeze blowing around her skirts and pulling at her hair as she stood on the parapet. London belonged to women like her again. The winter of terror was gone and she felt an assurance she had realised had been absent for so long. So much had happened, and as the small tendrils of her hair were pulled out of her bun and tussled at her face, she saw a familiar figure on the embankment below. Holding up a hand, she went to call out, but her voice was carried away behind her.

The figure, neat, sinewy and wearing an immaculate moustache, stood looking out across the river. His absolute stillness gave Fanny pause as if she felt she was intruding on something. He looked smaller, different somehow. Whereas before, she would have always found his presence reassuring, she felt no wish this time to draw his attention and watched as he paused and took something from a breast pocket. It caught the lamp light, sharp and thin, and flashed as it leapt in an arc into the water with only the faintest of sounds.

Albert reached down and picked up a large canvas bag, heaving it onto his back. Settling it into a comfortable position, he walked away to the east, towards the sea.

Epilogue

All he felt was pain in his head and body, which overwhelmed him. Everything he touched, each move and each breath caused sparks of pain like gunfire on top of the ceaseless gnawing. It was eating him alive.

Where was he? The floor felt soft and wrong, and the air smelled of chemicals. His mind, flowing away from him, was so full of the past that he had lost all sense of his present. He was picking up fragments of a lifetime ago in the mud of war and seeing them in the familiar streets of home.

He had lived a double life, one of battle in foreign lands which haunted his dreams and one of the battle on the streets of London. Which battle was he fighting? Who was he now? What was his name?

He could see the dark cobbles and walls of his city, his home, which writhed and pulsed with shapes and sounds that sometimes coalesced into battlefield faces. He could smell gunfire, rotting flesh and patches of the stones between his feet suddenly felt sticky and terrifyingly familiar. This sent a shaft of ice down his spine and the knowledge that his bones would never feel warm again. Napper put his hand out to hold onto a wall to try to ground himself, take a moment of stillness, and try to remember this new place, but it did nothing. Nothing was helping, and his lungs were on fire. He tasted a foul bolas which had risen in his throat, and he tried to swallow, but what his brain wanted, his body couldn't or wouldn't do. He spat a globule of green phlegm flecked with black and tried to hold back the vomit.

Where was the boy? Yes, Robert? The man? A small white figure that had turned red with her blood. Then, disappointment flooded his addled brain. That ungrateful son of a whore.

And her. The intoxicating sensation of her hair as it fell into curls flecked with fire from her never-tidy bun. The smell of violets always seemed to stay behind her in an echo of her presence. He could smell it now, rotting violets. That smell, her face, had disintegrated and joined the faces in the mud, haunting his nights and days. She had been smoke, sensation and a memory of the day they had killed each other.

But nearly twenty years after he had started to bury the memory of that bloody night after the last sack containing her remains had slid into the Thames, he had seen her face on the street. After all those years, she had somehow returned to claim him. So he had taken his knife, and like a soldier, gone to war on the streets of Whitechapel and sought her out.

Every time he saw he face, her cut her throat, cut out her rotting shame and stopped her from rising again and again. But she kept coming back like an army of corpses. She had been on the street, entering a house he didn't recognise, standing by a goods yard, and each time she pretended she didn't know him.

In a uniform, Napper the man was invisible, unremarkable, and unimpressive. Rage had risen, uninvited and unbidden, at her lack of recognition, and each time, he silenced her and hacked at her faithlessness with the skills of the butcher, honed in war. He no longer cared; every time she returned to haunt him, he picked up the knife Ripper had pressed into his hand when they left the Crimea and went back into battle. He was now killing demons and ghosts.

A blossom of pain raced across his chest, and he called out wordlessly. He tried again and heard the bellow of a beast in pain. Heavy footsteps approached, and he felt quick hands darting deftly around him, holding his arms and tightening his jacket. He wanted to tell them he couldn't move, but he struggled to catch his breath and form the words. Coins, his watch, his medal and Ripper's knife had all been taken at some point, leaving him without anchor or identity.

Defenseless and now alone, without the use of his arms, he tried to roll his body along the wall to find a way out and get somewhere, anywhere there might be help. These were his streets. He had played here as a boy, cleaned shop windows, run errands and when times were tight and the food so lively it had to be subdued before being boiled white in a pot, he would scan the foreshore in the mud for any bounty the river spewed up.

He'd had a trade, gone to war and returned a broken hero. Not broken like some who tied on rough wood to make up for missing limbs, but somehow in the head. He had joined the police like so many back from the war, and without a trade, they could return or didn't want to return to. Butchery had felt too near to war for him to want to continue with. So he joined his brothers and felt the security of the continued routine, the uniform, which was another form of armour and a clear enemy.

The enemy was close to home, and he knew many by face, name and family, but if they'd chosen to stay behind and break the law, they should be punished like the cowards they were. He was there to be a man of the city and for the city. No one was above the law, and in the back of his head, a small thought darted momentarily - Not her, not even him.

His foot gave way, and his body fell with a painful thump onto his hip, trapping his leg beneath him. He cried out briefly and involuntarily. His breathing was agony, and he tried to shift his position. Arms useless, he attempted to roll to the side and release his leg and in a small set of incremental movements, his leg came free, and he slid it out in front of him. The fall had broken something, and when he coughed, he vomited down his front, but he was below the line of enemy guns, and he could sit and wait for the medics. Ripper would find him, and they'd make it out. Maybe this would get him a pass home.

He looked up, and suddenly, the ceiling above him had faded. There was a sky above him, and it was clear. He looked up into the eyes of the gods. He'd never gone to church, but in battle, no one judges a soldier for talking to any available god and in a police melee, prayers are short and heartfelt. The Roman coves, like the victorious warrior on the back of his medal, had a lot of gods he'd heard. He'd gone to see the new British museum and the carvings of warriors killing a bull by cutting its throat. It was about blood, war, and perhaps the same bargain sealed in red to stay alive in battle. He respected that. In the end it was all about blood. It was a sacrifice. And as he looked down, he realised blood was covering him, baptising him. It was thick, sticky and familiar. As it caught what there was of the light, he regarded it with curiosity, wondering whose it was.

The stars above him blinked on and off and danced. Was it night? Had he been waiting here so long? He thought about his son, his wife, and the ghosts who never gave him peace. Sleeping, pale faces appeared when the rain washed away layers of mud, flesh which fell apart under the lightest touch to bones. Eventually, they would claim him. His chest felt tight, and the pain radiated around his body like a corona of light before exploding out of his chest like a grenade.

He threw back his head and howled as the darkness broke over him.

§

At daybreak, staff found the collapsed body of the old man in the corner of his room, wrapped in the confines of a grubby straightjacket. Blood covered him from neck to knee, pooling between crossed arms and splayed legs. His once imposing frame was strangely vulnerable, slumped and hollow. Sightless eyes stared into the distance, and the final grimace of pain frozen visible under his patchy stubble. In life, he had been an intimidating, influential figure and, in death, diminished.

He was taken to the morgue and placed on the same cold tiles as those whose lives he'd ended in the pursuit of silencing his ghosts. In the absence of light and air, death had rendered him sallow and unrecognisable. There was no need to check to investigate the cause. The end had been inevitable as the clock had slowly ticked away to the endgame of madness. His syphilitic body would be riddled with sores; his skull pitted with grooves, and his heart, the great engine which drove the beast, finally proved to be as brittle as paper. The disease of Venus and the curse from Rose.

So Napper Challen was sent for a pauper burial in an unmarked grave. He had remained unclaimed, and his son could not be found. No one could recognise this man, Soldier, Policeman and Murderer. Another soul, who had stepped off the speeding colossus of this city and was now lost beneath it.

As he was lowered into the ground on a day when the sky turned the earth to mud, he finally slipped beneath the opaque surface he had fought against for so long. He was not alone. Pauper burials were always in the company of at least six others, not even earth separating their stacked formation. The burial was deep to accommodate as many as possible and only covered when the last space was taken.

Napper Challen, a man of unspeakable and contagious horror created by poverty, war and finally madness, would lie in the company of the unknown, rotting and eventually mingling with them, sliding into history as the Ripper and his victims slid into legend.

§

" In the end we'll all become stories."
Margaret Atwood

A long time ago, in another life, I worked in the theatre. I was devoted to adrenalin, the lights, the camaraderie and the applause. Performances are like a bubble: short, intensely beautiful and magical. That sense of magic stayed with me, and many years later, while idly scrolling through my maternal family tree, I found an unexplored branch. One vaudeville actor became a whole dynasty of actors, singers, comedians and a treasure trove of the most extraordinary characters.

A picture caught my eye at the time, and it came back to me many years later in a *Writing for Procrastinator's* course with the author William Sutton. He gave us pictures to inspire us, and I found a Masher, a Victorian actress who played male roles. Immediately, I recalled that family of actors and a black and white picture of actress Fanny

Robina, leaning casually on a plinth, wearing breeches and a broad smile. So I researched her, and to my dismay, found she was always referred to with the preface 'and'- *'Vesta Tilley and Fanny Robina'*, *'Marie Lloyd and Fanny Robina'*. Someone who was a star in her lifetime had become an *'and'* in the better-documented lives of others. The more I read, the more I felt a sense of injustice for her.

Delving into research in places such as the British Newspaper Archive, I found the extraordinary details of the run of 'Faust Up To Date' and the 1888 Winter of Terror. That period was a short and intensive few months where the Ripper was murdering women in Whitechapel, London. Much still remains unknown, and until recently, the focus has been on unravelling the mystery of his identity. However, it has only been in the last few years that the lives of his victims are starting to be described in more detail and beyond the collective description of 'prostitutes'. At the time, actresses were also looked upon in a similar light and, even when lauded, were still viewed with some suspicion. In addition, it also became clear that the Ripper was not the only active murderer, and the Thames Torso Murderer was also killing unknown numbers of women, only one of whom was ever named. I became fascinated by the women of the time, how these terrifying circumstances affected them, and the impact of in-herited trauma. The Crimean War was still in living memory, leaving an enormous dent in a generation of men, and the Irish Fenians had just concluded their first bombing campaign in London. The city was in the middle of enormous physical change from the building of Embankments, tube line projects and on top of this the tension waves of murders. It was a city boiling over with stress.

The situation in 1888 was all too real, and so was the cast of the show, which consisted of Fanny Robina, Florence StJohn, and EJ 'Teddy Lonnen', to name but a few. I have tried to weave the story into the context of their lives so that it still makes sense before and after the story, even the sad and premature death of George Stone less than three months after the show finished. I have given them personalities that fit the narrative and try to honour their actions and motivations as real and complex people, but of course, this story is where reality meets fiction.

There is a joy as a writer in digging through an archive and finding morsels you would never think of. Mabel Love was a wonderful example. A true early Influencer, she chased PR, and nothing she did was invented for this story; it was all Mabel. Of course, some characters like Napper and Robert Challen had to be invented. They are both names lifted from my family tree, but the similarities end there. They are an amalgam of the reports of ex-soldiers returning from Crimea and my experience working with people with forensic pathologies. I can only look from the outside in, and what was done is horrific, but I have attempted to give some context as to why someone may undertake what are still unimaginable acts.

Tosher, Ida, Mr Free, Mrs Freeman, Mouse and Albert are also inventions based on stories of the time and characters who arose in research. Those behind the scenes were rarely thought necessary enough to be named, so I have tried to give them a name, life, and, in some cases, love.

Finally, William Pennett. William did exist; he was the officer who found the last confirmed bundle of human remains from the Torso Murderer. I gave him a background similar to that of Robert Challen, and he eventually became one of the early gangs which became the Peaky Blinders from Manchester, based on the photograph of a scarred young man arrested two years previously. His eyes stuck with me as being intelligent and dangerous, and I wanted to give him a happier conclusion in his future as a police officer and one committed to making a positive change.

In 1903, the Gaiety Theatre was demolished as part of the widening of the Strand. Reports at the time detail an enormous wave of rats rising from the basement and pouring down the street, bringing traffic to a standstill. This unusual event, even for London, gave rise to the idea of Robert Challen's underground world. A second Gaiety was built across the road as part of the redevelopment, replacing the first, and is now memorialised with two plaques on the wall of the office where it once stood. Today both Gaiety's have joined the ranks of London's 'Lost Theatres'. It is still possible to stand on the north pavement between number one, the Aldwych, and the junction with Waterloo Bridge where the first Gaiety stood and look west towards Charing Cross and Mrs Love's Boarding House and then east to the church of St Mary Le Strand and on to Whitechapel. While it has changed, there are still glimmers that can draw you back to 1888.

Please do your own research. The people are fascinating and have extraordinary stories. The libretto I have for 'Faust Up to Date' looks like it was raucous and tremendous fun and still had the power to make me laugh out loud. For the last year, the cast of the show has all become so real and vibrant. I have only visited this world, and there is so much more.

Thank you

Alexia

August 2024, looking out at a sunny day on the Solent.

Thank You

Looking at a finished manuscript for the first time is an extraordinary experience, and it will always be the result of the hearts, minds and generosity of the people around the author. My heart will always be with my mother, Katy, who has enabled everything: my dad, Tony Daniels, who always wanted to be an author and left us all far too early; John, miss you; Cher, Marjan, and Andy, who always keep it honest, grounded, and hilarious; and the Friends' Coffee Club. Courage in yourself has to start somewhere, and my thanks to AL, who wrote to me saying, "You should write. I mean, really write", at a time when I really needed it.

Via William Sutton and his fantastic course, I met the Portsmouth Authors' Collective and reconnected with Christine Lawrence and the powerhouse driver behind the group, Loree Westron. Their generosity, support, and absolute faith in me have been invaluable.

I would also like to thank Mary Torjusson for reading my early draft via the wonderful Jericho, Sam Pearce of SWATT books for helping me get this over the line and Benita Thompson of Kairos Book Design and Editing for this beautiful cover. And, of course, thank you to the British Music Hall Society and the Victoria and Albert Museum for your ceaseless patience with my questions.

I wrote this book at a crossroads in my life when I became ill with Long Covid, and suddenly, my physical world became small, so I decided to spend time in another. I have been between frustrated, angry, hopeful and the spectrum of emotions that happen when life launches a sizable lemon at you. This process kept me sane, and I suppose it is my Lemonade. I cannot thank those I have named, and those I have not, enough for the right words, pushes, and sometimes hugs.

This book is for all of us.

Milton Keynes UK
Ingram Content Group UK Ltd.
UKHW040305181024
449757UK00005B/336